Katherine
The ∧
rides again!

The
Mountain Man's
Bride

The Mountain Man Mysteries:
Book Two

Gary Corbin

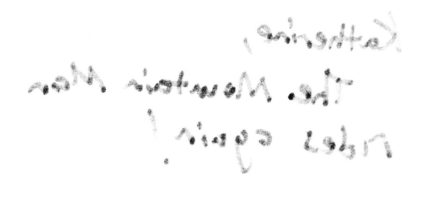

To Renée

CONTENTS

PART 1

Fallen Hero

CHAPTER 1

Lehigh squinted into the headlights of the oncoming car through the muddy mist on the windshield of his old pickup and navigated the tight curve of the old mountain road. Some part of his brain became aware of the fact that his beautiful fiancée, Stacy Lynn McBride, had just said something important, which he had missed, for the two hundredth time too many. And that was only this week.

"Sorry, hon." He adjusted his baseball cap, which didn't really need adjusting, but it gave him something to do while he thought of something smart to say. Which, unfortunately, didn't happen. As usual. "Say again?"

She crossed her arms and put on her I'm-being-patient-with-you voice. "I *said*, because of those stupid stores and their Byzantine sale policies, we're going to have to go back to some of those same shops tomorrow. I can't believe they wouldn't extend their sale prices one day early. Why, if someone came into the clinic with a sick cat or dog, and we had a special—"

"All the way back to Portland? Tomorrow?" Lehigh nearly drove off the road. Damned switchbacks. "Stacy, I can't. Not on a Monday. I have too much to do, and—well, I just can't."

"I see." She found something fascinating to stare at out the passenger side window. "I understand. I mean, there must be dozens of things more important than our wedding. How does one compare the health of a sapling against the mere union of our lives? Thinning a stand of fir, versus expressing the foreverness of our love? The—"

"Okay, okay, I'll go." He sighed. "I was hoping to get some work done. You know, to actually pay for all this wedding stuff? March is the busy season in the forestry world, and I—"

"Watch out for the deer!"

Lehigh slammed on his brakes and swerved in time to allow the doe to leap across the twin lanes of the highway to wooded safety.

"Maybe we should take this road a bit slower," Stacy said. "Unless you hate shopping so much that you can't wait to get away from it."

Lehigh bit back a snotty reply when a playful grin split her pretty face, framed by long black hair tumbling down around her shoulders. She sure knew how to push his buttons—good and bad.

"You know, I don't really mind the shopping," he said, "other than the driving, parking, expense, long lines, rude city people, the wandering around aisle after aisle of stuff I don't want to buy and can't afford, fakey-fake sales people pretending to be my friend, elevator music…"

"Other than that, it's your favorite contact sport." Her grin widened. She rested her hand on his knee, then slid it along his inner thigh, northbound.

"Second favorite." He clamped his hand over hers to arrest its progress. "But the first I can't do while driving, or *that* will become a contact sport."

"Prude." Her lips pressed together into a mischievous smile, her dark eyes sparkling. She leaned over and kissed his stubbly cheek. "You need a shave." She rested her head on his shoulder and took a breath. "Whew! And a shower, mountain man."

"Hey, I took a bath last week." He grinned and pulled her close, his fingers nestling in between her ribs. Still thin at thirty-seven, Stacy could pass for ten years younger, and still got ID'd in bars outside of Clarkesville. He could wrap one arm all the way around her if she stood in front of him, and her tiny waist had added to her frustration over the futile search for a wedding dress that fit right. The diet she'd started the day after he proposed had succeeded—too well, actually.

But he knew where to find soft flesh. He slid his hand further inside—

"Now look who's risking full contact driving!" She laughed and pushed his hand up to her shoulder. "And watch your speed. You're going ten miles over—oh, crap."

Flashing red and blue lights reflected in the pickup's rearview mirror. Lucky, their three year old yellow hound, sat up in the jump seat behind Stacy, growling. Diamond, a four month old Lab-Border Collie mix, sat up in the seat behind Lehigh and joined the chorus moments later.

"Down, dogs," Lehigh said. Lucky quieted first, followed by Diamond, as always.

Lehigh braked and steered the truck to the side of the highway. "Damn. Another ten minutes and we'd have been home." He fished in his wallet for his license.

"Just be polite, and maybe they'll let you off with a warning," Stacy said. Lehigh looked away. Being nice to cops wasn't his strong suit. Then again, they weren't often nice to him, either. He tucked his long brown ponytail inside of his hat. At least he'd shaved that morning.

The sheriff's cruiser, a blue Crown Victoria, pulled in behind his truck. A moment later a tall, athletic figure in a beige uniform emerged from the driver's side.

"Omigod," Stacy said. "It's Jared." She slunk down in the seat.

"Barkley?" Lehigh squinted in the rearview mirror. "What's he doing out on patrol?" He lowered the window, and a moment later, Barkley stepped into view.

"Evening, Sheriff. Dogs, be quiet." They stopped growling again in the back seat.

"Still Deputy, Mr. Carter. Do you know why I pulled you over tonight?"

Lehigh shrugged. "Because you recognized my car?"

Barkley scowled and shone his flashlight in Lehigh's face. "Speed limit's thirty-five here, Mr. Carter. You were going fifteen over the limit. That's a three hundred dollar ticket."

"Hey, Jared." Stacy sat up in the seat and flashed her trademark wide, toothy smile, the one that always melted Lehigh's heart. Flashed it, though, at Jared *frigging* Barkley.

Barkley shone the light on Stacy and his expression softened. He even smiled, for a change. "Evening, Ms. McBride. Is that Lucky and Diamond back there?" A puff of fog followed the words from his mouth.

"Sure is. Good memory!" She broadened her smile. Lehigh fought his impulse to block their view of each other. Stacy leaned closer. "Now, why is the Acting Sheriff of all of Mt. Hood County working traffic on a Saturday night?"

"Duty calls, Sta—uh, ma'am." Barkley cleared his throat, all official again. "Might I see your license, insurance, and registration, Mr. Carter?"

Lehigh groaned and handed his driver's license through the window. "Registration's in the glove box. Mind getting it for me, please, Stace?"

Stacy smiled past him and handed the registration card to the deputy. "Make sure to thank your mom for that strawberry cake recipe, Jared," she said. "You should swing by and try some on your day off. If you ever take one."

Barkley emitted a small cough. "Mighty kind of you to offer, but with Sheriff Summers' situation…well, don't let it go bad waiting on me." He smiled at Stacy, thought a moment, nodded once to Lehigh, then handed him back his license and paperwork. "Careful with your speed coming 'round these turns at night, Mr. Carter. That black ice'll get you this time of year." He tipped his hat and stepped back toward his car.

"Thank you!" Stacy waved out the back window, then turned to face Lehigh. "Well, that was mighty nice of him." She squeezed Lehigh's arm.

He wiggled away and rolled up the window. "*Awfully* nice. Next time you ought to make him dinner. Maybe then he'd let us *rob* a damned wedding store, and we'd be done with all this blasted shopping." He started the engine.

Her jaw dropped. "Lehigh, I'm surprised at you. Here you go acting all jealous when all I did was save you a three hundred dollar ticket."

Lehigh hesitated before putting the truck in gear. He couldn't put a finger on it, but something felt wrong about the way she'd interacted with Barkley. It seemed a little too…familiar. And Jared had seemed almost embarrassed once Stacy had made her presence known. Almost as if…

He gunned the engine and sped the truck back onto the highway. Gravel spewed from his rear wheels onto the front grill of the deputy's still-parked car.

"Slow down!" she said. "Are you trying to convince him to change his mind and write you a ticket anyway?"

They drove the rest of the way home in heated silence.

*****

Stacy stayed put in the passenger seat long after Lehigh parked his truck beside her car at the end of her hundred-foot gravel drive. Her modest two-bedroom bungalow needed painting and probably a new roof, projects she'd asked him to finish this year—and the source of too many arguments. "I have an entire house to rebuild," he'd pointed out the last time. "Or don't you remember how your last fiancé and his friends felt about me coming back into your life last fall?"

That cheap shot had earned him a night on the couch. Since then, he'd kept his thoughts about the relative priority of his and her house repairs to himself. And a lot of other thoughts, she reckoned. That had to change.

They sat in silence for several minutes, seat belts still buckled, his hands on the wheel, her arms crossed, both staring straight ahead into the misty darkness of the evergreens that bordered her two-acre property. A few times, she drew in a breath to speak, but no words came.

Finally Lehigh dropped his arms from the steering wheel to his lap and turned to face her. "Look, I'm sorry. This whole wedding thing…I don't know."

She faced him too. Took a deep breath. "Are you…having buyer's remorse?"

"What do you mean?"

She took a moment, choosing her words with care. "I mean, are you sorry you came up with this whole marriage idea?"

"*I* came up with the idea?" He sat flat against the seat and blew noisy air between his teeth. "I seem to recall a certain someone once cutting me out of her life for *not* asking."

"Oh, for heaven's sake. That was twelve years ago. What's next? Complaints about how I ignored you in high school?" Her dark hair whipped around her face as she turned away from him. Dammit. She'd gone and snapped at him—exactly what she'd tried *not* to do.

He sighed. "So much for trying to apologize."

"It just seems that ever since we started making plans to actually get married, you've been a total grump." She drooped her head and recrossed her arms, trying to keep the fear out of her voice. "It's as if you're...I don't know. Changing your mind."

"I'm *not*." He rubbed the stubble on his cheeks. "But I'll admit, this is becoming a much bigger deal than I ever wanted it to be."

"Getting married is a big deal."

"Yeah, but does the wedding have to be? Why can't we just get a couple of friends together, go to a justice of the peace..."

She bolted upright in her seat. "My father would kill you, that's why. And my mother would roast you alive first."

"Ain't that the truth." The first etchings of a smile crossed his lips. "I just thought that your dad might want a lower key event, now that he's dropped out of the governor's race."

She frowned. "Was *forced* out. By us."

"By his own bad choices." Lehigh looked away from her. "One of the many ways you don't take after him, thank God."

Stacy sighed. Her dad's role in ruining Lehigh's life six months before remained a serious bone of contention between them. One of many. Only, in the twisted way Senator George McBride told the story, it was Lehigh who'd ruined the other man's life. Taking ownership of mistakes was not in her father's toolbag.

"Still," she said, "it means a lot to him, and that means a lot to me." She took his hand. "I kind of hoped it meant something to you, too."

"Course it does. I just like things simple, is all." He squeezed her hand.

She leaned against him, rubbing his thumb with her much smaller, delicate fingers. "Maybe it can be, a little bit. Do you think, if we did something small, we could get your Pappy and Maw to come?"

Lehigh winced and dropped his chin to his chest. "Not even if we held the ceremony in their backyard, I reckon."

"Sorry, sweetie. Sore subject, I know." Stacy held him tighter, kissed his cheek. They sat in silence for several moments.

In the back seat, one of the dogs stretched and whimpered, followed by the other. Lehigh reached back with an expert hand and popped open the rear driver's side door. The dogs bounded out into the darkness, Diamond always two awkward puppy hops behind Lucky's lazy loping gait. Lehigh shut the door behind them. He reached around Stacy and pulled her close again. "What say we sit here a bit?"

She giggled. "It'd be warmer inside."

He hugged her tighter. "Yeah, but it's cozier in here. Besides, we'll be warm enough in a minute."

She slid her hand inside his shirt, onto the bare skin of his muscular chest. "You got a point there, cowboy." She leaned forward for a kiss. His hand slipped inside her suddenly unbuttoned blouse, and she wondered if they'd ever make it inside the house.

CHAPTER 2

Lehigh loosened his bolo tie and tugged at the collar of his starched, pressed dress shirt. The white cotton stuck to his neck, clammy in spite of the late winter chill, and he repressed a resurgent gag reflex for the tenth time that evening. But the uncomfortable clothes couldn't take all the blame for that. At least half the credit belonged to the stuffy dining room, paneled floor to ceiling in tobacco darkened walnut imported from the East Coast. For all of his local-yokel politics, Senator McBride's patrician past seemed to matter more than supporting the Oregon economy when it came to surrounding himself with luxurious creature comforts.

Stacy sidled up next to Lehigh and rested her hand against the small of his back. "You look wonderful," she said in a soft voice. "You should wear fitted shirts more often."

"Not if you want me to survive until our wedding day," he said. "But you look amazing. That dress—"

"Has cut off all circulation below my rib cage," she said. "But I'm glad you like it. It's Daddy's favorite too." She pecked him on the cheek. "I appreciate you coming tonight. I know being around politicians isn't your idea of fun."

"Speaking of your old man—"

"Shh!" She shook her head, a quick vibration back and forth, as if to hide the action. "He hates being called 'old.'"

"Okay, then. The esteemed senator. Where the heck is he?"

"Mom said he's in his—oh, here they come now." She

sipped from a glass of pinot grigio in her left hand. Lehigh drained the last of the melted ice from his own glass, now devoid of her father's prized eighteen-year-old Scotch. Best not let the senator see what his wife had so freely offered a half hour before. Bad enough that old George found Lehigh beneath contempt without him also knowing how much he'd had of his favorite liquor.

Catherine McBride, Stacy's mother, led the senator into the room. Despite her small stature—probably a full foot shorter than Lehigh's six foot, one-inch frame, if she kicked off her three-inch heels—her regal bearing and teased hairdo elevated her presence in the room. She wore a flowing, ankle-length dress that seemed to thin her matronly, if not stout, figure. She strode into the room with confidence and greeted them for the second time that night with hugs and smiles.

The senator, by contrast, seemed old and stooped, a half foot shorter than he'd appeared a few months before when the race to become Oregon's next governor seemed his to lose. His full shock of white hair lay flat against his scalp, and age spots dotted his bronze, wrinkled face. He mumbled a quick hello to Lehigh, kissed his daughter on the cheek, and shuffled over to the liquor cabinet to refill his glass.

"Dinner will be served in a few moments." Catherine took Lehigh by the arm. "And not a moment too soon, by the look of you. Stacy, don't you feed my future son-in-law?"

"I wouldn't want to spoil his appetite for your legendary dinners," Stacy said with a grin.

"That'll never happen," Lehigh said. "Who's the chef this week?"

"A new fellow from the culinary school in Portland. His name is Antonio. He's amazing—he has no sous-chef. He does everything himself." Catherine escorted him to his seat. She sat to Lehigh's right, and Stacy sat across from him. The senator took his customary position at the head of the long table.

Lehigh's stomach growled. Early dinners meant skipping lunch, and at that moment, he could have eaten one of the senator's retired show horses, medium rare.

Almost on cue, a short, chubby man with tufts of curly hair protruding from either side of a white ruffled chef's hat, dressed in kitchen whites and sporting a food-stained apron, whisked into the room. With nervous dispatch, he set a heaping salad plate in front of each guest, ground two twists of fresh pepper on top of the greens, and disappeared back into the kitchen, neither he nor the four diners having uttered a word.

Lehigh grabbed a fork and had nearly reached his quarry—baby green spinach leaves topped with thin slices of red onion, chunks of bright red strawberries, crumbled feta cheese, and crushed walnuts, all tossed in a vinaigrette redolent of chocolate and orange—when a sharp pain pierced his ankle. Catherine glared at him, her hands crossed in prayer. His stomach growled again, but he set down his fork, bowed his head, and folded his hands.

"Bless us, oh Lord, for these, thy gifts…" Catherine recited the prayer as if making it up for the first time, every word an intense plea for God's attention. Which made the damned thing take twice as long as it should. But he couldn't complain—it took four times as long when his Pappy meandered through it on Sunday mornings. "Amen," they said in unison at the end, and perhaps Lehigh said it a bit too forcefully, because Catherine kicked him again.

"I have an announcement to make." The senator stood, a laborious effort. Lehigh chewed the delicious greens and shoved more in. The guy wanted to talk, fine. *Some* people came to eat.

"Is it about the case?" Stacy asked.

"Only indirectly." The old man's face darkened, and he swallowed with some effort. Lehigh had already polished off half of his salad and would have offered half his kingdom for a crust of bread. Hell, a crouton.

The senator cleared his throat. "More to the point, it concerns your wedding plans."

Lehigh, about to shove a forkful of salad into his mouth, caught the warning in Stacy's eyes, and with great reluctance put down his fork.

"Because of my recent legal difficulties," McBride said, "largely due to your activities, I might add..." He gestured with his wine glass toward Lehigh.

Stacy pushed her chair back from the table, her face and neck muscles tight, her color drawn. "So that's your take on this?" She stood and pointed a finger at her father. "Well, it's not Lehigh's fault that you and Paul van Paten took cash bribes from corporate donors, broke into my veterinary clinic, poisoned animals, burned down Lehigh's house—"

The senator's face turned crimson. "How dare you accuse me of such outrageous—"

"Enough!" Catherine slapped the table with both hands, rattling glasses, plates, and silverware. She stood, her hazel eyes blazing. "There shall be no further discussion of this at my dinner table."

"But Mother—"

"Dammit, Catherine, it's *my* house, and—"

"Not one word!" Catherine pointed her fork at Stacy, then at her husband. "If we cannot discuss the matter civilly, we simply shall not discuss it. Nor anything else remotely related to it."

George glared at Lehigh and slammed his fist on the table. A chunk of walnut flew across the table onto Lehigh's half-empty plate. Lehigh suppressed the urge to scoop it into his mouth.

George waited for Stacy to sit, then continued. "Be that as it may, the legal fees incurred in my successful settlement of those scurrilous charges have drained my cash reserves. As a result, our ability to contribute to defraying the costs of your wedding has been seriously diminished."

Stacy covered her mouth with one hand, shock and worry clouding her eyes.

Lehigh chewed his salad, swallowed, and shrugged. "Understandable, sir. I know firsthand how quickly those legal expenses add up."

"Rubbish," Catherine said, setting down her fork. "We have

plenty of resources to draw on."

"I apologize to my wife for not briefing her on our financial condition prior to tonight's dinner." The senator glowered at his wife, and she responded with her own angry stare. He turned to Stacy. "I'm sorry, Pumpkin. I had hoped to be able to give you the big wedding you deserve. But," and he glanced at Lehigh, distaste evident, "my circumstances no longer permit it."

"It's...it's okay, Daddy." Stacy's eyes grew moist. "We've been thinking a smaller wedding might be a better idea anyway. Haven't we, Lehigh?"

Lehigh hurried to chew and swallow the last bite of his salad. For once, the smile he put on at the McBrides' home reflected genuine pleasure over something other than the food. "We don't need a big party," he said, "and we're plenty able to put on a modest celebration on our own for family and close friends. I'd kind of prefer it, actually."

"I don't think George is saying that we can't help at all," Catherine said with a hesitant smile. "Surely we could provide flowers and perhaps Stacy's dress, maybe some—"

"I'm afraid even that is out of the question." George frowned at his wife. "While criminal charges have been dropped, details of my settlement are still in negotiation. I may be facing stiff fines, which, while preferable to incarceration or the loss of my Senate seat, may leave us close to penniless, from a cash perspective."

"Baloney," Catherine said. "We have investments—"

"Non-liquid—"

"Trust funds—"

"Untouchable!"

"Dammit, George, I'll sell the damned horses if I have to!" Catherine said, her voice reaching top volume. "I'm buying my daughter's wedding dress, and that's final!"

McBride froze for a moment, then gave her a slight bow. "Very well. But that, I fear, may be all we can offer. Unless..."

"Unless what?" Stacy's voice betrayed a sharp edge of nervousness. Lehigh's ears perked up. Perhaps she knew something that he didn't?

George stared into his wine glass. "If the wedding could be, ah, postponed—"

"I knew it!" Stacy stood and threw her napkin onto her salad plate, knocking oily greens all over the pristine tablecloth. "This is all about trying to stop the wedding!"

"Pumpkin, how could you say such—"

"Don't you 'pumpkin' me. You've been against this marriage from the start!"

"On the contrary. I was very excited to hear of your engagement last summer. Wasn't I, Catherine?"

Stacy's jaw dropped open. "I wasn't engaged to Lehigh last summer!"

"Of course you were engaged then," George said with a wave of his hand. "I distinctly recall discussing the timing of it with you, so as not to interfere with the campaign."

"No, George," Catherine said in a low voice. "That was Paul, dear."

Lehigh scooped salad dressing from his plate with the edge of his fork. If he could crawl under the plate and hide, he would have.

Stacy gripped the edge of the table with both hands. "Ah, ha. I see what's going on here. Tell me, Daddy. If Paul van Paten were sitting here instead of Lehigh—"

"Stacy," Lehigh said, "please don't—"

"You'd find the money, now, wouldn't you?" Stacy leaned toward her father, her lower lip quivering.

George held up his hands. "Now, Stacy. If you were still engaged to Paul, we wouldn't be in this situ—"

"*I was never engaged to Paul!*" Stacy's voice echoed off the walls.

The door to the kitchen, which had edged open a moment before, fell shut again. Lehigh groaned. He could put up with family quarrels, but not on an empty stomach.

"Paul disagrees," George said in a quiet voice. "And I know him well. He would not lie."

"Of course he's lying! For heaven's sake!" Stacy raised her

eyes and hands to the heavens, pleading. "Oh, Daddy. Don't you think I'd know if I had ever been engaged to a man?"

"I'm just saying, my dear," George said, his voice still maddeningly calm, "that had the events of the last several months not transpired, we would not be having this conversation." He wiped his lips with a napkin, sat down, and took a tiny sip of wine.

Stacy glared at him. "I see. So. This is how it's going to be, then. Well, I don't need your money, and I don't need your blessing. I'm marrying the man I love, and that's Lehigh—with or without your support. Come on, Lehigh. We're leaving."

Lehigh's heart sank. He could smell bread, imagined a plateful of aged cheeses and salted meats, envisioned fresh pasta with spicy red sauce and melted cheese, and more—all behind that kitchen door. That now closed kitchen door. The limitless supplies of delicious food, with plenty of leftovers to take home, enough to live on for a week. He checked his fiancée's face, and found no sign of compromise there. He sighed. He had one last hope, and played it, making eye contact and a sad face in the direction of his future mother-in-law.

Catherine stood and reached across the table toward Stacy. "Dear, please don't—"

"I'm sorry, Mother. I can't dine with a man who so disrespects me and my life choices that he can't put aside his petty grievances for one minute—"

"Petty? Why, you little—"

"George! Shut up for one second!" Catherine glared at him.

Stacy grabbed Lehigh's arm. "Let's go, honey. We're done here."

Lehigh cast one last glance at the kitchen door, now propped open by Antonio, holding a tray loaded with steaming lasagna, the aromas of garlic and spicy tomato sauce wafting into the dining room. His stomach rumbled, and his eyes, fixed on the tray, watered in anticipation.

But one final glance at Stacy, and he knew he would taste no lasagna that night.

CHAPTER 3

Blue smoke rose from the mouths and nostrils of three of the four men seated around the low maple table in the center of the well-appointed library of the wealthiest and most influential man in Mt. Hood County. The owner of the space, a bloated, white-haired figure with a ruddy complexion, prided himself on his ability to wield the levers of power from behind the scenes, without the taint of having ever run for or held political office. Scowling, Everett Downey set out an array of shallow clay ashtrays, hand-crafted by locals whose tribal affiliations claimed the namesakes of his several casinos, each of which earned almost as much as his chain of "gentlemen's clubs" dotting small-town highway exits around the county. The ashtrays, however, went unheeded and unused, other than the one closest to Downey himself.

"So, where are we?" He waved a pudgy hand in the air to part the blue cloud hanging over their heads.

"We're in a world of hurt, that's where." The handsome, dark-haired thirty-something man, a Portland lawyer, and the only one of the group not indulging in the expensive Cuban treats, coughed into his fist. "We've lost control to a bunch of yahoos who couldn't find their own asses in a house of mirrors."

"Can we please forbear from the jailhouse vulgarity?" A slender man a few years' Downey's senior with a shiny pate, dressed in his customary black suit, pointed the lit end of his cigar at the younger man. "Unless you'd prefer to rejoin your colleagues behind bars...which I can easily arrange."

"Sorry, sorry," the Portland man said. So far as the people of Mt. Hood County knew, he still occupied one of their rustic jail cells, and he'd just as soon not give truth to that particular popular belief. "But the people around here view us as the bad guys in all of this. And until we can retake control of the sheriff's office, that message isn't going to change."

"Are you blaming me? Because that ain't my fault!" said the fourth man of the group, a middle-aged man with a bulbous nose and a salt-and-pepper crew cut. Alone among the four, he had never been to college, much less law school, and until recently had never been on the wrong side of the black bars in the county jail. "If you hadn't gone rogue—"

"Let's not start pointing fingers," Downey said.

"Exactly," Portland said. "We don't need blame. We need action. And a plan."

"And the first step is to get the right people back in charge of the sheriff's office," said the man with the crew cut. Dressed in khakis from shoulders to ankles, he gave the appearance of a man who never felt comfortable out of uniform.

"Agreed," said the bald man. "But how? Your successor—"

"Interim successor," Crewcut said.

"—Jared Barkley," the bald man continued, "is as popular with the voters as our esteemed senator once was. And why not? He's young, smart, handsome, courageous—"

"Who the hell's side are you on, dammit?" Portland said.

"Language! Please!"

"Aw, stuff it, Reverend!"

"Don't you call me that, ever!" The bald man stood, his entire head turning bright crimson except for his bushy white eyebrows. "Show some respect! Why, I've been locking up criminals since before you were born!"

"Easy, easy." Downey stood between them, arms extended. "Let's stay focused on solving the problem. Which is, how to restore control of this county's law enforcement to its rightful, traditional, responsible defenders. On this, we are all agreed. Correct?" He took a deep taste of his cigar.

The younger man glared at the other three. After taking several deep breaths through his nose, he nodded. "We'll need help. From the inside, and—well, from a lot of people."

Crewcut raised a hand. "I still have friends on the inside. They owe me. I think they'll help."

"You think," Portland said, "or you know?"

"I—I know. I think."

Exasperated, the Portland lawyer turned to their host. "We'll need some strings pulled."

Downey nodded. "Already in motion."

"Are we talking about the same man? *And* his daughter?" asked the bald man.

"You mean the man against whom *you* have filed charges? Against him *and* me?" Portland pointed a finger in his face. "Or has he been...*forgiven?*"

The man who hated being called Reverend gritted his teeth. "In terms of active support, no. But...I think he can be brought into play. And, with your help," he said with a nod to the Portland man, "the girl's opposition can be, shall we say, *neutralized.*"

"Assuming," Downey said, "we play our cards right and follow the plan."

All four heads nodded. Crewcut cleared his throat. "How, uh, far are we prepared to go?"

The Portland man furrowed his brow. "Perhaps it's best if you and I took up the operational aspects of this conversation in private."

"Great idea," the Reverend said, and Downey nodded his assent.

"And the girl?" Crewcut wiped sweat from his upper lip. "Your former fiancée?"

"Before we're done," Portland said with a crooked smile, "she'll be our biggest cheerleader."

***

Lehigh shut the snaps on his boxy old suitcase, a hand-me-down from when he had gone off to college at Oregon State. Since that day almost twenty years ago, he'd only used it a handful of times—mostly, like this occasion, on quick overnight or weekend trips to Portland.

"I'll be back on Sunday," he said to Stacy, who was applying make-up in front of an oval mirror in the bedroom. "Pappy and Maw invited us over for brunch, remember?"

"I'll be at Momma and Daddy's all day Sunday." She drew a perfect dark line over her left eye.

He paused, mouth open. "I thought you weren't speaking to them. After, you know—"

"Daddy came by the clinic yesterday and apologized. Didn't I tell you? Mom made him. They're also buying my dress, like Mom said. He's so full of bluster sometimes." She laughed and shook her head.

Lehigh shrugged, shook his head, and set the suitcase on the floor. "And he never does anything without a reason. What's up on Sunday? I take it, since I wasn't invited, it's something political."

"Yes, Daddy's having some people over—politicians, I mean—for the first time since the campaign ended. There's some talk about him running for the County Board."

"Already?" Lehigh shook his head. "His case hasn't been settled yet, has it? And I thought he already had a job lined up with the Oregon Lumber Council." He stood behind her and rubbed her shoulders.

"You can rub harder if you want." She slid back on the seat, closer to him. "Daddy would be bored if he wasn't involved in politics. And you know people around here. Him against the Feds—that practically makes him a local hero. As a recent victim of a police witch hunt, I'm sure you can appreciate that sentiment. Wow, that feels good." She melted back against him.

He squeezed her shoulders an extra long moment, then wrapped his arms around her and pressed his lips into her silky hair. "Give your Mom a kiss for me. And if there's any leftovers…"

"You're incorrigible. But I'll tell her."

"Tell her it's for the dogs. If you tell her it's for me, she won't include any prime rib."

Stacy laughed. "Who are you kidding? Mom loves you more than she loves me. Hell, you'll probably eat better than I will, knowing her care packages."

"I'm counting on it." He kissed the top of her head again. "I'd better go. My first meeting's at noon."

She tsk'd. "Most people *quit* working at noon on Fridays."

"You've been around government types too long." He breathed in the soft scent of her skin. "See you Sunday night."

"I can't wait." She pulled him closer. "Remember, take it easy around those curves, and don't drive tired. I want you back in one piece…and the sooner the better."

"Keep the dogs off the bed," he said on the way out. He pretended not to hear her uproarious laughter after he shut the door.

The drive took a little over two hours, thirty minutes of which he spent going practically nowhere on Portland's clogged city streets. Those media types could say what they wanted about how easy drivers could get around the city, but compared to Clarkesville, trafficwise, Portland might as well be New York.

Still, that gave him two hours to wait before his noon appointment with the lumber exporters from Astoria. He checked into his motel, ate an early lunch, and stopped by a big box store by the airport to restock on office supplies. Not paper, though—he bought paper only from Oregon mills.

The meetings filled Friday's daylight hours but left his evening free. He took in a second-run Matt Damon movie in one of Portland's renowned brewpub theaters and went to bed early, with the same plan for Saturday. But then, plans never seemed to make much difference in how his days went anymore.

***

"Where is he now?" the Boss Man asked.

"In his motel room. Looks like he's staying the night." The stocky, blond-haired man limped around his car to get a better view of the door to Lehigh's room. His leg still hurt from the gunshot wound he'd received at the hands of the very man who, once again, issued all the orders and did very little of the work. The man, that is, on the other end of the phone.

"Keep an eye on him. Let me know if he goes out, even if it's just for a cigarette."

"I don't think he smokes," the blond man said.

The Boss Man's voice dripped with contempt. "Just call me if anything happens." The line went dead.

***

The weekend in Portland passed in a blur. Lehigh skipped most of the dull workshops and panels that drew many to the conference and instead jammed his schedule full of meetings with buyers, bankers, and a few potential clients interested in having Lehigh manage their holdings. When Saturday night's social hour and banquet rolled around, exhaustion and a general discomfort with schmoozing led to a discreet exit— after a couple of quick passes through the buffet, of course.

He walked to his cheap motel a few blocks from the Convention Center and stopped at the front desk. A girl with ramrod straight, shoulder-length, blue-streaked black hair with light brown roots greeted him with a smile that failed to light up her hooded gray eyes. Her nose ring matched the one in her lip, and blue ink peeked out of the neckline of her blouse. Even at five foot six, she couldn't have weighed a hundred pounds.

"Help you?" she asked.

"I'd like to get an early start back home tomorrow," Lehigh said. "Okay if I check out in advance?"

She squinted at him, a disdainful look, and spoke in a monotone. "Just leave the key in your room. We have your credit card on file. We'll, like, email you the receipt."

"Thanks. Anyone open for breakfast before six around

here?"

Another condescending stare. "I have no idea. I'm never up that early."

He thanked her and returned to his room. He showered and packed, then lay in bed for half an hour, but couldn't sleep. He flicked on the TV. A Jennifer Aniston movie had just started. He'd seen it with Stacy once, a dumb romantic thing, but full of eye candy. Perfect for falling asleep.

Two hours later, an equally dumb Brad Pitt movie filled the screen, followed by a so-called 1950s classic he'd never heard of. He clicked it off, tossed and turned for another half hour, then gave up. He hated to admit it, but he couldn't sleep without the trio of comforts home represented to him: a familiar bed, snoring dogs, and Stacy.

He got out of bed, dressed, and loaded up the truck. He hit the highway about one a.m. He could make it home by three a.m. if traffic cooperated.

By one-thirty, though, his eyes grew heavy. The normally beautiful drive through the Cascades did him no good in the dark. He'd never last another hour. He should have left right after dinner.

Oh, well. Too late now. He pulled over onto the broad shoulder of the US highway at a place where truckers often stopped to rest or put chains on their massive wheels. He'd rest a bit, then head on.

Just a brief rest.

He closed his eyes.

***

"He stopped."

The Boss Man hissed into the phone loud enough to make the blond man's ears hurt. "Explain, please."

"He pulled over on the side of the highway. Looks like he's taking a snooze."

"Where are you?" The Boss Man sounded upbeat. Pleased, even.

"About a half mile past him, parked at a trailhead. If he goes by me, I'll see him. Where's the girl?"

After a long silence, The Boss Man spit out his reply. "Don't crowd that pitiful brain of yours with unnecessary information. Just let me know when something changes."

This time, the blond man hung up first. And punched the dashboard.

CHAPTER 4

Bright sunlight shocked Lehigh awake. He checked the dashboard clock. Seven-fifteen!

He started the engine, blinked boulders of sleep out of the corners of his eyes, and eased the truck back onto the highway. So much for sleeping in his own bed. Or, rather, Stacy's. His own bed had burned to cinders the previous November.

A flurry of snow greeted him out of nowhere some twenty minutes later. The late season skiers and snowboarders flying past him in four wheel drives toward Mt. Hood would love it, but Lehigh had forgotten to bring his tire chains. The snowfall intensified to a thick swirl, and he slowed to a safe crawl speed, hoping the alpine crazies wouldn't take idiotic chances passing him on the narrow highway. A few brave souls disappointed him, but most hung back until abandoning his tail at the first turn-off toward the ski resort.

The snow turned to rain on the eastside downhill slopes of the Cascades, then cleared to sunshine, allowing him to return to highway speed. He pulled into Stacy's driveway at 8:45, disappointed to discover her car gone. She'd no doubt joined her parents at church. That meant she'd silenced her cell phone, too, and would probably head straight over to their house for a mid-afternoon dinner.

Plenty of time for a nap to catch up on all that lost shut-eye.

He lugged his suitcase inside, left it by the front door, and headed upstairs to the bedroom. His clothes rained off his body onto the floor. The dogs danced around him and sniffed his discarded garments, but he didn't even pause to pet them. He collapsed onto the bed, face first into soft pillows, and drew the covers around him. So nice…

A sharp series of knocks followed by a duet of angry barking woke him. Bleary-eyed, he sat up. 9:20. Damn. He'd hoped for at least another hour.

"Just a minute!" He half-tripped down the stairs, let the dogs out back, and zipped his pants on the way to the front door. The loud knocks resumed.

"Mr. Carter? Are you in there?"

"Yes, yes. Just a sec." He grabbed a sweatshirt out of the coat closet and pulled it over his head, then opened the door.

A sheriff's deputy he didn't recognize stood facing him, holding a document. He stood about five feet ten, with tight red curls tucked under his hat, wore black-rimmed eyeglasses, and had the squat build of a wrestler gone soft. A taller deputy with a light brown crew cut, a few years younger and athletically built, stood behind him with one hand resting on his holster.

His unsnapped, ready-to-draw-a-gun-from-it holster.

"How can I help you?" Lehigh asked.

"We have a warrant to search this here premises," the red-haired deputy said, waving the paper at Lehigh. "May we come in?"

Lehigh stepped back. "Uh…I guess. What's this about?"

The two deputies pushed their way inside, stopping just inside the door, unable to squeeze past Lehigh. The bespectacled one said, "Mr. Carter, I'm Sergeant Cam Patrick, Mt. Hood County Sheriff's Office. This is Deputy Joe Flynn. Is that your truck outside?" Patrick waved a beefy arm toward Lehigh's Ford F150.

"Yes, sir. Why?"

"Been out driving it lately?"

Lehigh nodded. "Took it in to Portland this weekend. Just got back a half hour ago. But I still don't understand what this is all about."

"When is the last time you saw or spoke to Stacy McBride?" Sergeant Patrick asked.

"Am I under some sort of investigation? Because if I am, I'd like to call my lawyer."

"Please, Mr. Carter. If we could come in and get underway. It's all explained in the search warrant." Patrick again held the papers—two or three stapled sheets—out to Lehigh.

Lehigh scanned the pages, then furrowed his brow. "Says this is pursuant to the… Holy cow. Murder?" Lehigh took a step back. "Who died? And where's Stacy right now?"

Patrick and Flynn exchanged glances. Flynn bowed his head and Patrick spoke. "She's down at the station. Being questioned."

"As a witness, or…?" Heat filled Lehigh's cheeks.

"I'm afraid she'd have to be considered a subject of the investigation." Flynn gestured past Lehigh. "May we?"

"Subject of investigation? Are you guys crazy, stupid, or just plain ignorant?" Lehigh stomped into the room. The deputies, sensing an opportunity, spilled past him. "Hey!" Lehigh said. "Where the hell do you think you're going?"

Flynn entered the kitchen. Patrick pointed to the couch, stopping Lehigh from following him. "Please wait here. It'll be best for all concerned."

Lehigh planted his fists on his hips, feet shoulder-width apart. "Fine. If I can't stop you goons from tearing up my kitchen, at least let me go upstairs. I'd like to get a shirt on and call our lawyer, if you don't mind."

Patrick set his lips in a line, then nodded once. "I'll come with you."

"*Mighty* gracious." He stomped up the stairs to the bedroom, cop in tow, and peeled off the sweatshirt. He pulled a shirt off the tiny length of closet rod Stacy had allotted him in her walk-in and yanked it over his head. He checked by the bed for his cell phone, then the dresser. No go. "I'm gonna check my truck," he said to Patrick. "I'll be right back."

"I'd rather we all stayed inside just now, Mr. Carter."

Patrick's bulky frame blocked the doorway. In his youth Lehigh would have had no difficulty getting by him. On an open football field, speed beat size any day. But not in the tight quarters of the bungalow's bedroom doorway.

"Fine. I'll call from the kitchen phone."

"When Deputy Flynn is finished there." Patrick edged sideways, blocking the door.

Lehigh leaned into him. "Am I under arrest?"

Patrick shook his head. "Not at the moment."

"Then stop treating me like a damned prisoner and get the hell out of my way."

Sergeant Patrick glared at him a moment, then stepped aside.

Lehigh tore down the stairs, not bothering to look behind him to see if Patrick followed or not. What-*ever*. If they wanted to follow him around, they'd have to get ready for some exercise. He pounded into the living room and headed for the door.

Deputy Flynn intercepted him out of nowhere with a hand pressed flat against the closed door. "Going somewhere?"

"Yeah. Out to my front yard. Then maybe to the back, and perhaps I'll take a jog up the street. What do you care? The search warrant said you could search the premises. It didn't say anything about screwing around with me."

Flynn scowled and nudged Lehigh's suitcase, still sitting on the floor by the front door. "Seems maybe you were thinking of a longer trip."

"That's incoming, not outgoing. I went to Portland this weekend, remember?"

"So you say." Flynn pointed to the sofa. "All the same, we'd prefer if you'd stay close by and didn't touch anything."

"This is my damned house and I'll do whatever—"

"Mr. Carter, I believe this is Ms. McBride's house. At least, that's the one we intended to search."

Lehigh wrung his hands and exhaled with audible force. "Fine, then. Since it's Stacy's house and it's her things you're interested in, you won't need me. What's this all about, anyway? What's this about a murder? You never did tell me—who died?"

Flynn glared at him, then raised his gaze to the stairs. Lehigh turned to see what fascinated the deputy.

"You mean you haven't heard?" Patrick asked from the stairs. He trod with deliberation down each step.

"Heard what?"

"Ms. McBride didn't call you?"

"My phone's been off. What's up?"

"Mr. Carter." Patrick rounded the rail at the bottom of the stairs and leaned back against it. "You mean to tell me you haven't heard a single report, or rumor, or second hand story about the biggest tragedy to hit Mt Hood County in three generations?"

Big tragedy? Those didn't happen in Clarkesville. Area residents suffered occasional fires, landslides, or mild earthquakes, but—Lehigh's own house burning down an obvious exception, at least in his mind—nothing rose to the level of tragedy. Not since—

"Oh, good God." He stumbled to the couch. "Did somebody go shoot up the post office?"

"No, nothing so crazy as that." Patrick stepped closer to him. "But as far as we're concerned, it's equally bad. Mr. Carter, tell me. Could anyone you know—for that matter, yourself, or Ms. McBride—be fairly characterized as having a grudge against Jared Barkley?"

CHAPTER 5

"Barkley?" Lehigh slipped back down the few steps he'd climbed and collapsed onto the couch. "You mean to tell me that somebody's gone and gunned down an acting sheriff?" His head weighed a ton, and his heart weighed twenty. He held his head up with both hands.

Sgt. Patrick made his way down the steps and slid his eyes sideways to catch Flynn's eye. "You catch that?"

Flynn nodded and glared at Lehigh.

"Catch what?" Lehigh fought dizziness, tried to get up from the couch but collapsed back onto it. "What are you getting at?"

"Do either you or Ms. McBride own a gun, Mr. Carter?" Patrick asked.

"Am I under investigation? Do I need a lawyer present?"

"Good question. Do you?" Patrick crossed his arms, leaned back on his heels. "Where do you keep your weapon?"

Lehigh scowled. "Is my gun on that search warrant?"

Patrick chuckled. "Didn't you read it?"

Lehigh's dizziness passed and he stood up from the couch. Standing put him less than a foot from Patrick's flushed face. "Look. I understand you guys being upset and wanting to do a thorough investigation and all. And I want to cooperate as best I can, but if I'm a subject—"

"We appreciate that, Mr. Carter." Patrick spread his hands. "Now if you'd just show us where you keep your weapons—"

"But if I'm under investigation—"

"Things will go much easier if you'll just cooperate."

"I'm going to need to have my lawyer present."

Both cops froze and visibly darkened.

"So that's the way you want to play it," Patrick said.

"Hiding behind a lawyer," Flynn said.

"I'm not 'playing' or 'hiding' anything. I just want my rights protected, is all. As you probably know, I've been through this wringer with you folks before. And I want to know where Stacy's at, and whether we—"

"I told you. Ms. McBride is downtown." Patrick put a hand on Lehigh's chest and pushed him back toward the couch. "And as for your rights, you have the right to sit down, shut up, and stay out of the way of our investigation. Or you can help us. Those are your choices."

"I appreciate the advice." Lehigh pushed Patrick's hand away and stood up again. "But I reckon I'd be better off taking advice from my lawyer in this situation." He stepped around Patrick, then Flynn, and headed into the kitchen. Flynn followed him as far as the doorway. Heavy footsteps, no doubt Sgt. Patrick's, trudged back up the stairs. Lehigh searched his stack of business cards piled next to the phone, pulled one out, and lifted the receiver. He glared at Flynn. "You mind? This is supposed to be a privileged conversation."

Flynn shrugged and ambled into the living room. Lehigh dialed the evenings-and-weekends emergency number on the card.

"This is Constantine Richards," said the attorney in his familiar monotone.

"Mr. Richards, it's Lehigh Carter. I need your help."

"If this is in regards to the Barkley investigation, I may not be able to help you," Richards said. "I'm already representing another defendant in the case."

"Another defendant? Seriously? Who?"

Richards coughed, a delicate sound commensurate with his patrician bearing. "Your fiancée, Stacy McBride."

Lehigh stumbled to a ladderback chair, leaned heavily onto

its back with his free hand, and dug his fingernails into the varnish. He pressed the phone against his ear. "Is Stacy...do they think..."

"She has not yet been formally charged," Richards said. "Nor, to my knowledge, has anyone else. The police brought her in for questioning since, according to their allegations, she may have been the last known person to see him alive. That point, however, is still very much in question."

"Stacy was with Jared Barkley?" Lehigh pulled the chair away from the kitchen table and collapsed into it, bouncing off the edge of the table on the way down. A vase full of fresh flowers tipped over and spilled dank-smelling water all over the table. He let it drip onto the floor.

Barkley's interest in Stacy had grown more overt in recent months, especially since her engagement to Lehigh. She remained coy about their past, if they'd even had one. Lehigh suspected that past existed mostly in Barkley's imagination, and perhaps Stacy's. She seemed to enjoy his attentions, but never mentioned spending any time with the man.

But Barkley's star had risen recently in the public's eye, first as a key player in breaking Cal-Tex Lumber's bribery of George McBride's campaign manager, Paul van Paten, who also happened to be Stacy's fiancé at the time. The County Commissioners tapped Barkley to serve as acting sheriff after he exposed the complicity of his predecessor, Dallas "Buck" Summers, in covering up Paul's role in the arson of Lehigh's house. The public loved a giant killer, and Barkley had two notches in that particular gun barrel—on top of a squeaky clean record and a reputation for courage and integrity.

And on top of it all, the guy had chiseled good looks. Not movie star quality, but definitely the envy of most guys in Clarkesville.

"The police allege that they were seen together late Saturday evening," Richards said. "The veracity of that report has yet to be—excuse me a moment." A beep sounded in the receiver, then the line went mute.

Lehigh arched his back and cracked his neck. His head

pounded. Bad enough that Stacy went out with Barkley behind Lehigh's back. But him turning up dead—that complicated things on so many levels.

Lehigh refused to believe that Stacy killed Jared. She didn't have it in her. On the other hand, given the way she'd flirted with him recently, whoever did it may have done Lehigh a favor.

Not a healthy way to think right at that moment. He shook himself loose and recognized the remorse he felt over Barkley's passing. He never knew Jared well, but—other than Stacy's recent behavior, and now this—he never had any reason to dislike the man.

"I'm sorry." Richards' voice returned without warning. "The interrogation appears to be resuming. I'll need to go now. If you still need representation, please call my office in the morning and I'll refer you to reputable counsel."

"In the morning? As in tomorrow? Hell, I need a lawyer right now, dammit! I have cops crawling all over the house, making a damned mess!"

"Excuse me. Did you say they were at Ms. McBride's home now?" Richards sounded upset. "Why didn't you say something sooner? I'll send an associate over right away."

Constantine Richards' "right away" didn't match Lehigh's definition of the term. Lehigh spent the better part of an hour tossing a tennis ball for the dogs, hoping to wear them out before his lawyer arrived, but only succeeded in exhausting his throwing arm instead. Just as the dogs appeared ready to surrender, Deputy Flynn appeared inside the storm door, his hand on the knob. Lucky leaped high in the air outside the door, growling, teeth gnashing, with Diamond jumping around her in confused excitement.

"Get your dogs off me, Carter!" Flynn yelled, backing away from the door.

"Sorry, can't do much about it," Lehigh said, laughing. "Lucky here hates guns, attacks anyone carrying. It's liable to get her killed someday." He crossed his arms and watched the dogs exhaust themselves further, jumping higher unassisted than Lehigh could have with a trampoline.

"I need to check the backyard," Flynn said, waving the warrant.

"Suit yourself," Lehigh said. "All you're gonna find is some unscooped poop. You might want to watch where you step." He strolled to the side of the house, toward the gate.

"Where the hell are you going? Aren't you going to corral these dogs?" Flynn yelled from inside the house.

Lehigh laughed again, then whistled for the dogs. They gave up their harassment of the cop and chased after Lehigh to his truck. He lowered the windows and shared a few biscuits from his glove box. "Good dogs," he said in a soothing voice. "I don't trust those boys neither."

Constantine Richards' junior legal associate pulled up in his red Mercedes a half hour later. By that time, the two deputies—now joined by a pair of plainclothes detectives who'd driven down from Hood River—had turned Stacy's house and yard inside out and upside down. It looked like it'd take weeks to put the place back in order.

"I'm almost thankful my enemies chose arson," Lehigh said with a snarl at Deputy Flynn as they all gathered in the living room. "It's cleaner."

Richards' associate, a roly-poly, oily-skinned man named Farber, could have passed for a teenager. Dressed in a mismatched suit jacket and slacks, he wasted a good ten minutes ranting at each of the policemen participating in the search, then handed Lehigh a card. "We'll need to depose you," he said. "Ms. McBride says you can vouch for her."

"I bet she did." Lehigh scowled and calculated what this idiot had already cost them at two hundred fifty dollars an hour. "I might want to talk to her first, see what's what."

The young man shook his dark mop from side to side. "Best if we don't. We can't let her influence your statement. That could render it suspect in court, and—"

Lehigh rubbed his face with both hands. "Has Stacy been charged with anything?"

Farber bunched up his lips and narrowed his bulging eyes to slits. "That's privileged information."

Lehigh rose from the sofa. "Privileged from whom? If she's been arrested and charged with anything, it'll be in the damned newspapers tomorrow clear to Medford."

"Well." Farber picked lint off his paisley tie. No Constantine Richards, this one. "If and when it gets to that point, I'm sure Ms. McBride will bring you up to speed."

"Look, Farber. Stacy's my fiancée. Don't you think she'd want me to know what's up with her? If I didn't have these gray-suited monkeys tearing up our upholstery right now, I'd have been down to the station two hours ago. She's not answering her phone, nobody'll tell me squat about what's going on, and my own lawyer won't even speak to me. I wouldn't even have you here if the Keystone Kops weren't crawling all over my furniture. What do I gotta to do find some answers?"

"Got it! Found it!" someone yelled from upstairs. One of the plainclothes detectives dashed out of the kitchen and up the stairs.

"Dust it and bag it!" a second voice yelled.

"Check to see if it's loaded," another voice shouted.

"What the...?" Lehigh started up the stairs. One of the detectives met him halfway, coming down.

"Mr. Carter," the detective said, "you said you had only the one firearm, and it was with you this entire weekend?"

Lehigh nodded. "That's right. A Smith and Wesson .22 revolver. I showed it to your partner. Why?"

The detective smiled like a garter snake. "So any other weapon we find here would have to belong to Ms. McBride, then, correct?"

"Don't answer that," Farber said.

Lehigh shrugged. "So, I guess I've got an attorney present."

The detective's grin widened. "Good thing. I think you're going to need one."

CHAPTER 6

Stacy's back ached. Those stupid undersized wooden chairs in the interrogation room should be banned, if not burned. Making her sit in one for over three hours amounted to police brutality.

"I've told you a thousand times," she said to the graying, round-shouldered detective who'd spent the last hour with her. "Jared and I were friends. Not enemies. Not lovers. Just friends. We've known each other, but not real well, since high school."

"Well enough for him to buy your dinner on a Saturday night while your fiancé was out of town," said Detective "Gentleman Jim" Wadsworth. A frumpy, graying man in his forties, he'd long since surrendered the battle of the waistline, and another loss, the battle of the hairline, followed close behind.

Stacy grimaced and turned to her left toward Constantine Richards, a well-dressed, grey-haired man with perfect posture despite his stout build. "Mr. Richards, can't you make them stop saying that?" she asked. "Isn't there some sort of no-harassment rule? This is freaking torture."

Richards folded his hands and faced her tormenters. "My client has explained her relationship with the deceased to the fullest extent imaginable," he said. "She has, against my advice as her attorney, answered every one of your questions several times over. If you have nothing new to ask, perhaps our interview is over."

"She hasn't convinced me," Wadsworth said. "I'm still confused."

Stacy snorted. "Sounds like a permanent condition."

Richards placed a hand on her arm and gave her a tiny shake of his head. Turning back to the policeman, he said, "Your confusion is not my client's problem. Ms. McBride has the right to refrain from answering any of your questions, which will be her decision henceforth in response to any further haranguing. If you have anything new to ask, perhaps…"

"I still haven't gotten an answer to this question," Wadsworth said. "Did your fiancé, Lehigh Carter, know about your dinner with Jared Barkley? Did he know you were seeing him?"

"I wasn't *seeing* him!" Stacy said. "Why do you keep saying that?"

"The dinner, Ms. McBride. Did he know about the dinner?"

Stacy glanced at Richards. He took the cue. "My client chooses not to answer that question."

Wadsworth growled. "Hiding behind the Fifth Amendment won't help you with us, ma'am."

"I'm not hiding!" Stacy slapped the table in front of her, banging her elbow in the process. The chair they'd set her in must have been sized for a third grader. "I've been answering your stupid questions for hours. I've told you too much, if anything."

Richards nodded. "Besides, gentlemen. Any first-year law student would know, if you want to find out what Mr. Carter did or didn't know, you'd be far better off asking him. My client's assertions of what another person knows or doesn't know are not admissible evidence in any court."

"Well, we aren't lawyers, thank God," Wadsworth said. "Our job is to find the perpetrator. You lawyers can argue the technicalities. Now, Ms. McBride—"

"Is done answering your stupid questions." Stacy crossed

her arms and glared at the detectives in turn. "You know everything I know."

"I doubt that." Wadsworth smiled. "For instance, there are the phone records we haven't even discussed yet."

"What phone records?" Stacy bolted upright in her chair and faced her attorney. "Can they do that without my consent?"

Richards cleared his throat. "We would be most concerned if we were to discover Ms. McBride's privacy has been violated without due process. We have not consented to, nor received a warrant for, any such search."

"Relax." Wadsworth settled his bulk into a chair as tiny as Stacy's with an audible grunt. "We're not asking about your phone records. What we'd like to know is why you show up so often in the deceased's cell phone call history. Seven times in the ten days prior to his death."

Richards coughed into his fist. "I recommend you do not answer that."

Tightness gripped Stacy's throat. "So? I can't stop him from calling me."

Wadsworth's eyes narrowed. "No, but only four of those calls were outgoing—from him to you. Three were return calls, from you to him. Not exactly a sign of him pestering you with unwanted calls."

Stacy's clothes stuck to her skin when she tried to adjust her position in her uncomfortable chair. Her ears burned like fire. "So, I returned his calls. It's only polite." Richards held up his hand to silence her.

"Interesting point, and a possible explanation for some of the calls." Wadsworth cleaned a fingernail with a disposable pen cap. "But the first call came from you—before he called you." He lifted his heavy eyelids to gaze at her. "Seems to me, Sheriff Barkley wasn't chasing you. From the looks of things, you were chasing him."

Stacy clenched her eyes shut. Oh, this was bad.

CHAPTER 7

Lehigh smacked the double glass doors of the police station with flat palms, expecting them to swish open. Instead they shuddered back at him with a loud vibrating rattle. Only then did he notice the large white letters over the metal handles: "PULL." He yanked the door wide and strode up to the desk.

Dwayne Latner stood behind the counter, all six foot four, hundred and seventy pounds of him. Lehigh had seen thicker linguini at one of Senator McBride's Sunday dinners. "Can I help you?" Latner asked without making eye contact.

"Hey, Dwayne. I'm told Stacy's here with our lawyer." He refused to concede the loss of Constantine Richards' representation just yet.

"B'lieve so." Latner blinked, stepped back. Blinked again.

Lehigh leaned over the counter. "You want to tell me which room, or do I have to guess?"

Latner shook his head. "Won't make no difference, Mr. Carter. Can't let you in there while the interrogation's going on."

"For heaven's sake, Dwayne. She's been here five or six hours. Even Stacy can't talk that long." He strutted toward a pair of swinging doors. "Forget it. I'll find her myself."

"I can't let you through there." Latner beat Lehigh to the doors and stretched his long arms across them. "You'd best just wait here. Or go on home. We'll call you when she's released."

"Move it, Dwayne, or I'll take you out just like I used to do in football practice."

Latner's eyes widened and he seemed to choke. He cleared his throat. "Now, Lehigh, this ain't high school no more. I'm an officer of the law now. You can't—"

Latner's body slammed into the double doors and fell to the tiled floor beyond. Lehigh stepped over him and held up a foot to stop the doors from clocking the deputy's head on their return path.

"You never could take a block." Lehigh smiled and strolled down the hall, leaving Latner dazed and sandwiched between the heavy swinging doors.

He knew the layout well enough. Too well, in fact. A few months before, the police had locked him in an interrogation room, questioning him as a suspect in the arson of his own home, among other things. He hung a quick right, then a left, and passed a half-dozen identical doorways down the drab hallway.

Stacy's voice crept out of one of the rooms long before he reached it. She burst through the door, Constantine Richards in tow, some twenty feet ahead of Lehigh, her head turned toward her attorney. "And I want those idiots sued for invasion of my privacy, unlawful detention, improper conduct, and anything else you can think of." She faced forward again and stopped in her tracks. "Lehigh! What are you doing here?"

"I might ask you the same quest—oof!" All air left his lungs in the wake of Stacy crashing into him, spinning him around, and enveloping him in a vice-like hug. Her lips covered his, making it impossible to draw a decent breath to replenish his lungs. He placed his hands on her shoulders to push her away, then dropped them down her backside. If the price of getting smothered in kisses by a beautiful woman was asphyxiation, well then, he'd just have to suffer.

***

He drove her to Constantine Richards' office to pick up her car. They held hands the entire time, their fingers interlocked in the center of the truck's bench seat.

"We need to talk," he said after a bit.

"Uh huh." She squeezed his hand. "I didn't do it, Lehigh. I hope you—"

"Of course not." He flashed her a reassuring smile. "But I have a lot of questions. Why they'd even *think* you had anything to do with it. They said you'd been out with Jared—"

"Did you feed the dogs this morning?" she asked.

"Uh…I thought you did." He sighed, noted the change of subject.

"I never had the chance," she said. "The cops came by before dawn, threatening to arrest me if I didn't agree to come in for questioning. I didn't shower, eat breakfast, nothing."

"Looks like it's unanimous." Lehigh freed his hand for a moment to make a sharp turn. "Let's go take care of that, shall we? It's not quite two. Dot's will still be open, we can talk there."

"Ugh." Stacy screwed up her face, like she wanted to puke. "I'd rather starve. How about Shirley's?" She blinked at him—long, slow winks loaded with suggestion.

He grinned. "Like our first date."

"And our second first date, back in October." Her fingernails tickled his wrist. "But I think for dessert, we ought to skip the pie and go straight home."

He chuckled. "Hell, I'm fine with skipping breakfast and going straight to dessert. Don't tell Maw that, though—oh, hell!" He pounded the wheel. "Dang it, dammit, son of a bitch!"

"What?" Stacy squeezed his hand between her fingers. "What's the matter?"

He exhaled a burst of noisy air between his lips. "I clean forgot about going to Pappy and Maw's this morning for breakfast. Well, brunch. Hell, I'm four hours late now."

"They didn't call you?"

Lehigh curled an eyebrow at her. "When have you ever known Pappy or Maw to initiate a phone call?"

"Well, can't we go now and explain? I mean, it's not like we had a choice in the matter." She kissed his hand. "I do appreciate your coming to pick me up. It's so sweet of you."

"I wouldn't have been able to live with myself if I hadn't. Anyway, we're here." He turned into the lawyer's parking lot. "I'll call them in a minute. Where should we meet, then?"

She kissed him, hard. "Home. Right after you apologize to Pappy." She kissed him again, long and slow this time, and winked. "I'll be showered and scantily dressed. So…don't take too long. And after that, then, yes. Let's talk."

He smiled, noted the promise, and made a mental note to get back to that later. That was important, the talking part.

But then again, he never was much good at remembering to initiate a conversation.

***

Lehigh skidded to a stop at the end of Pappy and Maw's long gravel driveway. He pulled the keys from the ignition before the car's wipers could return to their home position at the bottom of the windshield, jumped out of the car, and hustled up the flagstone walk toward his parents' wrap-around porch. Rain splashed on his bare head, dripped in uneven rivers down the scraggly stubble of his unshaven face.

Pappy emerged from the dark house before Lehigh could reach the broad paint-chipped steps. "Best not come in, son. You know how Maw feels about people being late. 'Specially you." His flannel shirt and stained white bib overalls hung like loose laundry over his wiry body, and his wispy white hair danced in the breeze.

Lehigh paused with one foot on the bottom step. The board creaked beneath his weight. He'd meant to fix that for them—the nails had shaken loose due to dry rot. Without attention, soon the whole set of steps would need replacing.

"Pappy, I'm so sorry. This morning's been crazy. You wouldn't believe—"

"Got *that* damn straight." Pappy spit over the porch rail and fished a hand-rolled cigarette out of his shirt pocket. He lit it and tossed the match into the wet grass, joining several dozen others. "So don't waste your breath with one of your cockamamie stories."

"Just listen to me for one second."

"Did you hear what I just said?" Pappy blew smoke toward him, then leaned against the square white column connecting the rail to the porch's ceiling. "Where's that gal of yours? The skinny one with black hair. Thought she was coming too. 'Course, we *was* expecting you some five, six hours ago."

"That's what I'm trying to tell you. Stacy's been down at the sheriff's office answering questions all morning. I just came from there myself."

"What the hell trouble you in *now*?" Pappy inhaled again, and blew smoke out of his nostrils. "Maybe you don't need no new house after all. Seems like maybe you two ought to just live down there with the lawmen." He shook his head. "Don't understand where we went wrong with you, boy."

"Who's out there?" Maw's rail-thin frame appeared at the screen door, wearing a print knee length housedress and red fuzzy slippers. Her grey hair, as usual, looked like she'd just survived a hurricane. "Our so-called son finally showed up? The selfish one that don't know how to tell time?" She banged the door open and shook a flat spatula at Lehigh, who backed away a step. "I swear you look for new ways to aggravate me every damned day."

"Go on inside, Maw," Pappy said without looking at her. "I'll handle it."

"I knew we couldn't count on that good for nothing kid," she said, louder. "You been nothing but trouble your whole damned life, you hear me? Thinks of nobody except himself!"

Lehigh scuffed the grass with his boot, burying a few of Pappy's cigarette butts in the sandy soil. "Yeah, I know, Maw. I try, but—"

"You *try*." She gazed past him. "Where's that so-called woman of yours? Too good to show up, even late? Selfish, stuck-up, thinks her money buys her respect. Well it don't do her no good around here!"

"That's what I've been trying to tell you." Lehigh edged forward and placed his foot back on the bottom step. A flume of Pappy's smoke stopped him from climbing farther. "See, I had some meetings in Portland yesterday—"

"Always an excuse." Maw waved her spatula like a windshield wiper in front of her face. "Well, you can forget about your breakfast. I fed it to the raccoons."

Lehigh sighed. His rumbling stomach tempted him to see if the animals had left any of Maw's amazing cornmeal marionberry pancakes behind. "Well then, why don't we try again for next week? By then, things will have settled down, and—"

"Next week? Why not next year?" Maw slashed the spatula at him like an angry orchestra conductor. "I'm telling you, boy-o, you're on thin ice now. Very thin ice. I don't know how you got like this. Your brother sure never did this to me."

Lehigh's head jerked back like he'd been slapped. "My brother? Maw...oh, Maw." His stomach twisted into a tight knot. Maw's lucidity slipped in and out, and the made-up stories of his older brother, who died at three years old when Lehigh had just learned to walk, signaled a whole new phase of senile confusion.

"That's right." Maw stepped closer, almost to Pappy's side now. Pappy spread an arm to block her progress. "Augie never once disrespected me. Always such a good, kind boy. Always thought of others first. But you—you're nothing but trouble. Think of nothing except yourself."

Lehigh opened his mouth to speak, but a subtle shake of Pappy's head stopped him. He wiped his brow, took a step back, spit on the ground. Damn, damn. So that's why Pappy had warned him away. Pappy tried to hide Maw's worsening condition from the world, even from Lehigh, who'd picked up on it years before Pappy did. But her downward spiral—or, rather, her roller coaster ride between clarity and confusion, accompanied respectively by good natured curmudgeonliness and blind childlike rage—seemed to have deepened and accelerated in recent months.

Or, Pappy had succeeded in hiding her condition from Lehigh's distracted mind.

"Well, I'm sorry about this morning." He stepped back onto the grass and kept his eyes locked on Pappy's. "I reckon we ought to be the ones who host next time, to make it up to you. Maybe dinner this week?"

"I ain't going into no city for no dinner!" Maw scrambled around Pappy and perched on the top step, halted by her husband's hand on her shoulder. "You just get on home and think about how to show your elders some respect. Maybe ask your *brother*."

Lehigh shot Pappy a final glance and headed toward his truck.

Maw's raised voice followed him. "And don't come back 'round here until you do!"

Lehigh drove away, wondering what else could go wrong.

CHAPTER 8

"You're saying you found a gun at her house?" Former Sheriff Dallas "Buck" Summers grinned wider than the canyons striping the east slopes of Mt. Hood, visible through the windows of his office. "My, my. What a *coincidence.*"

"Is it registered?" Assistant District Attorney Ray Ferguson, dressed in a black suit and wearing the jacket even after five on a Monday evening, avoided eye contact with Buck. The less he knew about their investigatory practices, the better.

"No, sir," Sergeant Cam Patrick said. "It was reported stolen a few months ago. It was bought at—"

"You're still checking into that, aren't you?" Buck's grin hardened into more of a warning frown. He cocked his head toward Sergeant Patrick in a manner that brooked no disagreement.

"Y—yes, we are," Patrick said. "We ought to know pretty soon, though."

"Ballistics is analyzing it now to see if it's a match," Buck said, "but I fully expect it will be."

"And you think that because..."

"Same caliber, recently fired, and they had it hidden, right, Cam?"

The sergeant nodded. "Mr. Carter claims he had never seen it before. I think he was lying."

"'Course he was," Buck said.

"How do you know so much about this already?" Ferguson asked the former sheriff. "Were you on the scene?"

"I, uh, got a briefing earlier," Buck said, giving Sergeant Patrick an exaggerated nod. Patrick returned it, but with less certainty.

"So, what do we think, then?" the prosecutor said. "His, hers, or both?"

"Well," Buck said. "I ain't never seen a handgun been fired by two people at once. Personally I think they was working together. But as to which one pulled the trigger...we, uh, don't know enough. Yet."

"Well, then," Ferguson said, "we need to find out."

***

Late next morning, Lucky and Diamond erupted from their deep slumber into a crazed cacophony of barking, yipping, and running to and fro, destroying Lehigh's concentration. Moments later, tires kicked up gravel outside Lehigh's makeshift office, essentially a spare bedroom with an old computer resting on a second-hand desk Stacy overpaid ten bucks for at a garage sale. Lehigh swiveled in his chair—a cast-off remnant of an otherwise extinct dining set—expecting to see Stacy's car pulling in. She often liked to make excuses to come home for an early lunch, which often included luring Lehigh into the bedroom for what he preferred to call "dessert."

But to his chagrin, a black and white sheriff's deputy's vehicle occupied Stacy's preferred parking spot, closest to the house. A familiar-looking uniformed deputy about six feet tall with an athletic build and close-cropped sandy-colored hair got out on the driver's side. Lehigh recognized him as Joe Flynn from the prior day's search. A tall, balding man in a black suit exited the other side. Lehigh knew him only from newspaper stories: Raymond P. Ferguson, Assistant District Attorney for Mt. Hood County. He'd earned a derisive nickname, "The Reverend," for his tendency to cite Bible verse and preach homilies like an Evangelical minister to juries during closing arguments.

Then came the worst sight of all.

The back door of the cruiser opened, and out stepped a hulking figure wearing cheap aviator sunglasses, baggy navy slacks, and a camel-colored jacket: the recently disgraced, now-former Sheriff Buck Summers.

Lehigh groaned. Summers had it in for him, especially since the lawman's exposed involvement in the cover-up of the arson scandal that cost Lehigh his house and forestry business. Buck had destroyed, misplaced, and fabricated evidence to divert attention from Paul van Paten, now awaiting trial on corruption charges sustained while managing the finances of former gubernatorial candidate George McBride, Lehigh's future father-in-law. For that Buck had earned the right to resign as sheriff after fourteen years, two years before he'd reached full retirement, with twenty-eight years total service to the county.

Considering the drizzle that had been falling since bedtime, Lehigh considered leaving the dogs inside, but Lucky had already attacked a man once that she had, rightly, considered a threat. Since at least Flynn carried a weapon, that would just about guarantee that she'd go at least a little crazy. Instead he put the dogs in the backyard with fresh bones and water, and resigned himself to cleaning up their muddy mess after the three men left.

After another sharp triple-rap on the heavy wooden front door, he hurried to greet his unwelcome guests. He considered trying to fake being gone but decided against it. Pissing them off could only make a bad situation worse.

The triple-rap sounded again moments later when Lehigh reached for the door handle. He flung the door open wide toward him.

"What can I do for you guys?" Cold damp air rushed in and chilled his bare arms. Stacy liked to keep the house warm, so Lehigh rarely wore anything bulkier than T-shirts and jeans at home.

"May we come in, Mr. Carter?" Ferguson asked. The twenty-something uniformed cop standing next to the prosecutor stood at attention, as ramrod straight as the hair in his crew cut. Buck shifted his considerable weight back and forth behind them.

"Depends," Lehigh said. "You plan on staying long?"

"We have a few questions." Ferguson offered a crumpling smile that screamed insincerity. "Should only take a couple of minutes."

"In that case, why don't we talk right here?" Lehigh returned the fake smile and pushed the door halfway closed. "No sense you all having to take off your shoes and coats for such a short visit."

Deputy Flynn jammed his foot into the hinged side and pressed the door open one-handed without the slightest change of expression.

"I think we'd all be more comfortable inside," Buck said. "Maybe at your kitchen table, with a cup of coffee?"

"Is this a social call, Buck?" Lehigh let go of the door but maintained a spread-legged stance blocking the doorway. "If so, I'll have to check my calendar, see when I'm free. Maybe next October sometime, after your trial's over."

Buck's face turned pink, then red, then violet. Blue veins pulsed at graying temples. "Mark my words. There ain't gonna be no such trial. Bunch of bullcrap. And no, to answer your question, this is not a social call. I'm assisting the county on official business."

"Sheriff Summers has been hired on as a 'special consultant' to assist our investigation on the Jared Barkley case," Ferguson said. "Due to his, uh, knowledge and expertise."

Lehigh's jaw hit his chest. "Even though he's under investigation for obstruction of justice?"

"Innocent until proven guilty," Buck said through gritted teeth. "I ain't been indicted yet."

"Well, congratulations on the new job, Buck," Lehigh said. "I'll be sure to send you a card. But you didn't have to come all the way out here to deliver that news in person. Next time, just give me a call." Again he attempted to close the door. Again, Flynn prevented it.

"Like I said," Ferguson said, blowing into his cupped hands, "we have a few questions."

"About…?"

"About where you were this weekend—"

"Portland."

"And who you were with—"

"Potential clients. I'll send you a list."

"When you returned—"

"Sunday morning. Really, I've been over this with your investigators. Ruined my whole Sunday."

Ferguson cleared his throat and shifted his weight from foot to foot. "We'd like to go over it in a bit more detail…inside, if we could."

Lehigh crossed his arms. "Sounds like I might want my lawyer present."

Buck pushed between the prosecutor and Flynn and pointed a chubby finger into Lehigh's face. "Don't go getting all legalistic on us, Carter." Spittle flew from his chapped, nicotine-stained lips. "You don't need no lawyer. Unless you got something to hide."

Lehigh shook his head. "Sorry, Buck, no go. Either my lawyer sits in or you boys sit it out. I learned my lesson with you bozos last time."

Flynn's eyes widened and his flat nose flared wide. He edged forward, but Ferguson waved him back.

"If it's all the same to you, Mr. Carter…I'd always heard you were a civil, hospitable man, and you know, this sort of thing often gets taken into consideration during, uh…well, future *legalities* that may transpire." His expression darkened. Nothing about this man was subtle. But he did have the power to make good on his clumsy threats.

"If I let you in," Lehigh said, "it's only out of courtesy. I don't want you snooping around in here."

Buck snorted. "What you want us to do, keep our eyes shut? What are you trying to hide in there, anyhow?"

Ferguson pulled Buck aside and mumbled something in his ear. Buck shook his head and grimaced, but he stepped back behind Ferguson and shoved his hands in his pockets. A light drizzle dampened his hat and shoulders.

Ferguson smiled at Lehigh. "I'm perfectly comfortable with waiting for your attorney. But it sure would be a whole lot warmer inside." He shivered, and the deputy next to him did the same.

Lehigh scowled. He couldn't trust these guys. But no sense pissing them off. "Fine. You boys want some hot coffee?"

Buck's face split into a wide grin. "*Now* you're talking!"

The three cops took seats in the living room, filling the sofa and recliner with their massive collective bulk. Lehigh called Constantine Richards' office from the landline in the kitchen.

"Dammit, either you get over here or I'll get someone else," Lehigh said when Richards made excuses again. "No more greenhorn teenagers like last time. I don't see why Stacy gets dibs on your services when you were *my* lawyer first."

"We'll send a trusted colleague," Richards said. "My secretary will make some calls. It may take some time."

"Forget it," Lehigh said. "I know how to use the yellow pages as well as she does, and it won't cost me two hundred bucks an hour." He called the first attorney that came up with a four star rating on Yelp.

"We'll send our top attorney, right away," the man at Cascade Legal said after asking a few questions. "Expect Sam within the hour."

Lehigh hung up and filled the coffee carafe in the sink. He'd just filled the basket of the coffee maker with grounds when a pudgy hand grabbed his shoulder, spun him around, and pressed him backwards into the counter. The rank aroma of stale tobacco invaded his senses, and a wide expanse of beige khaki and ruddy flesh obstructed his view.

"You and me," Buck Summers said with a sneer, "we need to talk."

CHAPTER 9

Buck's considerable bulk closed to near-touching distance from Lehigh's chest.

"We'll talk," Lehigh said, "as soon as my lawyer arrives." He wiggled free, turned back toward the coffeemaker, and hit the "on" button. Buck spun him back around again.

"I mean *now*. Off the record." Behind Buck, Ferguson mumbled something to Deputy Flynn, who nodded and left the room. A moment later, the front door opened and slammed shut.

Lehigh shook his head. "I ain't saying nothing until—"

"I don't want *you* talking, Carter. I want you listening." Buck pulled a ladderback chair from the kitchen table and set it in the middle of the room. "Sit down."

Lehigh crossed his arms and leaned back against the wall. The last thing he wanted was big Buck Summers towering over him and delivering a lecture. "I'm comfortable standing."

"I said *sit!*" Buck grabbed him by the arms, but Lehigh shook him off. Eyes wide, nose flaring, Buck reached into his jacket and pulled out a dark cylinder resembling a long flashlight. On the end where the light belonged, four pointy probes extended outward.

Lehigh scowled. "Really, Buck? You gonna tase me if I refuse to sit?"

Ferguson stepped between them, arms extended, pushing them apart. "I think we'd all be more comfortable if we sat," he said. "Maybe in the living room?"

Buck snarled and pressed a button on his Taser. A low buzzing sound filled the room. "I say Carter sits. Now!" The Taser neared Lehigh's midsection. Lehigh tried to wiggle away, but he had nowhere to go.

BRA-AA-AP! A loud crackling sound echoed off the walls. Lehigh sucked in a quick breath, expecting pain to spread throughout his body, but none came. He opened his clenched eyes to discover an ugly grin splitting Buck's ruddy face.

Laughter accompanied the grin. "You pathetic little chicken." Buck spat. By some miracle his effluent landed in the sink. "I didn't even touch you and you practically crapped your pants. How do you think you're gonna hold up when I actually use it on you? Huh? Now, sit, boy!" He waved the device at Lehigh.

"Okay, Buck. I'll sit." Lehigh held up his hands in surrender and edged his way around Buck to the chair. Ferguson stood behind him somewhere, and Buck lumbered around in front.

"Now you listen to me, you little punk." Buck leaned over until his nose hovered inches from Lehigh's. The acrid aroma of stale chew polluted the air entering Lehigh's nostrils. "Let's get a few things straight. A man is dead. A good man, which is a lot more than I can say about you."

Tiny droplets of spittle stung Lehigh's eye. He blinked a few times to wash it clean.

Buck's jaw worked a wad of tobacco somewhere inside his gaping yaw. "That man wore a badge like this one." He tapped the spot on his chest where his sheriff's star used to rest. Buck sneered, daring Lehigh to comment, but for a change, Lehigh held his tongue.

"We who serve the cause of law and order in this county aim to find the man—or woman—who killed him. And we plan to put the killer into a chair." Another sneer. "But not a nice comfy chair like this one. We're talking a very specialized chair, Carter. One that plugs in to five thousand volts and shakes your bones for thirty-five seconds. You hear me?"

Lehigh cleared his throat. "I believe the preferred method

of execution in Oregon is lethal injection, Buck. Which ain't happened since—"

"Don't be a smartass!"

Tobacco-laced spittle covered Lehigh's face. Lehigh let it go this time.

Buck chewed with angry vigor, rested his broad boot on the edge of Lehigh's seat, and set his hands on Lehigh's shoulders. "Now, I know one of you pulled the trigger, Carter. You or your girlfriend. And the other one's just as guilty. You both hated him, and nobody else had a motive."

"Buck, I—"

"*Shut! Up!*" Buck shoved Lehigh by the shoulders and pushed the seat with his foot. Lehigh's chair skidded backward, ramming into the counter. His head snapped back, rapping the countertop. Pain ran down his neck.

Buck stepped toward him. "Now I aim to prove you done it. And I know I can. But I also know that you and your fancy lawyers have ways of getting you off on technicalities. So let me just warn you right now, off the record. If you try any of that techno-legalistic crap—if you and your girlfriend somehow walk free after all this—I guarantee you, Carter. The people of this county will have their revenge. For you, and your pretty little girlfriend. Are we clear?"

Lehigh wiped the spittle off his face and found Ferguson, arms crossed, leaning against the wall a few feet away. "I take it you're in agreement with the former sheriff," he said. Ferguson's eyes narrowed and his lips curled into a tight smile. Lehigh brushed off his jeans, taking his time. "Well, I see. So, even if I prove both of us innocent—"

"You can't because you ain't." Buck pointed a finger in Lehigh's face. "And just to make sure you understand how serious we are, remember this. We're keeping cells at the jail empty for the two of you. *Separate* cells."

"I'm crushed, Buck. No honeymoon suite?"

A mean growl erupted from somewhere deep inside Buck's considerable gut. He squeezed Lehigh's face in his hands. "I'm warning you, Carter. If you so much as jaywalk, if you so much as fish without a license, if you so much as use the wrong postage on a piece of third-class mail, you're gonna find yourself behind bars with no hope of ever seeing daylight again. And we got some rough boys locked up in that jail. A pretty boy like you might not last too long in there. You understand?"

Buck forced Lehigh's head to nod. Lehigh decided not to resist.

"And remember. If you try anything stupid, like leaving the county or messing with our investigation...well, we might just have to *assume* that pretty little girlfriend of yours is the guilty one. Understand me, Carter?"

Lehigh answered in a low, level voice. "I understand, Buck."

"Good." A relaxed grin spread over Buck's face, and he stepped back a foot or two. "Now, how's about that coffee?"

***

Lehigh had just served the three men a second cup of coffee when a dark gray Lexus sedan pulled up behind the police cruiser. He answered the knock on the door a moment after it sounded. He swung the door open wide to meet the man who would represent him—

And stared open-mouthed at the blondest, prettiest woman he'd ever seen wearing a suit, standing on his doorstep.

Part 2

Surprise Suspect

CHAPTER 10

"Mr. Carter?" the blonde woman said. "I'm Samantha Pullen with Cascade Legal. Please call me Sam." She extended her hand, a fragile wisp of bones in pale, delicate skin. She enveloped Lehigh's hand in both of hers and held on a moment or two too long.

"Come in." He tried to say more, but no words would come. All the blood seemed to have left his brain, or at least the part that controlled speech.

The other men stood when she entered. Ferguson and Summers exchanged knowing glances.

"Gentlemen, this is my attorney, Samantha—"

"We've met," Ferguson said with a growl. "Morning, Counselor."

"Mr. Ferguson. Mr. Summers. I don't believe I've met Deputy…Flynn, is it?" She stepped over to the uniformed cop and extended a hand. Flynn gave it a quick, formal shake, and stared at her lithe, well-proportioned figure a little too long— long enough to earn a glare in return. He stepped back, his face reddening.

"Coffee, Ms. Pullen?" Lehigh suppressed a smirk at Flynn's discomfort. Stacy often responded to similar treatment with less diplomacy than Pullen showed them. Then again, Stacy didn't have to work around cops all of the time.

"Please. A touch of milk, no sugar." Pullen flashed him a juror-wowing smile. Lehigh stared at her a moment, almost hypnotized. He broke away and stumbled into the kitchen to fetch her coffee.

When he returned to the living room, his new attorney had taken a seat on an ottoman next to his vacant rocking chair and rested her briefcase on her lap. The black leather case blended into the pitch-hued skirt that extended a few inches below her knees. She sat at a right angle to the sofa occupied by Summers and Ferguson. Deputy Flynn stood at attention by the front door, his gaze most decidedly averted from her legs—unlike his more senior compatriots.

Sam accepted the coffee with a polite smile. "Gentlemen, let's set some ground rules," she said. "All questions shall be addressed to my client, Mr. Carter. He will answer any question he likes, after conferring with me—or refuse to answer, which is his constitutional right."

"I knew it," Summers said. "We're wasting our time here if he's just gonna take the nickel defense."

"Nickel defense?" Lehigh sat in the rocker.

"He means your Fifth Amendment right not to answer questions that could incriminate you," Sam said. "But since they haven't charged you with anything, or even explained the purpose of their visit, they will no doubt appreciate our reticence. Won't you, gentlemen?"

Summers and Ferguson shrugged. Sam adjusted her sitting position, and their idiotic gazes followed.

"Let's start with that. Why *are* you here, Mr. Ferguson?" Pullen clicked a pen and jotted the date and time on a legal pad, using her briefcase as a lap desk.

"We, ah, have some questions pertaining to Mr. Carter's whereabouts this past weekend," Ferguson said in a hesitant monotone.

"Are these questions pertinent to a particular case under investigation?"

Ferguson sipped his coffee. "The homicide of Sheriff—er, *Acting* Sheriff Jared Barkley."

Buck's grimace eased into an easy smile. "Just some clarifying questions."

"Is my client a subject of the investigation?"

Buck glanced at Ferguson. The prosecutor hesitated, then surrendered a curt nod. "Potentially," he said.

"May I ask who is in charge of this investigation?" Sam's gaze remained fixed on her notepad.

"Detective Wadsworth is," Buck said.

"And he isn't here because...?"

"He, er, couldn't be here today, but we are coordinating our efforts," Ferguson said.

Pullen glared at Buck. Impatience crept into her voice. "What, then, would your role be?"

"The former sheriff is a kind of consultant on the case." Ferguson's voice trailed off under Samantha's hot stare.

"Deputized?"

"Not officially," Buck said.

Sam turned her body to face Ferguson. "Mr. Ferguson, far be it from me to tell you how to do your job. But if you want maximum participation from my client to help you solve this case, you might consider assigning *consultants* who don't have a prior history of bias and hostility toward Mr. Carter."

"Bias? Why, you cheap ambulance chaser!" Buck struggled to his feet.

Sam rose faster and, with a hand pressed onto his large head, pushed him back onto the sofa. "*Mister* Summers, please. There's no need to insult everyone in the room." She flashed him a dimpled smile, as if she'd just cracked a private joke between old friends. "Now, Mr. Ferguson, did you have questions prepared for this interview that I could review in advance for Mr. Carter?"

"Now, listen, Ms. Pullen, you know I don't operate that way," Ferguson said. "I have questions, sure, but—"

"In that case, we'll have to take them one at a time. Now, Mr. Carter—"

"Lehigh, please."

"Lehigh. Thank you." The dazzling smile flashed again. "Keep in mind, you are not required to answer any question, or volunteer any information, if you feel it may appear to incriminate you. As a potential subject of the investigation, that applies to any question at all, even the most mundane. I advise you to confer with me before answering any question so I can advise you of the legal ramifications. Understood?"

Lehigh grinned and nodded. Maybe Constantine Richards' potential conflict of interest had worked to Lehigh's advantage after all. Samantha Pullen knew her stuff and knew how to take charge, even in a room full of cops.

She faced Ferguson again. "Fire away, gentlemen."

"Not sure I see much point anymore, given the gag you just shoved in your client's mouth," Buck said.

Ferguson rolled his eyes. "Be that as it may, we shall try." He focused his gaze on Lehigh. "Where were you between the hours of midnight and five a.m. this past Saturday night?"

Lehigh opened his mouth to speak. Sam raised a delicate hand in front of him. "I advise you to refrain from answering that question until we've had a chance to confer."

"Damn you!" Buck exploded off the couch. "How in the hell are we—"

"Mr. Summers." Sam flashed him a smile—that sexy, amazing, you're-the-only-man-I-see smile that Lehigh had enjoyed only moments before. "It's procedure. And I know you are a man of procedure." Her smile faded, replaced by a flat line, her full red lips disappearing into seriousness. "Besides, you wouldn't want evidence collected here to be tossed out by a judge on some *technicality*, would you?"

Summers turned purple from his open-necked shirt up to the tips of his ears. He clamped his mouth shut and turned away. "Go ahead and confer," he said in a dull voice.

"Mr. Carter—Lehigh." The smile returned. "In the kitchen?"

Lehigh nodded and strode in ahead of her. When she arrived behind him, he held up both hands in surrender.

"Ms. Pullen—"

"Sam. Please. I insist."

"Sam. I appreciate what you're doing, but I'm afraid you may only be piss— uh, ticking these guys off."

She shrugged. "That's their problem. Here's my take on it. These men are here for a reason. They haven't been very forthcoming with that reason, and I suspect it's because they're fishing. We don't know what for, unfortunately, and they're unlikely to tell us. So your best bet is to tell them nothing until you and I have had a chance to talk."

"But I'm innocent." Lehigh paced around the kitchen and combed his fingers through his hair. He considered telling her about their earlier threats but didn't want to risk them overhearing. "Wouldn't it be better to explain all that sooner rather than later?"

"You don't understand." She pointed a finger toward the living room, then pressed it against her lips for a moment. She took a step toward him and waved him closer. Lehigh leaned in to her. She smelled like freshly bloomed roses. No wonder Ferguson and Summers sat so close to her. She said in a near whisper, "Last fall, when they accused you of arson. Did talking to them help then?"

He could barely hear, so he shuffled toward her. Her delicate flower scent filled his senses. He tried to hold his breath, but he had to talk. "Uh, no," he said. "No, it didn't. How do you know—"

"I do my research. Did they even once try to help you?"

"No," he said, his voice hoarse. His throat tightened and his breath grew heavy. He edged closer, almost touching her. This woman, this stranger, his attorney for God's sake, charmed him by just standing there, asking intelligent, strategic questions. "No," he said again, "they just tried to paint me as...as guilty. They never once tried to help."

"And now?" Her blue eyes, large as the coffee cups in the open cabinet behind her, searching, came to rest on his own. "Their colleague—their friend, a fellow officer—is dead." Her whisper dropped half again its volume, now just a breath of air against his face. "Do you think they're here to help you now? To prove your innocence—you, the man the police harassed to humiliation just a few months ago? Does that make sense to you?"

"No." He cleared his throat, uncomfortable with her proximity to him. "No, I think they're here to arrest me and throw me in jail."

"Which only can happen if you tell them something incriminating. The trouble is, at this point, I don't know enough to help you avoid that." She paused a moment. "Lehigh, do you trust me?"

He met the gaze of her fierce blue eyes. He barely knew her, but confidence, intelligence, and power exuded from her every pore. Unlike Constantine Richards' associate, she'd gone to bat for him from the moment she walked in the door. He nodded.

"Then I need you to do something you're probably not very comfortable with." She rested her hand on his forearm. "I need you to put your fate in my hands—a perfect stranger you've just met. Can you do that?"

Lehigh took a deep breath. For someone who'd just met him, she'd figured him out pretty well. "I should probably tell you what happened before you got here, then," he said.

"Please." She sat at the kitchen table and broke out a pen and notepad. By the time Lehigh finished talking, Samantha Pullen was furious.

CHAPTER 11

"You told me his lawyer was downtown!" Buck Summers shoved his hands in his armpits and glared at the tall prosecutor's bald head. "I wouldn't have bothered if I'd a thunk she was anywhere near this place."

"Last time, his lawyer was Constantine Richards," Ferguson said. "He *is* downtown. Since when did he enlist the services of Samantha Pullen?"

"The Barracuda? Hell if I know. This is your department." Ignoring Flynn's smirk, Buck shook his head and reached for the door. "He ain't never gonna talk now. We might as well just leave."

"We can't just walk out of here," Ferguson said. "All that would do is raise suspicions."

Buck fumed, but he conceded Ferguson's point. "So what are our options?"

Ferguson thought a moment. "We test him. Catch him in his lies. Men like Carter *want* to talk. They can't help themselves—they feel they have to clear their names. We'll repeat some of our questions from before, and see if his answers are consistent. Push him a little, challenge him on some details he's already shared with us. If he changes his story at all, we focus on that."

Buck grinned. "I like it. I like the way you think, Mr. Attorney General."

Ferguson dipped his head in false modesty. "Not yet, my good friend. Not yet."

"They're coming!" Flynn said in a hoarse whisper. The men broke their huddle and hurried toward their seats.

***

Lehigh followed Sam Pullen into the living room. Reverend Ray Ferguson and Buck Summers turned from a huddle with Deputy Flynn by the front door. The prosecutor scurried back to the couch as if they'd caught him doing something naughty, but the former sheriff remained standing.

"You ready to answer some questions now, Carter?" Buck asked, thumbs hooked in his belt. "Or you still gonna hide behind your pretty little lawyer friend?"

"I appreciate the *compliment*, Mr. Summers," Sam said, in a tone that made it clear she didn't consider it a compliment at all. "But no one here is hiding anything—except, possibly, you. For instance, we still don't know for sure whether my client is under investigation as a suspect, or if his fiancée is, and what evidence you'd base that on."

"That depends," Ferguson said. "If Mr. Carter cooperates and is forthcoming with the information we need, perhaps we can clear up the matter of his innocence right away. And that of Ms. McBride."

Sam glanced at Lehigh, who shrugged. "Ask your questions," Sam said. "We'll decide together whether Mr. Carter will choose to answer."

"Good." Buck stepped into the middle of the room. "Now Carter, you said you was in Portland overnight on Saturday night. Ain't that right?"

Lehigh nodded. Sam narrowed her eyes but said nothing.

"Where was you staying?"

"At the Comfort Inn, near the Convention Center. I told you that on Sunday."

"Both nights?"

"Yes. Well…" Lehigh leaned over to whisper in his lawyer's ear. "Technically I checked out early…late Saturday night. Should I tell them that?"

Sam shook her head and whispered back, "Do you have

your receipt?"

Lehigh nodded. Sam turned to Ferguson. "Surely, as a well-trained, competent investigator, you've already checked the hotel registry."

Ferguson shook his head. "Not me." He stole a glance at Buck, who wriggled in his seat.

"See here, the hotel says you checked out Saturday night," Buck said. "You coulda had plenty of time to make it back to Clarkesville by midnight."

"I did check out early," Lehigh said before Sam could cut him off, "but not *that* early. And I did start driving home, but I got too tired and had to pull off to rest awhile."

"What time did you leave?" Ferguson asked.

"Mr. Carter will have to check his notes," Sam said before Lehigh could answer.

"His notes?" Ferguson asked, eyebrows arched.

Lehigh leaned closer to Sam, tried to ignore the fact that she smelled like heaven, and whispered, "I did make a call just as I was leaving. It ought to be in my phone's memory still."

"This is a bunch of bull–loney." Buck's voice rose. "You didn't stop and rest nowhere. You were on the way home to see your girlfriend. I know you, Lehigh. You'd have never stopped."

"But I did, Buck."

"Bullcrap. Here's what I think," Buck said over Ferguson's half-hearted protests. "You drove home early Saturday night, right to Clarkesville, and found Stacy McBride with her old flame, Jared Barkley, and killed him. Didn't you?"

"Outrageous," Sam said. "But very informative. Apparently, Mr. Carter *is* the subject of the investigation."

"Buck, for God's sake." Lehigh swallowed a mouthful of warm spit. Outside, and out of eyeshot of his lawyer, he'd have drenched the idiot with it, lawman or no. "Stacy ain't hooked up with Jared Barkley, first off. And second—"

"My client is advised not to continue, although that is, of course, his choice." Sam placed a gentle hand on Lehigh's shoulder. "After he consults with me."

"This is ridiculous." Buck huffed, arms crossed, then turned his back on the room.

Ferguson glared at Buck, exhaled a gallon of air, then eased his long, lean body off the sofa. "I suspect this conversation might proceed more effectively if we give Mr. Carter a chance to confer at length with his attorney."

"Precisely." Sam stood and shared another amazing smile with the Reverend. No jury could resist it, Lehigh guessed. She gave Lehigh a gentle push toward the kitchen. "Why don't we all meet tomorrow morning at your office?"

"I had this afternoon in mind," Ferguson said, trying in vain to match her smile. "Say, one o'clock?"

"I'm not sure Mr. Carter will be able to fully brief me by then."

"Mr. Carter is a man of few words," Ferguson said. "I'm sure you can get the full story from him in…" He checked his watch. "The next three hours or so." He buttoned his coat and faced Lehigh. "Two o'clock, then. You know how to find us. Come along, gentlemen."

Lehigh leaned over to whisper in Sam's ear. Golden locks parted around her lobe, and diamond studs reflected what little light found its way into the room. He hesitated a moment, then choked out his words, barely audible even to him. "Can't we delay this? I'd like to talk to Stacy before I go in."

Sam shook her head and half-turned toward him, muttering, "We're lucky they gave us three hours. Very unorthodox. What it tells me is they've got nothing. Good for us." She caught up with the departing policemen at the door. "Thank you, gentlemen. We'll be prompt."

"Just be ready to talk," Buck said over his shoulder. "This is ridiculous. Waiting for a suspect. In over twenty-five years of law enforcement, I never…" He strode down the sidewalk and his voice faded into the chill wind. Flynn trailed behind.

Ferguson paused at the front step. "You know, this *is* pretty unusual," he said over the attorney's shoulder to Lehigh. "It's only because of the mistakes made in your previous case that you're getting any leeway at all now. Consider it a favor."

"Much appreciated, Reverend," Lehigh said. "I do want to help. But I screwed up last time, too, by talking too much, and I don't need to repeat that, either."

Ferguson grimaced and walked to his car.

Pullen turned to Lehigh, her charming smile gone. "Now, let's talk," she said. "Start at the beginning."

CHAPTER 12

An hour later, Sam nodded in response to the conclusion of Lehigh's story and scrawled another mess of notes on her pad, illegible upside down and no doubt right side up, too. The woman finally had a fault, even if it only amounted to bad handwriting. Otherwise she remained perfect—looks, brains...hell, she even had perfect posture. Not even a strand of her long blonde hair fell out of place.

"From what you've told me, we should be able to establish a solid alibi for you," she said, stretching in her chair at the kitchen table. "Hotels, or at least the cable providers, usually keep a time record of pay-per-view movie viewings, so we should be able to establish your being in Portland until nearly the estimated time of Mr. Barkley's death."

"Nearly?"

She shrugged. "Nearly is good enough. You couldn't have driven here in under an hour, which is what it would have taken, based on when you left the motel. Barkley was dead long before you woke up from your little roadside nap. Now, tell me what you know of Ms. McBride's whereabouts while you were away."

Lehigh stood and paced about the cramped kitchen, hands knitted behind his back. "Just what she told me yesterday. We weren't in touch much Friday or Saturday. I was pretty busy with my meetings, and she was at the clinic, daytimes anyhow."

"And nights?" She left a thin residue of dark red lipstick behind on the rim of the ivory-colored mug. The contents of her cup, more cream than coffee, nearly matched the paleness of her skin.

"I, uh...well." Lehigh halted his pacing. "She said Friday she'd be at her folks' house, and Saturday night, uh, out with some friends."

"Names?"

"I'm guessing Donna Arbuckle. I'm not really sure of who else."

"Ms. Arbuckle will vouch for her?"

"I'm sure of it." His stomach sank. Stacy had not actually said who she'd been out with—he'd just assumed.

Sam's eyes held his for a moment, then slid away. "Good. We'll interview her immediately. Now, tell me, what was your relationship with Jared Barkley?"

Lehigh shrugged and thrust his hands in his pockets. "Okay, I guess. We played football together in high school. Jared was a year behind me and Stacy. He played backup quarterback my senior year when I was first string wide receiver—"

"The relationship, Mr. Carter, not a box score." She smiled and her eyes twinkled. Teasing, but with a steely edge.

"Right. I'm getting to that. Jared and I didn't socialize much, but we knew each other. Hell, I still don't socialize much with anyone. Neither did he, from what I gather."

"And after high school?"

"I went to Oregon State, he went to Eugene. He played some college ball—"

"And in recent years?"

Lehigh shook his head and spread his hands wide. "Barely crossed paths. I'd see him now and again in his cruiser. Until last fall."

"The arson?" She scribbled on her legal pad.

"And the break-in. Jared seemed to cut me more of a break than these other yahoos. Not favoritism. Just being objective where the others seemed always ready to blame me first." Lehigh scowled and stared out the window at nothing. "Stacy's ex turned out to be behind all that."

"Paul van Paten?"

Lehigh nodded, again ready to spit.

"Good. That gives us someone else with a possible motive, along with Sheriff Summers." Sam looked up from her notes. "Which brings me to a difficult subject. Lehigh, what was Stacy's relationship to Jared Barkley?"

"Stacy and Jared? They're old school pals." Lehigh fought the bile rising in his gut.

"Just friends, eh?" Sam's blue eyes froze on Lehigh's. Her coffee cup rose to her perfect red lips. She took a tiny sip, returned it to the table.

He tore his gaze away. "It's what she says."

"And you believe her?"

"Why shouldn't I?" For some reason his voice sounded tinny and hollow. "She's as honest a person as I've ever known. Honest to a fault, really." He said it like he meant it— and he really *wanted* to mean it. But, against his will, doubts crept in.

"Mr. Carter, honest people lie. *All* people lie, when forced to." She tapped her pen on her notepad.

"Why would she be forced to?"

Sam took a slow, deep breath, and exhaled. "What would you think of her if you found out that she *was* hiding something?" That steely blue stare froze him again.

He coughed. "There's no reason to suspect that." But his voice betrayed him.

"Lehigh, answer the question. How would it affect your relationship if you found out she'd been spending time with Jared Barkley while you were gone?" Unmoving, rock-still, her eyes bore a hole into his forehead.

He pushed his chair away from the table, stood, and walked to the window, arms crossed. "Where are you going with this, Sam? If it's where I think you're headed—"

"I'm exploring all plausible explanations. And believe me, so is the district attorney."

Lehigh glanced to his side, following the soft scent of rose petals, the aroma of femininity. She stood less than two feet away, arms behind her back, framing the soft curves of her waist and hips. He tore his eyes away, back toward the window. "I believe her. She says it, so that's the truth." His voice cracked, losing strength.

"We need to verify that." Sam's voice seemed farther away. He snuck a peek. She'd crossed back to the table and stood over her notepad, flicking through the pages. "When can I talk to her?"

"Soon as she gets home. Or you can call her, I guess. If the prosecutor suspects her, why's he still busting my chops?"

"Don't be surprised if he charges you both and adds a charge of conspiracy." She lifted her long lashes at him. "And if that happens, she'll need her own lawyer."

Lehigh snorted. "She has one. Mine." To her puzzled expression, he said, "Constantine Richards was my lawyer, anyway, on my last case. Then he became her lawyer when she got arrested, and he said he couldn't represent me anymore. What I don't get is why."

Sam stepped closer, hands folded in front of her. "Too often, the way this works in two-suspect cases, one of them turns state's evidence against the other." She took a deep breath. "The question is, which one of you will it be? Are you willing to testify against her?"

"Never!"

Her lips curled into a faint smile. "Then you have to assume she will be the one to testify against you."

"She wouldn't!"

Sam shrugged. "Are you sure?"

"One hundred percent." Again, he wanted to believe.

"Ms. McBride loves you, I'm sure, and you love her. But are either of you willing to go to prison for the other?"

Lehigh turned to face her full on. "She's my fiancée. Yes, I'd…I'd die for her."

Sam nodded. "Of course. But remember, you don't see a lot of each other from prison."

Lehigh opened his mouth to reply, but he could think of nothing to say. His head drooped toward his chest. Somehow this whole situation had gotten so screwed up.

He wiped his sweaty hands on his jeans and faced his attorney again. Entertained the notion. Conjured up the words. "Let's say she did like him as 'more than friends.' Then what?"

Sam pointed an open palm to his empty chair. Lehigh sat down and leaned both elbows onto the table. He rubbed his face, his eyes, his neck. Fatigue swept over him like a tidal wave.

Sam sat down at ninety degrees to him. Her skirt rested an inch below her knees, spread an inch apart. He looked away. "That provides each of you with motives," she said. "For you, jealousy. For her, a desire to hide the relationship. Or perhaps it started going bad. Possible blackmail on his part. A creative mind could concoct any number of possibilities."

"If creativity's the issue, our sheriff's office will give us nothing to worry about." Lehigh smiled at his own joke and elicited one from his attorney. He cracked his neck and shoulders. "I reckon there's other folks to worry about, though."

"The only one I'm concerned about is you." Sam's smile faded.

"What's next?" he asked.

"I need all of the details—of everything. The night of Barkley's attack and as much as you can remember of the days and nights leading up to it—both your activities and Stacy's."

"All the details? Even when we... How personal do you need me to get?" His cheeks warmed.

She smiled and blushed. "You can omit, uh, *those* details...unless anything changed. Any change in the frequency, or any, um...surprises? New...proclivities, shall we say?" Sam's eyes locked on the pen in her hand, poised over the yellow pad.

"Well, she always...um...no, no change." His hand rested on the nape of his neck, the spot that had a little scrape, possibly from fingernails, or teeth, or...

"Nothing at all?" The tip of her pen pressed onto the paper.

His lower back ached. No lumbar support in these damned chairs. That, and the memory of Stacy rolling him underneath her, propping him up, tearing at his clothes—

"Nothing," he said in a mumble. Then, louder: "No."

She drew in a slow breath, exhaled. "I know this is awkward. But trust me, it'd be even more awkward for me to hear it for the first time from her in court."

Lehigh's gaze dropped. Paused on the way down, just for a moment, on the curve of her calf. Smooth. Slender. He forced his gaze toward the floor.

Then he remembered some things. And then his mouth refused to obey his mind's bidding to shut the hell up.

"Okay," he said, "a few things were different."

And in that moment, everything changed.

CHAPTER 13

It took the rest of the morning to bring Sam up to speed, and by the time the noon hour approached, Lehigh's head ached. But worse, his heart weighed a thousand pounds.

"I don't want you taking any of this the wrong way," he said, walking Sam to the door. "We've been arguing a bit, sure. And yes, some things have changed a bit recently. But overall, we're very happy together. Ecstatic. And that goes for both of us."

Sam nodded. "I understand that you're feeling like you've betrayed her, but trust me, you have not. If anything, I think you've helped her. In fact, if it's okay with you, I would like to confer with her attorney to see if they'd like to coordinate our efforts."

"Makes sense to me." Lehigh sighed. "Still…this whole thing is such a mess. I'm really glad you were available to represent me. When Constantine Richards told me to bugger off, I started to feel pretty desperate." He exhaled a long, slow breath. "I just wonder if Buck Summers and that whole gang will ever leave us alone. And now I've dragged Stacy into it, and if anything happened to her…I don't think I could live with myself." His voice cracked, and he sealed his mouth shut before any more nonsense spilled out.

Sam's smile set him at ease again. "We're in good shape, Lehigh. Really."

He eyed her sideways. "For real?"

She nodded and rested her hand on his forearm. "For real."

"I'm so grateful to you, I..." His voice trailed off, and he stood a foot away from her, feeling foolish, not knowing what to say. The moment dragged on, his discomfort building.

He was about to speak—he needed to thank her, at the very least—when his cell phone rang.

***

Stacy pulled her car into the long gravel drive at the slowest, quietest pace her Volvo wagon could travel without stalling, then veered over onto the trimmed lawn for her final approach. No sense spoiling the surprise too soon by kicking up loose rocks against her car's underbelly.

Sure enough, Lehigh's pickup remained where he always left it—one space over from the door, leaving room for her car, ten feet less for her to walk through mud in her heels.

Which she appreciated, especially given her current set, a pair of four-inch "knock me down" spikes that matched the outfit she had on—if you could call it that.

Then she did a double take. And saw the other car—a shiny, dark gray Lexus—in her spot.

She sighed. The car probably belonged to a lumber buyer—and with business so slow of late, Lehigh could ill afford to turn away any clients. So, it was a good thing.

But it definitely spoiled her plans. She'd have to back out without being noticed. If they spotted her, she'd have to go in, and she couldn't go in dressed like *this*.

Before scooting out of work for a long and early "lunch"—one in which she'd hoped to burn calories with the love of her life, rather than consume them—she'd closed her office door, slipped into a sexy shred of black silk and lace, Lehigh's favorite, and covered up with a boot-length overcoat. No sense shocking Ann Marie, her dowdy and ever present volunteer clerk, into a premature exit to the sweet hereafter.

The plan she'd entertained the entire ten minute drive over was to whip the coat off as soon as she entered the house, and hope like hell that Lehigh had already let the dogs outside. Wet noses had interrupted unbridled passion too many times already in the past six months.

Time for Plan B.

Then again…maybe not. Maybe with a little encouragement, his client meeting could come to a swift, businesslike close.

She halted the car amidst the trees some twenty feet from the big picture window in front and speed-dialed Lehigh's cell.

"Hey, Stacy," he answered. Not "honey," or "lover," or any of the other sweet names he often used. He seemed tense.

Hmm.

"Are you in a meeting?" she asked.

"Just finishing up," he said. "Want to get some lunch in a bit?"

Yay. At least he wanted to see her. "Great minds think alike."

"And so do we."

She laughed. Sweet, funny man. "I'll swing by and pick you up. Ten minutes?" No sense letting on where she was.

"Better give me fifteen or twenty. Gotta go, I'm paying her by the hour."

"Okay…see you soon." She hung up, then gripped the phone in her fist when she realized what he'd just said.

Paying *her*…by the hour?

She peered into the picture window. A figure came into view. Blonde hair down to her shoulders, pulled back. The top of her head reached about eye level on him, her back to the window, facing Lehigh. They seemed to be talking. The woman turned toward the door. The shadows made judging tricky, but Stacy would have had to call her pretty.

Too damned pretty.

The blonde stopped, faced Lehigh again—he'd spoken to her. Kept speaking. Moved a little closer. They moved out of sight, then the inside door opened. They remained visible through the glass of the storm door—the back of her off-white overcoat fit ever so perfectly around her hips, drawn in at the waist…

The woman extended a hand to Lehigh. He took it, shook it, paused. Held on a second or two. Their hands dropped to their sides, and they edged closer, as if some magnetic force pulled them back together, resisted by some invisible shield. Lehigh nodded at her. Smiled.

Oh, God.

That smile...it was *that* smile. The one Stacy knew all too well. That folksy, charming, aw-shucks kind of smile, the one he used when he was...

Say it...

Flirting. Wooing, even. Damn him!

"Get a grip," Stacy said aloud. She took a deep, calming breath. "They're just ending a long meeting, probably have some unfinished business, a new business relationship—"

Their hands joined again. This time Lehigh enveloped both of her hands in his. He held on again, for too long.

The blonde's head moved. She was talking. Earnestly, it seemed. Looking straight into his eyes. Her other hand came up, clasped his. The act drew them closer together. He nodded. Then, out of nowhere, he hugged her. Her face disappeared into his shoulder. His face appeared over hers, eyes closed.

They stayed there for a second, ten minutes, an hour— Stacy couldn't tell. Time froze when those two bodies touched. When he held her, her lips near his face, his hand around her back, so close to her waist, her hips...holding her...still holding her...

They broke the embrace, the embrace of a moment or a minute or a lifetime, and the woman pushed open the door, got into her Lexus, started it, and backed up past Stacy's car, still idling to the side in the tender spring grass.

The doorway now housed only blackness. No tall man in a T-shirt holding a pretty blonde woman, who in turn had Stacy's man in her own arms, her own well manicured hands.

And maybe his heart as well.

Maybe.

Stacy wanted to find out. But not in her current state.

She spun a one-eighty on the grass, jammed the accelerator to the floor, and raced toward the street, spewing mud from her tires onto the big picture window.

CHAPTER 14

Detective James Wadsworth—"Jimmy" to his wife of seventeen years, Gwen, the light of his life and stay-at-home mother to their three wonderful children—never could abide cheaters. Of any kind: tax cheaters, cheats at sports and games, crooked politicians, and worst of all, people who cheated on their spouses. Or fiancés. Or boyfriends, girlfriends, steadies—hell, even a john cheating on his regular prostitute bugged "Gentleman Jim," as his colleagues in the sheriff's department called him when they thought he'd drifted out of earshot.

Which is why this whole Jared Barkley case got under his skin. Too many damned cheaters: Stacy McBride, her father, Buck Summers, Paul van Paten, even Jared himself. Get that many cheaters together and something bad always happens.

He'd parked his cruiser on a blind curve of Brady Mountain Road, relegated to filling in on traffic duty for an ailing deputy, and set his radar gun to capture the county's frequent speeders coming into town, who ignored the posted fifteen mile per hour speed limit reduction about a quarter mile back. He didn't mind the sentry duty—it helped him catch traffic cheaters. A cheater's a cheater's a cheater.

But one cheater—Barkley—didn't fit the pattern.

Barkley had been something of a local hero twice already—first as a high school quarterback, leading the team to all-state glory in his senior year in Division III. Good looking, smart, athletic, personable if a bit shy, and unfailingly polite, Barkley was the poster boy for wholesome Americana as a Clarkesville teen.

Then this past year he'd cracked the George McBride-Paul van Paten scandal, sending two powerful politicians into humiliating retreat, hopefully ending their crooked political careers and probably sending at least one, van Paten, to a well deserved stay in Hotel Round Bars wearing orange pajamas. Barkley had even nailed Buck Summers as a co-conspirator and briefly occupied the big man's chair as interim sheriff at the tender age of thirty-six. Hell, Jared probably could have been elected mayor, sheriff, and prom queen if he'd wanted. People in Mt. Hood County loved heroes.

But then he got plugged. And while the Golden Hero lay in a tiny cool chamber in the county morgue, his ugly secret life came to light. To Wadsworth, anyway.

Dating Stacy McBride, of all people. While she was engaged, no less. Engaged not just once, but twice—first to Paul van Paten, if anyone could believe a word that scumbag ever said, then to the hayseed Lehigh Carter. Boy, she really knew how to pick 'em.

But no surprise on her part. Picking losers seemed to be a McBride family tradition. For the women, anyway. How old George had conned a woman as elegant and kind as Catherine into marrying him, Wadsworth would never understand.

But Barkley's entanglement in Stacy's mess surprised Wadsworth. Mr. Clean, Eagle Scout, Mr. Good Boy. He shook his head. Crazy.

For almost anyone else, it might have made sense. A looker like McBride loved to command the center of attention. Apparently Barkley had a thing for her since high school. And that whole "forbidden fruit" thing—a lot of guys go for that.

But not Jared Barkley. At least, never before, that Wadsworth knew of.

For some reason, van Paten never caught on to his fiancée's dalliances with Barkley—only her later idiotic choice to hook up with Carter. Lehigh, though, maybe wasn't as dumb as he looked. Barkley didn't last long once that hot-tempered mountain man entered the picture.

The trick, as always, was finding proof. Court-admissible

proof.

Wadsworth swallowed the last of his apple-pear Danish and washed it down with pure black Joe, the way God intended coffee. If He'd wanted cream in it, He'd have sprouted coffee beans in cow pastures. And as for sugar—

A familiar looking green Volvo wagon zoomed past him, kicking up dust and gravel.

"Well, I'll be damned!" Figures that'd happen when he'd set his radar gun down. And the McBrides may have thought they were above the law, but for Stacy to flaunt it like that in front of a cop—well, that needed correcting.

He slapped the red and white flasher on top of his blue Crown Victoria sedan and blipped the siren, then sped onto the highway, already a few hundred yards behind her. She'd sped up, if anything. If that didn't just beat all.

He flicked on the flasher and the siren, full bore this time, and floored the gas pedal. Great thing about police cruisers— they always had oversized engines, full of pop, with great handling. He hit sixty in seven, maybe six seconds. He grinned. He didn't get to do this sort of thing often enough anymore. Too long behind a desk chasing down stolen license plates.

He closed the distance behind the Volvo to thirty yards before she pulled over. He parked behind her on the shoulder, left the lights flashing, and killed the siren. He waited ten, twenty seconds. That always raised their anxiety a bit, got people talking, admitting things they shouldn't. Usually talk themselves right into a ticket instead of out of one. Just for grins, he turned on the hood-mounted floodlights. Even at midday, they had the desired effect.

Pro forma, he called it in to Central. Make, model, license plate.

"That's Stacy McBride's car," Dwayne Latner radioed back. "What's she done?"

"Never mind," Wadsworth said. "Stand by."

He got out, lumbered up to the driver's door. His bulky shape cast an extra wide shadow on her pretty little car. Dang it. Tomorrow, no Danish.

"What seems to be the problem, Detective?" Sweet little voice, a smile his Daddy always would've called "purty." No wonder she got away with murder around here.

Well, not anymore. Not literally, anyway.

"Morning—er, should I say, afternoon, ma'am. Might I have a look at your license, registration, and proof of insurance?" He kept his aviators over his eyes so she couldn't see where they landed. Not that she could really doubt what any red-blooded man in God's country would be looking at in his position.

Especially with that low-cut thing she had on. Crap on a cracker, it looked more like a nightie than a dress.

"Of course," she said. "It's in my purse." She fumbled inside her handbag next to her on the seat. Wadsworth stepped closer so he could watch her, his right hand resting on his holstered weapon. Probably unnecessary, but who knew? After all, somebody—maybe even Stacy McBride—put two slugs in Jared Barkley's chest. If she got scared...

She turned back, handed him the license and insurance card. "Here you go, Detective."

"Registration?" He didn't even glance at the cards in his hand. He knew by feel what was missing.

"Oh. Right." She leaned across the seat, opened the glove box. Something black fell out.

"Freeze!" He unsnapped his holster and drew his weapon. She turned her body, hand frozen in the air, leaning forward in her seat. A generous swell of pale flesh bulged against a lacy black cup, now exposed by the gap in her overcoat.

Dang. If she wanted to, she could have plugged Wadsworth right then and there. He'd have never noticed. And unless she shot him below the waist, he might not have bled a drop.

"Is there a problem, Detective?" She glanced down, closed her overcoat over the nightie. Yes, definitely a nightie.

He gazed past her. The black object that had fallen out lay on the floor—a square, book-shaped thing, resembling very much the faux leather case for an owner's manual. Not a gun.

"Just move slow," he said.

She picked up the black book-shaped case, zipped it open, slid a small rectangle of paper out of it, unfolded the page, and handed it to him.

He took it between two fingers, as if it might explode in his hands. "Thanks, ma'am. You just sit tight." He lumbered back to his vehicle, sat inside awhile. A minute at least, maybe two.

He couldn't get that image out of his mind. The image of her. Dressed like that. Mid-day. Nobody goes out driving like that. Not unless they had been caught in the act of you-know-what with someone that nobody knew about—or should know about. No time to dress, just put on her coat and fly out the door.

That explained the fast driving, too.

Cheater!

It all made sense. And the crazy, nasty, over-the-top piece of news was, she'd already found a new lover. Jared Barkley's body hadn't even grown cold yet.

Which meant another body could likely follow, if she went loose now.

The only question remaining: did she pull the trigger? Or did Carter?

Hell. Carter may have found her cheating a few minutes before. In which case he'd likely pull up any minute now. If Wadsworth kept her here a few minutes, he could just ask the man. With Carter's hot temper and her being caught red-handed, he'd likely rat her out right then and there.

He called her data in and waited. "Take your time," he told Dwayne.

Sure enough, an old Ford pickup truck crested the hill behind him, moving fast.

***

Lehigh slowed to sixty when the cop car came into view, right behind Stacy's Volvo. The blue and red flasher blinked at an awkward angle on the driver's side of the road. A portable

unit, slapped onto an unmarked Crown Victoria, a car driven
only by cops and grandmas in Iowa, so far as Lehigh knew.
And he'd never met an Iowan of any sort, much less an Iowan
grandmother.

He pulled in behind the cop, parked, and waited a moment.
Lucky poked her wet snout over the seat and drooled on his
shoulder. Scrambling noises suggested that Diamond wanted
to try the same thing on the empty passenger side. Hard to
imagine a dog any cuter—or dumber.

The cop car's driver door popped open. Gentleman Jim
Wadsworth got out. From appearances, even that much effort
put a strain on the big man's heart. He wore a dark suit a size
too small over a white shirt, a wide 1980s style tie, and a
raincoat that skirted his knees. Only the traditional cop's cap
was uniform-issue.

Wadsworth signaled Lehigh to roll down his window.
Lehigh complied. "Problem with my fiancée, Officer?"

Wadsworth grimaced. Probably passed for a smile in his
world. "You tell me."

Lehigh craned his neck to get a better view of her car over
the Crown Vic. "You must've had some reason to stop her."

"That's police business. Unless you're her lawyer—"

"C'mon, Detective. This ain't *Miami Vice*. We know each
other and we all know what's going on in this town. So cut the
crap. Why'd you stop her?"

Wadsworth's face reddened and his nose flared. "You're
overstepping, Carter. Back off."

Lucky growled in the back of the pickup. Diamond, of
course, followed suit.

"Shush, dogs." He reached back where he knew Lucky's
neck would be and gave her collar a brief shake. "Lie down
and be quiet."

"That's good advice all around," Wadsworth said. "Why
don't you just wait here until—"

"Lehigh, what in the hell are you doing here?"

Wadsworth spun toward the front of the truck, where Stacy
stood in an open coat over what appeared to be her slinkiest

nightie and a pair of stiletto heels.

Lehigh's mouth fell open. "Stacy!" he said, perhaps loud enough for her to hear. "What in the hell are you doing here in your underwear?"

"Long story," she said. Then, in an accusing tone: "Who were you meeting with back at the house?"

Wadsworth stared at the heavens, hands clenched next to his head. "Could we hold this family meeting some other time? And Miss McBride, would you *please* get back in your car? For God's sake."

Stacy rolled her hands into fists and used them to hold her coat closed. "If *you'd* kindly get a move-on and decide whether you're going to let me go on about my business or drum up some fictional charge—"

"Lady, you were going seventy-five miles an hour in a fifty zone," Wadsworth said. "For starters. Now get back in your car."

"No way," Lehigh said. "Her car couldn't do seventy-five falling off a cliff. Did you clock that on radar?"

"Carter, I'm warning you. Back off. And Miss McBride, for the final time, get back in your car. Now!" Wadsworth pointed a thick trunk of an arm at her car.

Stacy glared at Wadsworth, then glanced at Lehigh. A cold breeze kicked up and she shivered, pulling her overcoat tighter around her. "All right. But get on with it, will you? This is taking all day." She stomped back to her car. Lehigh covered a wry smile with his hand.

Wadsworth pointed a finger at Lehigh. "You stay put, too."

Lehigh help up his hands in surrender. The detective's comical authoritarian demeanor made it that much harder to keep from grinning like a maniac. Particularly with his fiancée prancing around in the mud in high heels and skimpy underwear, for whatever reason.

Wadsworth lumbered back to his cruiser. Lehigh flicked on his police band radio, a Christmas present from Stacy he'd only gotten around to installing a few days before.

"Got that plate and registration for ya, Jim." Lehigh recognized Dwayne's voice, perhaps the most likeable sheriff's deputy after Barkley, though not half as smart. In his youth, Dwayne showed great athletic promise, but couldn't keep his grades up—even in Clarkesville's permissive pro-jock environment. He'd blown a full ride football scholarship to Oregon State by becoming academically ineligible midway through the season during his senior year of high school, even though he took mostly gym and shop classes.

But he'd also dated the prettiest girl in school (other than Stacy), a buxom blonde named Julie he knocked up and married three months after graduation. This past fall, Dwayne's son Earl accepted the scholarship Dwayne long ago forfeited and led the OSU Beavers in receptions his sophomore year.

"Go on." Wadsworth's voice crackled over the radio speaker.

"It's all clean," Dwayne said. "Nothing outstanding. It's her car, insurance checks out. But…"

Lehigh sat up from his slouch. "But what?" he said at the same time as Wadsworth.

"Bring her in," Dwayne said.

"For what?" Once again Lehigh and the detective spoke in unison.

"There's a bench warrant out on her. Apparently she missed a court date."

"What court date?" Lehigh asked this time without Wadsworth's help.

"Details," the detective said.

"A grand jury hearing yesterday. She never showed."

"She never mentioned any jury summons." Lehigh's stomach turned to jelly.

"Roger. Thanks, Dwayne." The detective swung his car door open and stepped out. He walked with a pronounced swagger to Stacy's car. Lehigh turned off the radio and lowered his window to listen.

"Ma'am," Wadsworth said, loud enough for the next county to hear, "get out of the car."

CHAPTER 15

Stacy froze in place, her eyeliner pencil an inch from her face. That stupid cop sounded like he wanted to arrest her.

And for what? Nobody got arrested in Clarkesville for going a few miles over the speed limit. More important, she hadn't exactly dressed for the occasion.

She lowered the driver's door window and put on her best "helpless female" face...which wasn't very good. Stacy didn't do "helpless" very often. "Excuse me, I didn't quite hear what you said."

"Get out of the damned car!" Wadsworth spread his feet into a wide—some might say shooting—stance, leaning forward from the waist, hand on his holster.

His unsnapped holster.

She pushed open the door and stepped out. Her coat flapped open in the breeze. She pulled the two sides closed and grabbed the loose ends of her belt to tie it.

"Hands up where I can see 'em!" Wadsworth's hand shook, pointing at her, six feet from her face.

She raised her hands and let the coat flap open again. Freezing cold, scared, and half naked, plus getting arrested right in front of her fiancé for God knows what...this, she could tell, would go down as one of the worst days of her life.

"My eyes are up here, Detective."

His gaze snapped up from her chest. No doubt the thin, lacy fabric and cold air gave him quite the show.

The detective reddened further, if that was even possible.

"I'm, uh, going to have to check you for weapons."

Stacy snorted. "In this outfit? Where would I hide a weapon? In my butt?"

"Procedure, ma'am. Please face the vehicle and place your hands on the roof." He gestured toward the car.

She rolled her eyes but obeyed. "Careful where you put your hands. Remember, my fiancé is watching."

He patted her sides, then reached into her coat pockets. Stacy grinned when he pulled out a fistful of used tissues, as well as some lip gloss and a half-pack of gum. He ran his hands up over her hips and legs, too fast to feel anything. She could have smuggled a cannon past him.

"You're under arrest for driving in excess of the posted speed limit, and for failing to appear in response to a court-ordered summons."

"What summons?" She turned her head toward him.

"Eyes forward, ma'am. You have the right to remain silent. You have the right to an attorney." He cuffed her—for God's sake!—and led her to the cruiser.

Where Lehigh stood, waiting, at the front bumper.

Humiliation fought with love and gratitude for control of her emotions. The only daughter of a recently disgraced politician getting arrested in her underwear on the side of a highway in front of her fiancé—God, it sounded like the worst tabloid headline imaginable.

But to have him there, blocking this cop's path, sticking up for her, taking care of her, making sure the cop didn't do anything stupid, felt like an answer to a prayer she hadn't even uttered.

"Call my lawyer," she said to Lehigh.

Then the humiliation and rage returned. *Lawyers.* Like her disgraced father, and the piece of garbage she'd broken up with a few months before, Paul van Paten—the source of so much pain in her life. Freaking *lawyers.*

"Where are you taking her, Detective?" Lehigh, his voice firm, kept his feet planted in their path to the cruiser.

"Headquarters, first off. I think you're familiar with the

location?" Wadsworth dragged Stacy forward. She ⌄⌄ against the edge of the pavement, unsteady in the skinny spike heels. Wadsworth's grip loosened on her arm, and she tipped sideways. With both hands cuffed behind her, she had no way to break her fall. She landed hard on her side, and her knee and head bounced on the wet tarmac.

"For God's sake, Wadsworth!" Lehigh bent down and reached for her.

"Stay back!" The cop pushed Lehigh away from her and stood at Stacy's feet—feet splayed wide, that is, providing a full view of every inch of her skin from the top of her shoe straps to the sliver of black thong underwear bunching up at her waist. With her hands cuffed, she couldn't even close her coat.

She struggled up to a seated position. The nightie *probably* covered her crotch at that point. Wetness seeped through her coat, soaking her butt. Blood seeped from scratches on her knee, and something warm trickled down the side of her face.

"Don't bother fixing your dress, ma'am," Wadsworth said. "Where you're going, nobody's going to see it anyway."

***

Stacy wrapped her coat tight around her body, trying to conserve some body heat in the walk-in freezer of an interrogation room at the sheriff's office. Still, having sat there for the better part of an hour, her unprotected bare legs felt like ice cubes, and she couldn't even feel her feet. Which was probably a good thing, since she still wore the ridiculously uncomfortable pumps whose sole purpose in life was to get kicked off the moment something amorous happened. Which it hadn't, of course, making everything just a little more frustrating.

Detective Wadsworth pushed open the door, and a young, athletically built deputy named Flynn followed him into the room. Flynn closed the door and stood with his back to it. Wadsworth ambled over to the interview table, stood next to Stacy, and glared down at her. "You're in my chair."

Stacy scoffed. "You snooze, you lose."

Flynn grabbed her arm. "Move it!"

Stacy shrugged him off and stayed put in the somewhat more comfortable swiveling desk chair, which had at least a tiny bit of padding and was the right height for her, after she'd spent several minutes fussing with the flat black levers under the seat. No mean trick for a person in handcuffs. The undersized metal-framed job on the other side of the table, into which she'd been pushed a half hour before, remained empty and uninviting. She glanced up at Wadsworth. "You want a better chair, go get one. I'm stuck here, remember?"

Wadsworth took a deep breath and let it out through his nose. He shook his head at the deputy to back him away from her. "You're not helping yourself here, Ms. McBride."

"Where's that phone you promised? I need to call my lawyer."

Wadsworth snorted. "Figures. Well, actually, you *don't* need a phone to call him—just raise your voice a bit. Constantine Richards has been in the building since about five seconds after you arrived. He's not a terribly happy person, by the way."

"That makes two of us. Why haven't I seen him yet?"

"You're about to." With a heavy sigh, Wadsworth gestured to Flynn, who unlocked the shackles on Stacy's wrists, then stepped aside. "You're free to go. I, uh, apologize for the inconvenience."

"*Inconvenience?* What the hell?" Stacy jumped to her feet. "Why was there ever a bench warrant out on me, anyway? Why didn't I know I was supposed to be at a grand jury hearing yesterday?"

"Because you got juked. You, me, a lot of people." Wadsworth walked to the other side of the table and sat on the edge of it. The table creaked under his weight, but held.

"Forgive me for asking, but what do you mean by 'juked'?" Stacy rubbed her sore wrists where the handcuffs had pressed hard into her skin.

"It means, someone got into our very secure computer

system and secretly removed key documents that should have been hand delivered to you and your attorney by marshals of the county court," Wadsworth said, voice glum. "Several times over the past several months, as it turns out, not just in your case. Lucky for you, it was rather clumsily and incompletely done, so it became obvious, once we looked for it. But, unfortunately, not in time for you to appear as a witness for the hearing."

"What hearing? Where? How do I—"

"We're still tracking that down. That information, too, got scrubbed. The key thing is, it's obviously not your fault, and you're now free to go."

Stacy huffed and headed to the door. "You don't have to tell me twice. But I'll tell you this once, twice, or a hundred times if need be: this place stinks deep down to the core, and I'm not talking about your toilets. Whoever's responsible for this mess had better watch out. You've crossed the wrong person, buster."

Wadsworth stared at the floor and nodded. Stacy left the room, slamming the door behind her.

CHAPTER 16

"Lehigh, I swear. I never even got a traffic ticket before today," Stacy said to Lehigh a few hours later, as he drove her home from the sheriff's headquarters. "Much less a grand jury summons."

"They pulled the same type of crap on me last fall." He checked his speed—five miles under. "This thing has the stench of Buck Summers all over it."

"And Paul van Paten." She shivered and cranked up the heat. She wished she'd brought her jeans, blouse, and sweater on her surprise visit home that morning. "He's threatened to get me back for landing his sorry butt in jail. I'm sure his thuggish friends in high places are pulling strings to make my life miserable."

"Reckon you're right. But I doubt Paul will stop at manufacturing tickets and making subpoenas disappear." He scowled and downshifted into his turn. "It's criminal. We're not safe, even with him in jail."

"I asked Mr. Richards if there was anything we could do." She sank down in her seat. "I didn't like his response."

"No doubt. Legal methods won't scare a guy who's already behind bars." He pulled into her long gravel drive and parked in his usual spot alongside her empty spot closer to the door. "We gotta figure out how to get your car home."

"I can't believe they took my license!" She jumped out of the truck and slammed the door hard enough to rock the truck on its wheels. "How am I going to get to work?"

"I'll drive you, of course." He followed her to the front door and inside. The dogs scooted in ahead of him.

She sat on the couch, still wearing her coat, and patted the seat next to her. "We need to talk."

Lehigh nodded and sat a foot away. She took a deep breath.

"Who was that woman with you in here today?"

He licked his lips. "Woman? Oh, you mean my attorney. She—"

"I need you to hire a new attorney, then."

Lehigh blinked. "Why?"

Her eyes bored into his head. Her dark irises burned. "I saw you holding her. It wasn't a brotherly hug."

Lehigh lay back on the couch and blew out a long, slow breath, eyes closed. He lay there several seconds. "There's nothing going on between Sam and me."

"Oh, it's 'Sam' now? Let me guess. She's really smart, and she's starting to make real headway on your case. You two are becoming 'good friends,' and she really understands you. You're ever so grateful and just wanted to show some appreciation. Oh, and is she pretty? I bet you hardly even *noticed*. Right?"

He drummed his fingertips on his chest, opened his eyes. "Something like that. And I suppose I should just ignore the fact that you've been dressed only in a nightie all day?"

Her shoulders drooped. "No. Lehigh, I was trying to surprise you, and...everything got all messed up."

Lucky stuck her wet nose into Stacy's folded hands. She brushed the dog away. The hound curled up on the floor between them, joined by Diamond.

"All right, I get that," Lehigh said. "Now, about Sam. The thing is, she *is* really sharp, she's a great strategist, and *has* done a ton of work already. A new lawyer would have to repeat a lot of it—and I can't afford it."

"Think about this. Can you afford to lose *me*?" Stacy stood, stomped into the bedroom, and locked the door behind her.

***

Lehigh parked outside of the sheriff's office about ten minutes before their scheduled appointment. A dark gray Lexus pulled in next to his pickup seconds later. Samantha Pullen got out and waved. He joined her on the walk up to the double doors of the entrance.

"I understand you had another little adventure since I saw you last," she said with a smile.

"Stacy did, anyway." He held the door open for her. "How'd you hear?"

"I spent much of the last hour at Constantine Richards' office." She waited outside the door and lowered her voice. "By the way, he called in a favor with his old buddy Jim Wadsworth, and convinced him to return her license to her. You can pick it up from Deputy Latner." She nodded in the direction of the reception desk, where Dwayne stood, staring at his computer screen.

"Good afternoon, Mr. Carter," Latner said. "You got an appointment, or have you found yourself some new trouble to get into this fine day?" He grinned like a mischievous third grader who'd just gotten away with something. Odd behavior for Dwayne, but then, everything seemed weird these days.

"I just figured I'd check on my room, see if it's still as comfy as my last visit," Lehigh said. Dwayne blinked, confusion written all over his face. Lehigh sighed. Sarcasm was a lost cause on simple minds. "I'm told you've got something for me?"

Dwayne searched under the counter and produced a white letter-sized envelope with Stacy's name written across it in a neat, elegant script. "For your fiancée, but I reckon it's okay to give it to you." He handed Lehigh the envelope.

"We're here to see Mr. Summers," Sam said. "We're a few minutes early."

Latner squinted at the screen and shook his head. "I don't see you on his calendar. Hold on a sec." He picked up the desk phone receiver and dialed a few digits. Waited. "This is Dwayne. Mr. Carter and, uh, what's your name, Miss?"

"Pullen. I'm Mr. Carter's attorney."

"Carter and a Miss Pullen are here to see Buck...oh. Okay. I'll let 'em know." He hung up and shrugged. "Sher–er, Mr. Summers regrets to have to cancel your meeting. Urgent business."

Lehigh leaned on the counter. "What kind of urgent business?"

Dwayne shrugged.

"Are you sure?" Sam asked. "He and Mr. Ferguson were quite adamant that we resume our interview at precisely two o'clock."

Dwayne shrugged. "The Reverend ain't here neither. I'd a seen him come in."

"Fine," Lehigh said. "Their loss. I really didn't want to talk to them anyway. I just wish they'd have called and saved us the trip." And an hour of his lawyer's expensive time. He bolted for the door.

"Lehigh, wait," Sam called after him. Outside the door, she smiled. "This is good news. It means they're probably not serious about pursuing you as a suspect."

"Then who are they after?"

Her face clouded. "You're not going to like my answer."

She was right. He didn't.

***

"Speaking of Stacy," he said a few moments later, standing between their parked cars, "*she's* not happy about you being my lawyer."

"May I ask why?"

He shrugged. "Basically—and I don't mean this in a bad way—you're too pretty."

Sam's face darkened. "That's a pretty poor reason. I wish I could say it's the first time someone's made assumptions about me because of my appearance. But you're the client—you choose who represents you. What do you think?"

He coughed. "Well...she's right about you being very attractive. But I also think you're a good lawyer. And I don't want to start over with someone else. I'm...I'm kind of in a bind."

Sam dropped her briefcase into her car, closed the door, and crossed her arms. "Did she give you the option of choosing *her* lawyer?"

He chuckled. "Nope."

She nodded, deep in thought. "I tell you what, then. I'll keep working until you tell me not to. If for any reason you're unhappy with my work—and I mean *any* reason—you just say the word, and I'll find you a replacement myself. Deal?"

Lehigh hitched his thumbs into his belt. "Will my replacement lawyer be as good as you?"

She grinned. "On that question, *I'll* plead the fifth."

Lehigh returned the grin and stuck out his hand. "You got a deal, counselor."

***

The next morning, Wadsworth pushed open the swinging glass door into the tiny foyer of Dot's Diner. Even with the inner door shut, the smell of grease, stale coffee, and burnt bacon overwhelmed him. How people could stomach this joint, when Shirley's down on the strip served up such great hash browns and burgers—and pie to die for—he'd never understand.

He stepped inside. Two or three groups of old men, no more than three in a group, clustered around chipped Formica tables in each corner. No one sat at the long counter.

"Evening, Detective. Coffee? On the house." Dot, the frumpy matron with brown Brillo for hair and the hairiest arms of any woman he'd ever seen, volunteered a cheery smile and a chipped porcelain cup half filled with thin, light brown fluid.

"Many thanks, ma'am." He never turned down free coffee or an available restroom. He never knew when the next one might come along. He sat, sipped, and forced himself to swallow. As many times as he'd frequented Dot's, he managed to forget every time that she made the worst coffee in the entire Pacific Northwest. As much as he hated to do it, he waved at her and formulated his request. "Could I trouble you for some—"

"Cream and sugar, coming right up." The desired condiments appeared from nowhere. Dot stood in front of him, staring. He stirred in two heaping scoops of sugar and as much cream as coffee. Which made it almost drinkable.

"Lehigh Carter been here today?" He set his spoon down on the counter.

"Nope. He ain't been here in weeks. Not since before…" She turned, busied herself at wiping the counter.

"Since before what?"

Wipe, wipe. She hummed something, not really a song.

"Since Jared Barkley died?"

She froze mid-wipe, then resumed, and nodded.

"Why were you so reluctant to say that?" He sipped his coffee and somehow did not choke. Horrible stuff.

She opened her mouth to speak, then closed it and found a spot farther down the counter that needed wiping.

"Dot—can I call you Dot?"

She shrugged. "It's my name."

He followed her down the counter, sliding a finger along its greasy surface. "He was a regular here, wasn't he?"

"Who?" She flipped over her rag, wiped harder.

"Suppose you tell me."

She glared at him from beneath her bristly curls. "I got lots of regulars."

Wadsworth grabbed her counter rag and yanked it out of her hand. He grabbed her wrist with his other hand and held it in space between them. "Don't be coy with me, lady. Or would you like your next official visit to be from the Health Department?"

She stared at him, eyes and nostrils wide, then shook her arm free. "Fine. Yes, they both used to come here. Jared Barkley and Lehigh Carter. Not together, even though…"

Wadsworth drew a heavy breath. "Even though?"

"They used to come here at different times…with the same

girl."

Wadsworth's jaw dropped. "Which girl?"

"That politician's daughter. With the black ponytail. McBride. Stacy McBride."

CHAPTER 17

Wadsworth plunked his heavy frame onto the closest stool, the tall spinning metal kind with cracked red vinyl over a thin layer of compressed foam. The stool spun under his weight, and he had to rotate it back to put Dot back in his field of vision.

"You saw them in here together? Stacy McBride and Jared Barkley?"

"Lots of times. They almost always sat in that corner." She pointed to a tiny square-top with two chairs at right angles to each other. A wiry man wearing overalls and a large-truck manufacturer's cap over a thinning scalp sipped coffee and stared back at them. Dot wiped her hands with the counter rag. "Seems they liked their privacy."

"Did they ever do anything…romantic?" Wadsworth made air quotes around "romantic," but Dot shook her head.

"They wanted privacy, I give it to 'em. You don't get a lot of repeat customers if you go spying on people." She set the rag down and shuffled toward the kitchen.

"Wait. One more question." His favorite and most effective fib. He *always* had more questions. "When did they come in? Late at night? Daytime?"

"Afternoons, evening…maybe a few mornings. Last time was a couple of days before you found him." She walked faster toward the swinging door.

"Which days of the week?"

Dot shrugged. "I take Tuesdays off and sometimes Mondays. So, the other days, I reckon."

"Can you possibly be more specific?" Pleading rather than commanding.

The corners of her lips lifted from her near-permanent grimace to a flat line. Almost a smile for her. She glanced at the empty counter. "No." A twitch of her eyebrow, then she turned on her heel and disappeared into the noisy kitchen.

***

Wadsworth checked a number of other likely meeting places in town, including several fast food chains along the strip of highway that served as Clarkesville's main drag, but none of the employees on duty had worked there long enough, or were observant enough, to have noticed whether the illicit couple had patronized the establishments, together or alone. Exhausted, he returned to headquarters to document his findings.

To his surprise, Deputy Dwayne Latner did not greet him at the front desk. A junior recruit did, an early-twenty-something boy he'd once arrested for shoplifting. Back then the kid sported a loose ponytail, fuzzy moustache, and a nose ring. He'd cleaned up since then—crew cut, clean shaven, no face jewelry, and now, the beige uniform of the Mt. Hood County Sheriff's Office.

"Where's Dwayne?" he asked the kid, whose nameplate read "T. Roscoe."

"In his office." Roscoe grinned like a kid eating ice cream.

"What office? Since when does Dwayne get an office?"

The kid's grin widened. "Since he became the acting sheriff."

"He *what?*" Wadsworth steadied his weight against the counter. "When the...how did... Holy mackerel!"

"The County Commission appointed him today, on my recommendation." The booming voice of former Sheriff Buck Summers echoed across the room. Buck stood in the doorway to the back offices, thumbs hooked on his size forty-eight belt. "They met in executive session yesterday afternoon."

Dwayne Latner. Sheriff. Holy smokes. The commission

could not have found an emptier vessel to pour their hopes into for "cleaning up the department." Only Buck's patronage—and Dwayne's loyalty to the corrupt, well-connected old coot—kept him on the county payroll all these years. He sure hadn't made it on brainpower.

And now, sheriff.

Wadsworth rubbed his temples. "Why didn't he mention it when I talked to him this morning? And, not to be rude, Buck, but what the heck are you doing here?"

Buck grinned. Only then did Wadsworth notice the silver deputy badge pinned to Buck's camel-colored suit jacket. "Come on inside," Buck said. "Let's talk about Stacy McBride."

***

Amazement. Shock. Incredulity. Wadsworth couldn't find a strong enough word to describe his reaction to Buck's news and his sudden return to active duty status in the sheriff's office.

"The grand jury refused to return an indictment against me earlier this week," Buck said once he'd led Wadsworth to his new office, the opulence of which doubled the detective's shock level. Already decked out with Buck's old oversized desk and memorabilia from twenty-five years in uniform, it looked like he'd somehow managed to beam up his old office from down the hall, Star Trek style. "It appears they lacked a key witness—one that you arrested yesterday morning, I believe."

"That was *your* hearing she missed?" Wadsworth steadied himself with clammy hands on the arms of Buck's uncomfortable vinyl guest chair.

"Yep. Key witness fails to show, the jury had no choice but to set me free. At which point, the sheriff had no choice but to reinstate me on the force."

"But there was no sheriff yesterday."

"Exactly. So they had to appoint one. With all the recent goings-on, they didn't feel comfortable appointing me yet.

Wimped out, if you ask me."

Wadsworth grunted. Only Buck could see it that way.

"But they took my recommendation to pick Dwayne—someone they know will only want to hold the job on an interim basis, until the election this fall."

Wadsworth grunted louder. Stupid politicians. Well, he couldn't blame them for picking one of their own kind. Idiots, that is. "So how does this affect your status on the Barkley murder case?" he asked. "I assume that since you're no longer a contractor—"

"I'll be taking charge of it." Buck's slimy grin chilled the air. "You'll report to me now."

Wadsworth's stomach tightened. "I see. The new 'acting sheriff' made this decision?"

"I did indeedy." Dwayne's lanky figure occupied the open doorway of Buck's office. The shiny five-pointed gold star, Mt Hood County's traditional badge of honor for the chief occupant of the sheriff's office, occupied a prominent space on his beige uniform. "My first official decision."

"And a good one," Buck said, with an even larger, slimier grin. "You're off to a great start, Dw—I mean, *Sheriff* Latner."

Dwayne straightened his slack stance and lifted his chin, giving him a comical, almost cartoonish man-in-charge posture. "Thank you, Sher—I mean, *First Deputy* Summers."

Wadsworth stood, breath hissing from his lips, and extended his hand to Dwayne. "Congratulations, Sheriff. Best of luck to you. Well, I guess I should get back to investigating."

"On that note, Detective, I have some new information for you." Buck pulled a manila file from his desk drawer and slid it across his desk. "My notes from some recent interviews with witnesses."

"What witnesses?"

"It's all in the file. Along with some other very interesting tidbits."

"Give me the five cent tour."

Buck's grin curled into an evil sneer. "We've got motive, means, and opportunity on a suspect. Seems Jared Barkley had made a real enemy out there, based on some of his own investigations into the seedier businesses here in Clarkesville."

"Really? Jeez, Buck, you could have spared me a heck of a lot of wasted effort today if I'd known this sooner."

"Don't worry, Jim. Your efforts have not been wasted one teeny tiny little bit. It all helps build the case."

"Only if...wait a sec. Who was the suspect Barkley was investigating?"

Buck tapped the folder with a stumpy finger. "It's not who he targeted with his investigation. It's the collateral findings—what he found on other people."

"Like who?" Wadsworth's blood pressure rose to the bursting point. Patience was never one of his strongest virtues.

"What Jared Barkley found—and what certain people didn't want brought to light—was the secret past of a certain someone which could prove very embarrassing and damaging to the reputations of some very important people in this town."

"Namely?"

The evil grin returned. Buck patted the file with a beefy hand. "None other than Stacy Lynn McBride."

***

Back in his own office, Wadsworth paged through Buck's typewritten notes—word processed, technically, but Gentleman Jim remained a steadfast old-schooler—about Barkley's investigation of Stacy McBride. Barkley's own notes—a mix of neat handwriting, instant print photos, and bullet-point typed pages—painted a damning picture.

While investigating Paul van Paten's role in the intimidation of Lehigh Carter the previous fall, Barkley stumbled onto some evidence of a connection between Stacy McBride and Everett Downey, a local businessman who liked to call himself an "entrepreneur," but whom Wadsworth preferred to call a smut dealer. Downey owned a series of cheap motels, casinos, dive bars, adult video stores, and strip clubs in the county. Photos and notes showed that Stacy often used a luxury suite in back of one of Downey's dance clubs as her own private getaway—often for trysts with whomever she happened to be dating at the time, including, at different times, both Paul van Paten and Lehigh Carter. Barkley's file created a convincing picture of van Paten's hand in the arson of Carter's home and the break-in at the animal clinic the previous fall, but also one that raised serious questions about the reputation of the beautiful daughter of the county's most powerful politician.

But the proof, and the investigation, didn't stop there. The file also included documentation—some of it almost twenty years old—that Stacy had secured access to this suite the hard way: as a dancer in one of Downey's strip clubs.

Well, she sure had the body for it. Especially back then.

Wadsworth closed his eyes, tried to put that evil, tempting image out of his mind. In twenty-five years of marriage to the same wonderful woman, he'd never once strayed further than the occasional purchase of a *Sports Illustrated* swimsuit issue—which he'd hidden from his wife with the utmost care, so as not to offend her. Gwen would have never forgiven him, and he'd have never forgiven himself for hurting her if she'd found them. She never had that kind of body, nor the shameless urge to display it in such a crass, corrupt way.

He reopened his eyes, flipped through the pages to the back of the folder.

Then things got weird.

The "evidence" Barkley had collected included some dark, faded photos from nearly twenty years before from, apparently, the inside of Downey's club. In one, a somewhat skinnier, much younger, red-haired woman with an otherwise striking resemblance to Stacy McBride, wearing essentially a black G-string, fishnet stockings, and four inch heels, sat on the lap of a much older gentleman. A man who had since risen to a powerful position in the county, prosecuting criminals. A man who had ambitions of rising higher in the halls of power—Attorney General, according to some rumors. A man whose reputation would suffer mightily if such a picture ever hit the newsstands.

A man whom, because of his Bible-citing ways, others often called "The Reverend."

In the photo, Stacy had her arms wrapped around him, her lips an inch from his ear, as if propositioning him. The man's hand rested on her thigh. He was smiling.

Wadsworth was not.

CHAPTER 18

Stacy fished a chunk of gooey orange chicken out of the take-out container with her chopsticks and plunked the glop into her mouth. She savored its over-the-top sweetness, its melt-in-your-mouth overcookedness, its warmth.

"Thank you for picking up dinner, honey." She leaned over on the couch and pecked Lehigh on the cheek. After she'd cooled off from the shenanigans of her arrest and Lehigh's too-cozy relationship with his gorgeous attorney, they'd talked for hours into the night, falling asleep fully dressed in each other's arms. As he'd promised, Lehigh drove her to work in the morning and picked her up in the evening, dinner in hand. Only afterwards did he confess that he'd had her license in his possession the whole time. She laughed to herself. Such a sweet man.

He finished chewing a mouthful of beef lo mein and squeezed her knee. A welcome, loving touch after too many days of either separation or, when together, constant bickering. "My pleasure. Sure beats having me cook my usual."

"Oh, I don't know. I love having pancakes for dinner." She smiled and speared a piece of beef from his container. "This is good. Let's trade."

He scanned both containers and put on a half-frown, half-smile. "I think I'm getting the worse end of the deal here. How can such a small gal like you eat so much faster than me?" But he slid the beef toward her and reached for the chicken.

She plucked a small bite of beef out of the container and

sucked the savory sauce from it before chewing. They still hadn't yet discussed the one thing she most dreaded: her meetings with Jared over the past several months. Never a man of words, no doubt Lehigh simply hadn't found a comfortable way or convenient time to ask the tough questions, and she wasn't going to bring it up if she could help it. But it occupied heavy space in the room, creating long periods of silence where difficult, but open and necessary, conversation belonged.

Clearly he was waiting for her, so… She took a deep breath and opened her mouth to speak. But before she could come up with the right words, a knock sounded on the door. The dogs, quarantined out back so the couple could eat in peace, erupted into a cacophony of crazy barking. "I'll get it," he said. "You keep eating, Miss Piggy."

"Hey!" Relieved, she swatted his butt on the way by. Her hand stung. Lehigh needed to add some padding to that bony tush. Maybe she should slow down after all and give him a bigger share of dinner. Besides, she couldn't afford to gain any weight now that the dressmaker had begun her work for the Big Day, thanks to her mom's generosity.

"What the hell are *you* doing here?" Lehigh's body blocked the doorway.

"Who is it, honey?" she shouted above the noise of the dogs.

"You're not gonna believe it. Hell, I don't believe it."

The barking ceased for an inexplicable moment, and a far-too-familiar voice responded. "That's always been your problem, Carter. You're too stupid to believe what's right before your eyes."

Stacy froze. Oh, God no. Please, no.

Lehigh slid to one side and the tall, handsome figure in the doorway became visible, grinning his guilty-but-I-don't-care grin, and tipped his white cowboy hat. A brand new hat—he'd never taken to them before. Not in all the years she'd known Paul van Paten.

"Well," he said, "aren't you going to invite me in? We have

so much to talk about."

Lehigh, eyes ablaze, slammed the door shut in Paul's grinning face, and the dogs erupted once again.

***

Loud, obnoxious knocking began moments later, almost inaudible over the noise of the dogs. "Quiet, dogs!" Lehigh settled back onto the couch and picked up his chopsticks. Stacy sighed and set hers down.

"He's not going away, you know," she said.

"He ain't coming in, neither." Lehigh snagged a mouthful of beef from her box.

The knocking stopped, and moments later, so did the barking. Seconds later the phone rang. Stacy stood. "I'll get it."

"If it's Paul, ask him why he's not in jail."

"If I can get a word in edgewise. You know how he can get. All the world's his soapbox." She walked into the kitchen at a deliberate pace and let the phone ring for the fourth time. The answering machine clicked on.

"Stacy, it's Paul. Pick up, I obviously know you're in there." Knocking resumed at the front door.

She picked up the receiver. "When did they let you out?"

"Hello to you, too. Aren't you going to let me in? It's cold out here."

"I'd rather we talk privately." Never mind that the machine would record it all, and that Lehigh could hear it all on the machine's speaker.

"Fine. Actually, that's probably best. I only came by to tell you that you really ought to rethink what you're doing. Protecting Lehigh Carter is only going to bring you down."

"Protecting...? What do you mean?"

Paul laughed. "Come on, Stacy. It's me you're talking to, not that hayseed ignoramus farting on your couch. We both know Carter plugged Barkley."

"He did no such thing. He was a hundred miles away from here." She glanced at Lehigh, who nodded and pointed outside, then gave a questioning shrug. Stacy picked up on the hint. "Speaking of which, where were you last weekend?"

"Playing poker on the Oregon coast. Lots of witnesses will back me up. Not so for your backwoods boy. I heard he got lost on the highway."

"You heard wrong. Anyway, what reason would Lehigh have to kill Jared?"

"The same reason all of your men do crazy dumb-ass things. You drive them to it." Another laugh, this one low and hollow.

"You're the only one that's ever acted like a lunatic." She made a fist with her free hand. Good thing Lehigh hadn't let Paul in. She'd have slugged him by now.

"I beg to differ. Lehigh's as jealous as the next guy, and we both know Jared's been trying to get into your pants for years."

Stacy raised the phone over her head, ready to smash it into the wall. She counted to five, then brought it down to her ear, her hand shaking. "Regardless of what you think he may have wanted, nothing ever came of it."

"Yeah, you keep telling yourself that, and the bonehead in the living room. I know better, and it's all going to come out sooner or later. If it comes out wrong, you're going to prison. Do it right, and that lamebrain logger friend of yours—"

The front door slammed shut. Loud crashing sounds echoed in Stacy's ear, full of static, and the dogs' barking resumed in stereo, coming from both the phone and the backyard. A second man's voice sounded in the receiver, muffled and distant, but fully recognizable…and echoed in through the walls as well.

"Get off this property before I break your damned neck."

"Let–go–you're–choking–me—"

"On purpose, too. If you ever speak one more word to or about Stacy or me, I'll rip your throat out and tie your mouth shut with it. Understood? Good. Now *get*!"

After a loud, crunching sound, the phone went dead.

***

Stacy rolled onto her left side, facing away from Lehigh in the spacious king-sized bed, for the five hundredth time in the past ten minutes. Or so it seemed. Her much-needed beauty sleep proved an elusive quarry after the day's tumultuous conclusion.

Lehigh slumbered next to her. The man could sleep through earthquakes, physical or emotional. She considered waking him—talking to someone right now could really help—but resisted the urge. It'd just make him as miserable as she, and what good would that do?

Paul's visit had unnerved her more than the prospect of being arrested again. She'd retained the best lawyer in the county in Constantine Richards, and if the cops wanted to play dirty, well, so could she. She was not above using the influence of George Lindsay McBride if it came to that.

But the fact that Paul had somehow gained his freedom changed the whole equation. That meant he'd worked the system somehow, using, and thereby tainting, the very same levers of influence available to her. No doubt he'd poisoned those waters and filled them with his own version of events—none of which would favor her case.

Nor Lehigh's. Definitely not Lehigh's.

Plus it meant Paul's harassment would pick up where it left off before his arrest. His visit earlier in the evening proved that, even after Lehigh had dusted him up a little. He simply couldn't resist taunting her, and he'd never forgive her for dumping him. If he truly believed it yet, even after almost six months. Sometimes she doubted it. Paul could convince himself, and others, of the most outrageous falsehoods. Like the way he spread the tale about them being engaged, even though he'd never formally proposed and she'd never accepted.

Still, his message scared her, implying that the police had uncovered some new damning information about her—something she could, if she chose, use to divert suspicion to Lehigh. A jealousy angle of some sort, involving Jared Barkley.

Which meant that somebody had done some serious

digging into her past. Hers, Jared Barkley's, or both.

Which reminded her: she never did get back to telling Lehigh why she'd met with Jared so often in recent months. Paul's intrusion had left Lehigh in a sour mood for hours, and he only calmed down in time to announce he needed to go to bed. The conversation would be tough enough with him in a good mood. No way would she try when he was already furious.

She rolled over again, facing Lehigh's broad back. Most sleepless nights, she'd spoon up next to him, and his regular heavy breathing and warm, strong body would lull her to sleep. But somehow cuddling him felt wrong right then—awkward, even dishonest. He trusted her, in spite of everything pointing to reasons he shouldn't. Meanwhile, she'd suspected him of the worst at the first opportunity.

Of course, he never actually denied any of it.

She shifted again and faced the window. Faint moonlight trickled in through the drapes. The digital alarm clock emitted a faint hum. The furnace kicked in, sending a whoosh of warm air into the room.

A hand curled around her waist from behind, and a muscular leg grazed against hers.

"What's up, honey?" he whispered.

She placed her hand over his and pressed it into her abdomen. He squeezed her close, moved his hand northward over her ribs to seek out softer, suppler flesh. His lips caressed her neck, her ear, her face.

Maybe being awake wouldn't be so bad after all.

***

Lehigh shook himself awake at his makeshift desk and wiped drool off of his chin with a shirtsleeve. Dang, twice that morning he'd dozed off sitting up. At this rate he'd waste the whole day without getting a thing done.

But then again, so what? He had no deadlines to meet— nothing firm, anyway. And the reason for his exhaustion—

Stacy jumping his bones at the slightest provocation. Well, small price to pay.

He stared down at the draft blueprints in front of him, plans for rebuilding his house up on Brady Mountain. The house seemed small, even though he'd added a hundred square feet to the existing footprint. More important, it blew the budget he'd set for it, the amount of the insurance settlement, by fifty thousand bucks. On top of the legal bills, he couldn't afford to increase his mortgage debt any further, at least not until some of his forest stands matured. Which, being trees, he could do little to accelerate.

He stood, stretched, cracked his back, and headed into the kitchen to get some coffee. It had gone cold, so he put a cup in the microwave. While the machine whirred, he took creamer out of the fridge and sniffed it. On its last legs, but drinkable.

The phone's sudden ring echoed off the walls. Lucky and Diamond emerged from nowhere, barking their fool heads off. "Quiet, dogs!" That worked until the next ring, three seconds later. He kicked open the back door to let them outside and picked up after the third ring.

"Mr. Carter? Please hold for Constantine Richards."

"Screw that," he said to the efficient young woman at the other end of the line. "Tell him to call when he's—"

"Mr. Carter?" Richards sounded irritated. Maybe he'd heard Lehigh's rant. Good for him. That might teach him to dump a good client. "I'm afraid I have some bad news."

"More bad news? What the hell else could go wrong this week?" Probably not much, since it was almost Friday.

"Your fiancée was arrested once again this afternoon."

"Oh hell. Now what for? Another speeding ticket?"

Richards cleared his throat and his voice lowered to a thunderous rumble. "I'm afraid this time, it's much more serious. Mr. Carter, Stacy has been charged with murder."

CHAPTER 19

Lehigh pounded the steering wheel for the fifth time since dashing unshaven and unshowered out of the house. This time it hurt his hand, which pissed him off, so he smacked the wheel again, this time with his other hand. It hurt even worse when he gripped the wheel for a NASCAR-style pass of a crappy little Toyota hybrid whose driver apparently cared more about his dashboard readings than what went on around him on the road. Probably a freaking Portlander. Never mind that other people had places to go, things to do.

Like strangle Buck Summers, for starters.

He skidded to a stop in the parking lot at the Sheriff's office, startling a uniformed deputy into spilling his coffee, a new recruit Lehigh didn't recognize. Probably one of Buck's nephews or some such. He slammed the truck door shut behind him and stalked toward the entrance.

The young deputy hustled to intercept him. "Sir? That was not a safe entry into this—"

Lehigh held up an open palm. "Stow it, kid. I'm in a hurry." The kid's name tag read "T. Roscoe."

"Sir, I'm going to have to ask you to show some identification. Your driver's license, regist—"

Lehigh spun on one heel, smacked the foam coffee cup out of the deputy's hand, and pointed a finger in his face. "One more word out of you and I tell your mother you're skipping algebra to smoke cigarettes. Now get out of my way or I'll feed you to my dogs. In pieces. Starting with your balls. *Get!*"

The deputy, already at least four inches shorter than Lehigh, shrunk further under the taller man's fierce glare. He opened his mouth to object, then shut it and stepped aside. "I'll let you go with a warning," he said. "This time."

Lehigh rolled his eyes and pulled open the double glass doors. Nobody sat behind the desk—probably T. Roscoe's job, the slacker. He walked over to the door labeled "Staff only beyond this point" and pushed the door open wide.

"Sir, you can't go in there!" The kid again.

"In that case, you guys should invest in some locks." Lehigh kept walking. Where to, he had no idea.

"Sir? Sir?" Fast footsteps grew louder behind him.

Lehigh spun to face the huffing, red-faced Roscoe. "If you insist on being part of this party, at least make yourself useful. Where's Stacy McBride?"

The kid stopped, mouth open. "You must be Lehigh Carter."

Maybe the kid wasn't as dumb as he looked. "Suppose I am. Does that help or hinder?"

"Wait right here." The deputy disappeared behind the double doors again, then returned with an envelope in his hand. The return address read "C. Richards, Attorney at Law." Lehigh's name appeared in neat typewritten letters at the center of the envelope. The bottom read, "Private Correspondence."

"Thanks." Lehigh tore open the envelope and scanned the first page. Halfway through, vomit surged up his throat. He clamped down and swallowed it, then re-read the page.

Somehow, though he'd never have predicted it, things had gotten a whole hell of a lot worse.

***

"What do you mean, I can't see her?" Lehigh balled his hands into fists and resisted the urge to pummel the bobbing Adam's apple of Constantine Richards.

"You will need to be deposed," Richards said for the twenty thousandth time. "It is best if you two do not have the opportunity to share information—or even appear to have that opportunity."

"How idiotic. Need I remind you that we live together?" Lehigh grabbed at his long locks and stomped around the room. "At least we did, until she took up residence at old Iron Bar Hotel here, courtesy of crooked cops!" His shout strained his throat, already sore from thirty minutes of "talking" with his former lawyer.

"I might recommend, for her sake, a change in your arrangements in that regard." Richards blinked a few times. Dandruff stuck to the tips of a few of his eyelashes. "Assuming she is released, of course."

"What changes? And what do you mean 'assuming'? Aren't you here to spring her out of this hoosegow?" Resist. Urge. To. Strangle.

"That matter is pending. It appears she will be detained until a hearing, tentatively set for Friday morning. Before then, you should find suitable alternative living arrangements." Two more blinks, and a tuft of white flakes floated onto the lapel of his otherwise immaculate dark blue suit.

"You're telling me I gotta move out of our house?"

Richards brushed the speck off his lapel and cleared his throat. "Of course it is not legally required. But with the potential for you being called as a witness for both sides, not to mention the possibility of being charged separately as an accomplice—"

"What?" Lehigh's screech hurt his own ears. The wince on Richards' face indicated he shared the injury. Lehigh stomped in circles around the small meeting room, bumping into extra chairs and thrusting them aside in wanton disregard for noise and breakage. "This is so damned screwed up. How the hell could you let this happen? We pay you big bucks, mister, to keep this sort of crap from happening. Well, I ain't moving out. You're just going to have to deal with it."

"If you'd consider the ramifications for her defense—"

"If you'll consider the ramifications of me firing your ugly butt!"

Richards grimaced. "Mr. Carter, if you'll forgive me. Only Miss McBride can make that decision."

"And she will. Let me see her, and—"

"Mr. Carter, the decision not to discuss any of this with you was also her decision. As was the decision for you to change residences."

Lehigh stopped pacing and stared.

Richards pointed to the phone on the table. "Perhaps now would be a good time for you to consult with your own attorney."

***

Lehigh emptied the contents of his bathroom drawer into a shoe box, tossed in the toothbrush and razor blade he kept by the sink, and slammed the box's lid over the opening. Some space remained in the box, but he had no time or patience for efficient packing.

All of his stuff fit in the back of the pickup with ease, one benefit of having lost most of his possessions to fire six months before. He whistled for the dogs. Lucky appeared from nowhere, bounded into the open door of the king cab and hopped into the open jump seat in back. A second later, Diamond scrambled in behind her.

His stomach rumbled. He hadn't had time to eat since breakfast, some seven-plus hours ago. He craved a burger and beer. He knew of a place where he could get both cheap, pretty close to the motel on the highway. Lucky would be fine in the cab of the truck.

He hadn't seen Stacy since before her arrest, nor heard from her, other than through her pompous-assed lawyer. He realized he'd blown his chance of getting her to talk about her dinner dates, or whatever the hell they were, with Jared Barkley. He'd waited too long for the right moment, and now—well. Maybe cutting him off *was* her idea, after all.

Even so, she couldn't have been the one to decide that Lehigh should leave. It had to have been Richards—but she'd gone along with it. Unbelievable. Three months before their wedding and things were unraveling with gale force. The wedding would have to be postponed, if it could happen at all. She might still be in jail, if her hearing the next day didn't go well. Even if it did, Lehigh didn't feel inclined to marry someone who kicked him out of the house, met secretly with other men, and wouldn't speak to him, no matter what some big-bucks lawyer advised.

Fifteen minutes later, he pulled into the parking lot of the Roadhouse Grill and skidded to a stop. Two men in cowboy hats looked up from their cigarettes, eyes squinted. A steady drizzle blurred their images through the windshield in seconds.

"I won't be long, dogs." He lowered his windows a crack and opened the back slider window a few inches. They wouldn't mind if a few drops of rain got in. He locked the truck and headed to the entrance, nodding at the two men on the way by. One of them nodded back. The other stared at him, holding smoke inside puffed cheeks.

The Roadhouse could get rowdy on a Friday night, but early Thursdays drew a more sedate crowd—truckers wolfing down an early dinner, locals grabbing a quick shot of whiskey after work, the occasional hungry tourist looking for local color on their way between Mt. Hood and Mt. Bachelor. A few locals, men who appeared to be in their twenties, laughed around a pool table, their equally young and jovial wives or girlfriends sitting on benches gossiping or admiring their manly men. A few held pool cues. All held drinks.

Lehigh sat on the short side of the L-shaped bar so he could keep his eye on things. Only the hallway to the restrooms and a few small tables remained out of his line of sight. He signaled the barkeep, a skinny, pony-tailed brunette with lines on her face whose gravity-defying bust practically provided chin support. She smiled, scurried over and slapped a beer coaster and paper menu in front of him. She stood at an angle to him, no doubt to make sure he could obtain the best possible view of her oversized boobs, skinny legs, and non-existent butt wrapped in a skirt as tight as sausage casings.

"Get ya something, handsome?"

He assumed she meant only food and drink. "A pale ale, one of them Portland ones," he said. "And food, in a minute." He picked up the menu.

She moved closer and leaned over the bar. So much for assumptions. Her cleavage didn't move, but she gave him a much better view of it. "Our specialty's the chicken dinner," she said. "All breast meat." Her eyes flickered downward. With great effort, his did not.

"Chicken sounds good. With the potatoes." He set down the menu.

"Save room for dessert." She wiggled away and shouted his order into a two-foot stainless steel opening to the kitchen and poured his beer. She help up an index finger to another customer—"wait"—and sauntered back to Lehigh.

"I know you." She set the beer down. A few drops splashed onto her fingers. She wiped her hands on a bar rag. "You're that Lee Carter fella, ain't you?"

He blinked. "Sorry I can't say the same. Have we met?" He sipped the beer. Cold, full-bodied and bitter. Kind of like her.

She winked. "Let's just say we have mutual friends."

At that moment, a hand clasped hard on his shoulder.

CHAPTER 20

The hand squeezed and pulled, whipping Lehigh around on his bar stool. Three men faced him—men he hadn't seen, or noticed at least, on his way in.

But he'd seen them plenty of times before.

To one side stood a short, overweight man wearing a black fedora over dark curls. On the other side slouched a taller, blond-haired man with a muscular build, leaning on a walking stick. Lehigh remembered their names: Thornburgh and Brockton. Thugs for hire, most recently in the employ of the dark-haired, smirking lawyer standing between them.

Paul van Paten cocked his head, hands on hips, and said, "I'd say you're a long way from home, but I hear home is a bit undefined for you at the moment."

"News travels fast in the underworld." Lehigh slid off the chair toward the blond one, who, though muscular, leaned on a cane. Thornburgh, the dumpy, curly-haired guy, a half-foot shorter than everyone else, stepped in front, blocking his path, and the other two slid over to box him in.

"We like to stay informed of what goes on in our backyard," Paul said. "For instance, when we see someone in here that doesn't belong, we pay attention."

"Can I get you gents a beer?" the barkeep called from behind Lehigh.

"No thanks, Babs." Paul kept his eyes on Lehigh. "In fact I think we're all set for a while. You may want to check on your food orders in the kitchen."

"Don't break anything," she said. Brockton's eyes followed what Lehigh guessed was the barkeep's skinny butt into the kitchen.

"Sorry, gentlemen," Lehigh said. "I didn't realize this was a private club. I'm happy to take my business elsewhere."

"Too late." Spittle flew from Thornburgh's mouth and landed on Lehigh's shirt. The blond guy, Brockton, snickered.

"I'm afraid my associate is correct." Paul edged toward Lehigh and dropped his hands to his sides. "They've probably already started cooking your dinner. You seem to be suggesting that you'd run out of here and stiff them for a half-made food order and a bar tab."

"That's bad," said the curly-haired guy.

"Real bad," Brockton said. The two of them edged closer.

"See, these folks, they're our friends," said Curly. Er, Thornburgh.

"We don't like people who mistreat our friends," Brockton said.

"Oh, I fully intend to pay." Lehigh reached for his wallet.

"Look out!" Brockton shouted. "He's going for his gun!"

Before Lehigh could protest, the two thugs grabbed his arms and pinned him to the bar.

"What the—"

Pain and lack of air—both phenomena centered around his abdomen—made further speech impossible. Fists pounded his stomach, kidneys, and other organs he could not name. Lehigh struggled to free his arms, but the two brutes hung on, and more blows rained on his midsection.

After eons, the punching stopped. The thugs loosened their grip on his arms. Lehigh's rubbery legs gave way and he crumpled to the floor. His head bumped the bar on the way down. When he could think again, he found himself kneeling on all fours on the filthy floor, aching all over and barely able to breathe. A pair of work boots connected to baggy, dirty overalls occupied most of his field of vision. Fancy black dress shoes and argyle socks blocked his view to the right.

Paul's voice cut through the ringing in Lehigh's ears.

"Consider that a down payment on what I owe you." He sucked in air—delivering the blows had winded him, apparently. "You ever come back in here, you'll get a double payment." Another noisy intake of air. "Anywhere I see you alone, in fact anywhere I happen to think you shouldn't be—same thing goes. You hear?" Another noisy breath.

"He shouldn't be anywhere, boss," one of the thugs said.

"True," Paul said. "You hear that, Carter? You shouldn't be anywhere—except maybe in prison. You and that lousy bitch you were hoping to marry. You hear me? *Were* going to marry. Because that isn't going to happen."

Lehigh held up one hand, half in surrender, half to shut his slimy mouth. "Oh…kay. Just…back up…a step. Let me get up."

One of the fancy dress shoes jabbed hard into his ribs, slamming Lehigh's body into the bar. Loud laughter echoed around the tavern. "You'll get up when I say so."

Lehigh sat against the bar, holding his sore gut. The blond thug held his walking stick like a baseball bat. He drew it back, swung it toward Lehigh's head—

He ducked, not quite in time. The cane's shaft glanced off the top of his head and smacked against the bar. Lehigh reached behind him and got lucky, catching the cane on its return swing. He yanked it out of the blond's grasp, then used it to jab its owner in the groin. The thug went down with a loud grunt.

With no wasted motion, he swung the cane and connected with the side of a well dressed knee. Paul howled and collapsed on top of the blond thug. Another hard poke of the cane crunched Paul's nose and elicited another howl.

The curly-haired man's thick boot landed another direct hit in Lehigh's ribs, and then it was Lehigh's turn to howl. He swung the cane wildly, missed. The thug kicked again, a glancing blow off Lehigh's bent knee. Lehigh cursed, grabbed a nearby bar stool and threw it at Curly. It fell far short, but forced Thornburgh to back up a step. Lehigh scrambled to his feet and roundhouse-punched him in the temple. His nemesis collapsed on top of his blond companion like a deflating balloon.

Paul, on his knees, held his bleeding nose a few steps away, pointing at Lehigh. "That's the one, deputies. Arrest him!"

Two uniformed sheriff's deputies hustled around Paul, clubs raised. "Hands up!" one of them shouted. A familiar face—Sergeant Patrick of house search fame. Next to him, another familiar face—Deputy Flynn.

Lehigh raised his hands to ear level, panting. "Gentlemen, do you really believe I attacked three guys?"

"He's got a gun!" Brockton pushed Thornburgh off him. "Check him for weapons!"

"I ain't got no—"

"Turn around! Hands on the bar!" Patrick shouted.

"But—"

"I said turn around!" Patrick's face flushed deep red.

Lehigh sighed, turned, leaned forward, and spread his hands on the bar. Someone kicked his heels apart and he almost fell. Hands patted his sides, legs, and arms.

"He's clean, Sarge."

"He musta dropped it somewhere," said Brockton. Or maybe a groggy Thornburgh.

"I saw him reach for it," said someone who sounded a lot like Babs.

"Search the area," Patrick said. "Lock that door. Nobody leaves until we find the weapon."

"There ain't no gun," Lehigh said.

"Mr. Carter, you're under arrest," Patrick said. "You have the right to remain silent."

Lehigh thought it best to exercise that right.

CHAPTER 21

Someone pounded on Detective Jim Wadsworth's office door. He glanced at the clock and cursed under his breath. He should have gone home an hour ago for dinner. If he remained quiet, maybe the intruder would believe that he had.

"Detective?" Sgt. Cam Patrick's voice yelled through the door. "You in there? We need your help, or at least, your office."

Wadsworth cursed again. Stuck. "Yeah, I'm here. What's up?"

Patrick stuck his head in the door. "We got a bunch of guys in a bar fight and we need to separate them and talk to them. Buck's not here, so we've got van Paten in there—"

"Paul van Paten was in a bar fight? With whom? Oh, hell. Don't tell me. Lehigh Carter."

Patrick nodded. "He had some help. Two guys. They're here too."

"Who had help? Carter or van Paten?"

"You kidding me? You think Lehigh Carter needs help fighting anybody?"

Wadsworth grunted. "Good point. Okay, bring Carter in here. Separate the other grunts in the interrogation rooms. Who else we got?"

"Roscoe, Flynn, and Latner. The Reverend's on his way over."

"What? Why is he coming? Who called him?"

"Dwayne did. Says he wants the big boys here anytime van

Paten's involved."

"Crap. Anyone make a statement yet?"

Patrick shrugged. "Carter says they jumped him. The waitress says he pulled a gun on them, but we searched him and the whole bar and didn't find one. I should mention, one of the guys, Brockton, is her boyfriend."

"Let me talk to van Paten first." Wadsworth lumbered down the hall toward Buck's office. Moments later, Deputy Flynn escorted Paul van Paten into the office. Paul held a bloody gauze against his nose.

Wadsworth glared at Flynn. "No handcuffs?"

Flynn shrugged. "He's got a nosebleed. I didn't figure him to be running, or slugging anybody." Under Wadsworth's angry glare, he slunk toward the door and pushed it shut.

Wadsworth settled into the chair behind Buck's desk and grabbed a pencil and paper. "All right, Mr. van Paten. Take a seat. What happened?"

Paul settled himself into the guest chair and leaned his head back. "I like this chair. Seems like I've been in it once or twice before. Oh, yeah, now I remember—it was the *last* time you guys arrested me for no reason. No, wait. Maybe it was when the sheriff asked for my help in putting Lehigh Carter in jail. Which, if we'd succeeded, might have prevented him from assaulting me tonight."

Wadsworth grunted his disagreement. "According to witnesses, *you* started the fight."

"Which witnesses? The ones who saw Carter pull a gun on me?"

"Funny. The gun seems to have disappeared."

"Sounds like sloppy police work to me."

Wadsworth turned to Deputy Flynn. "Is the Roadhouse pressing charges against anyone?"

Flynn shook his head. "Nobody's done nothing yet."

"*I'm* pressing charges," Paul said. "Assault and battery, assault with a deadly weapon—"

"Do you really think that's wise? Your story doesn't really add up." Wadsworth counted off on his fingers. "Three guys against one, no weapon, no corroborating witnesses—"

"I'm telling you, he started it."

"Then he's stupider than he looks," Wadsworth said.

"I keep trying to tell you guys that," Paul said with a sneer.

Wadsworth stood and took slow steps around Buck's desk toward Paul. "Where were you the night Jared Barkley was killed?"

Paul waved the question away. "I've told you guys this a hundred times. At the Oregon coast, playing poker. I've got witnesses. I've given you their names. What does that have to do with Carter picking a bar fight?"

Wadsworth sighed. "Stay here. Flynn, keep an eye on him." He walked to the door. Time to put some pressure on Carter, see if his story added up.

Before exiting, he glanced back at Paul. Leaning back in the chair, the young lawyer looked relaxed. Like he owned the place.

Wadsworth frowned and shook his head. That, unfortunately, was too true for comfort.

**

Deputy Roscoe escorted Lehigh to Wadsworth's office and instructed him to take a seat. "The Detective will be here shortly to ask you some questions," he said. "If you behave yourself, I won't have to put the cuffs back on you."

"I'll be a good boy." Lehigh settled in to the stiff padding of the ancient chair and waited.

Ten minutes later, Wadsworth entered and motioned Roscoe outside. "I'm seeing far too much of you lately," he said, settling into the chair behind his desk.

"Not by my choice."

"You gonna talk to me, or hide behind that cute lawyer I heard you hired?" Wadsworth sat on the edge of his desk, his bent knee close to Lehigh's face.

A knock on the door pre-empted Lehigh's reply. Samantha Pullen poked her head in the door, dressed, as usual, in an elegant skirt suit, every strand of her blonde wavy hair in place. "Thank you, Deputy," she said over her shoulder.

"Guess that answers that," Wadsworth said.

Lehigh stood and extended his hand. She shook it, caught his eye, and held his gaze an extra moment, as if in warning—or perhaps disapproval.

"Gentlemen, let's get right to work here." She took a seat next to Lehigh and flipped open her notepad. "I am prepared to advise my client to press charges only against the principal instigator of this unfortunate event, Mr. van Paten, and withhold from suing the sheriff's office for unlawful arrest, if you're willing to cooperate."

Wadsworth's jaw nearly hit his desk. "Say *what*?"

Lehigh smirked. He liked this woman.

"We'll need all charges, if any, against Mr. Carter dropped and expunged, of course, and I'll need to depose the two accomplices—er, witnesses—immediately." Sam flipped back through a few pages of notes. "Of course, I'll share my witnesses' statements as soon as my staff types them up."

"What witnesses?" Wadsworth's face flushed red. "I hope you weren't intending to interfere with a police investigation, because if you are—"

"Of course not." Sam's trademark smile reappeared, focused on Lehigh, and an embarrassed heat rose in his neck. She winked at him, then faced Wadsworth. "We did, however, locate a few witnesses that you officers could not apparently locate or convince to speak—I'm not sure which. Their eyewitness accounts diverge remarkably from the accounts your office shared with me and completely undermine the allegations you've made."

"Wait a sec," Wadsworth said. "How did you find these so-called witnesses so fast? And what allegations? What the hell's going on here?"

"Like I said, I'll be sharing that information as soon as possible. For now, here are their names and contact information." She pulled a folded page out of her notepad and held it out to Wadsworth. Lehigh could not make out the typewritten words, but the page appeared to contain six or seven names, addresses, and phone numbers. She'd clearly done her homework.

"Thank you." Wadsworth scanned the page. "Hmm. Very interesting." He picked up his phone, pressed a few buttons, and waited. "Jim here. I've got something for you. No, you send someone to make a copy. Anything from your guy? Yeah, I thought so." He hung up. "Okay, Ms. Pullen. Give me the nickel tour."

"My witnesses agree that Misters van Paten, Thornburgh, and Brockton initiated this fight, and even got the bartender— who, apparently, is dating Mr. Brockton—to help, uh, *distract* Mr. Carter while they snuck up on him." She shot Lehigh a glance at the word "distract" but otherwise seemed to ignore him. "Mr. Carter tried to leave, but they jumped him."

"That's the exact opposite of what our witnesses say."

"I'll need to see their statements, but I wouldn't be surprised to discover they're all friends of the three attackers. Which begs the question: why would Mr. Carter pick a fight with three men in a bar chock full of their friends?"

"I agree with you there. But still, there are a few things—" A knock interrupted him. "That'll be my messenger. Come in!"

The door opened a foot or so. Deputy Roscoe stuck his head in. "You have something for us?"

Wadsworth held up Sam's list of names. "Make a copy of this for everyone on the team and one for the file. Then start calling people. I know it's getting late, but see how many you can reach."

Roscoe nodded and grabbed the page. He scanned it a moment. "Wow."

Wadsworth's eyebrows curled into a giant furry "V" on his forehead. "What in the world about a witness list could warrant a 'wow'?"

Roscoe lowered the page. "Two of these people are my first cousins. Another one used to work for us. The sheriff's department, I mean."

"Start with them." Wadsworth waved him away. After the
door clicked shut, he gave Samantha a long look. "Pretty
impressive…if you knew about those connections."

She shrugged. "Just lucky, I guess."

Lehigh covered his grin with a cough. As far as lawyers
went, Lehigh was the one who felt lucky. Stacy could keep
Constantine Richards.

***

"So what you're telling me is, you had me followed."
Lehigh held the white porcelain coffee mug an inch above the
saucer. He'd forgotten whether he'd been picking it up or
setting it back down, so he just held it there.

"Essentially." Samantha Pullen kept her voice low, a habit
of hers, it seemed, when she didn't know who else could be
listening. They occupied a corner booth at Shirley's and had
just polished off a quick, greasy dinner and ordered a slice of
pie—apple for Lehigh, lemon meringue for his attorney.
"Once I heard of Paul van Paten's release from jail, I figured
he'd try to confront you, sooner or later. Following him isn't
quite kosher, but you're my client. Besides, I couldn't be sure if
he'd show up to mess with you personally or send thugs."

"It might've been nice to let me know," Lehigh said. "In
advance, I mean."

She winced. "That tends not to work so well." Their pie
arrived, and Lehigh dived right into his. She picked at hers,
then set down her fork. "You'll need a place to stay. Have you
patched things up with your parents yet?"

Lehigh spit out a laugh and scooped another huge chunk of
warm apple filling and flaky crust onto his fork. "Pappy'd just
as soon see me sleep in jail. Hell, I know Maw would."

"I expected as much, so I reserved a hotel room for you in
Twin Falls."

He swallowed a massive mouthful of warm, sweet apple.
"That's a half hour away. I can't drive that every day."

"Why would you?" She nibbled at the puffy white topping
of her pie. "You have all of your work files with you, plus a cell

phone, and your dogs. If you stay in town, there'll only be more trouble. Up there, you'll be closer to my office." She looked right at him. "And I'll have much better access to you."

Lehigh's protests did no good, and he found himself unable to argue with her for long. Nor did he regret giving in, in the end. The hotel turned out to be a standalone cabin at an outdoorsman's resort, complete with a furnished kitchen, living room, and separate bedroom. The resort's tiny restaurant served breakfast and dinner on fisherman's hours—five to eight, a.m. and p.m.—and the room even included internet service. Best of all, they allowed dogs.

"You get to stay," he told the dogs after brushing his teeth, "but not on the bed." Moping, Diamond slunk down off the pillowy comforter and curled up with Lucky on a shag throw rug.

Despite the bed's welcome comfort, Lehigh couldn't sleep. The arrest, the strange environment, missing Stacy, and worry over what the hell she could possibly be thinking kept him awake until the first hints of gray light peeked through the windows around six a.m. He took a quick shower, dressed, and shaved, even though he had no appointments scheduled. He'd made up his mind—strategy or no strategy, and Constantine Richards be damned, Lehigh had to see Stacy.

He had just finished breakfast when his phone rang. He glanced at the caller ID and groaned. "You're up early," he said into the phone.

"We have a lot to do today," Sam said in a businesslike voice. "Can you be in my office at nine?"

"Maybe before nine, or well after," he said. "I'm going to Stacy's hearing in Clarkesville."

"You are doing no such thing." Sam's voice grew sharp, commanding. "My clerk will attend and take notes. We'll know exactly what happens ten minutes after it's over."

"I want to see her," Lehigh said.

"I understand, but you have to come to grips with the fact that she doesn't want to see you." Her voice grew softer. "I'm sorry. I don't mean to come off as harsh, but the reality of the situation is, she's a murder suspect, and her lawyer takes no prisoners. Constantine Richards is about to throw you under a bus, and your fiancée is going along for the ride."

"Hell, I don't care if she's driving the bus. I'm going. Besides, wouldn't me being there help? Maybe it'll shame them into a less mercenary strategy."

"It might make them cloak their strategy, but not change it," Sam said. "Please, take my advice. Stay away from that courtroom."

Lehigh drew a heavy breath. Dammit. He held a losing hand, which left him only one way to win: bluff. "Okay. I'll be there in twenty minutes."

"Um, nine a.m. is better. I'm not even out of bed yet."

Lehigh laughed. "Nine, then." He hung up and grabbed his coat. "C'mon, dogs. We still have time to make a quick trip into town."

CHAPTER 22

"You looking for your girlfriend?" Deputy Roscoe leaned against the brick wall, smoking a hand-rolled cigarette considerably less than the legally mandated twenty-five feet from the front door of the sheriff's office.

Lehigh considered walking the long way around his truck to avoid him, but that seemed silly. He took his time approaching the deputy. "Actually, I was hoping to talk to Paul van Paten. He still here?"

Roscoe squinted at him through the smoke. "Nope. Long gone."

Lehigh grunted. "Well, he didn't spend much time in lockup, then, did he?"

Roscoe laughed. "You kidding me? Not with Buck back on the job. Paul van Paten wouldn't serve time if we videotaped him slitting the throat of Mother Theresa. I'm more likely to go to jail than him."

"And his two pals?"

The deputy shrugged. "Can't exactly keep *them* if we don't keep *him*. Say, what'd you do to piss him off, anyhow?"

"Stole his girl, I guess." Lehigh waved away Roscoe's exhaled smoke. Usually tobacco didn't bother him, even Pappy's foul pipes and cigars, but this deputy's strange-smelling crud made him gag.

"Really? That McBride gal? Well, I guess I can see it, kind of. She's a looker. Especially at her age." He drew another deep drag and held his hands up in surrender. "No offense. Sorry, man."

"No, it's okay." The deputy seemed friendly, unlike the ones who'd paraded through Stacy's house, looking for evidence of Lehigh's guilt. "She still here?"

Roscoe pointed down the street at the courthouse. "She's about to head across, couple minutes from now. They'll cart her over in a county rig from the back door. Sorry, you can't go there. Security." He finished his cigarette, if that's what it was, and crushed it under his boot on the pavement.

"Can I talk to her?"

Roscoe shrugged. "Not likely. Your best bet's to head down there, by the prisoner's entrance. You might be able to shout hello. Well, I gotta get back to work." Roscoe pulled open the double glass doors of the sheriff's office and shuffled inside.

***

Stacy exited the county van outside the courthouse, escorted by Sergeant Cam Patrick and Deputy Joe Flynn, both wrists handcuffed in front of her, dressed in a pale blue one piece jumpsuit. They guided her into a secure entrance on the side of the building amidst about a dozen or so reporters and photographers shouting questions and flashing pictures in the most obnoxious way possible. She kept her eyes glued to the ground and let the officers guide her to the door, where Constantine Richards and a young female assistant joined her. The lawyer leaned in close to her ear. "I have the outfit you asked for. You can change into it once we're inside." A dry cleaning bag lay draped over the young assistant's arm.

"And my makeup kit?"

Constantine raised an eyebrow at the assistant. She nodded.

The courthouse door opened. Stacy turned her body at an angle so she could pass through without bumping into the lawyer's generous belly, or his assistant, who had scooted in ahead of her. As she turned, she caught a glimpse of a handsome, smirking face out of the corner of her eye.

Paul.

And behind him, some forty yards away, a familiar, beat-up

old truck, with a long-haired man at the wheel and two dogs panting next to him in the passenger seat. What had been, until very recently, *her* seat in the truck.

She looked down again, and scurried inside.

***

After changing and applying the scantiest bit of makeup imaginable in the dank, smelly restroom attached to the prisoners' holding area, Stacy called her attorney's young assistant over. The young woman nearly dropped an armload of folders and papers scurrying to Stacy's side. "Do you need help with your hair, Ms. McBride?" she asked. A female guard glowered at them from the exit, but kept her distance.

"My hair's fine…actually, it's never really fine," Stacy said with a frown, "but that's not what I need. I was wondering if you could do me a teensy little favor."

The aide blinked and averted her eyes from the tangled black mop on Stacy's head. "I suppose. What is it?"

"I need to send a note to someone, but I don't have a pen or paper."

The aide's eyes grew wide. She couldn't have been more than twenty-two, but at that moment, she looked about nine. "That's not allowed. Nothing that could be considered a weapon, and a pen—"

"Perhaps you could write it for me, then, if I dictate it to you?" Stacy smiled at the girl—er, *young woman*—and forced tears into her eyes. The girl's face softened.

"Yes, ma'am." She pulled a legal pad and pen from her oversized purse. "Whenever you're ready, ma'am."

Stacy cleared her throat. "My dear…" Ugh. That sounded so formal. Would he get the wrong idea?

"Go on," said the aide.

"I'm sorry for all the grief I've caused you these past weeks. No, scratch that. Months."

"…Months." The aide scribbled, then waited.

"I hope there's a way I can make it up to you."

"Up...to...you."

"When this is over, I hope—no, wait, I *look forward to* being with you again. Until then, however, we must maintain the impression that we are no longer a couple."

"...Impression...couple. Okay."

"Please forgive me for this necessary evil." Stacy's heart ripped in two. This was a dangerous, sad path to follow, but she had no choice.

"...evil. Anything else?"

She swallowed hard, but forced out the words. "Love, Stacy." She resisted the urge to spit, despite the sharp, astringent taste filling her mouth. "I'll need a second note, too."

"Yes'm. Uh, to whom should I address the one you just wrote?"

Stacy's heart shattered like glass on concrete. She bit her lower lip, hard, then uttered the name she dreaded hearing the most:

"Paul van Paten."

CHAPTER 23

Lehigh crumpled the note from Stacy into his fist and threw it to the floor of his truck. He clenched his teeth so hard, he could taste shavings from the filling in his second molar. Pain shot down from the tooth into his jaw.

Good. He needed that pain as a distraction from the heavy ache rising in his chest.

Diamond sniffed the note and licked at it. He loved to chew paper. Lehigh opened his mouth to stop him, then changed his mind. His first inclination had been to make Stacy eat her words, but perhaps it would be better if the puppy did it for her.

Besides, he'd read the note a hundred times. He knew it by heart already.

"*Dearest* Lehigh." Yeah. Bull crap.

"I'm sorry for all I'm putting you through lately. I know how difficult it must be for you."

No, you don't.

"I haven't been able to communicate very much of what is going on, and I'm sorry for that, too."

Blah, blah. He could just see the crocodile tears running down her perfect little face. Part of him wanted to wipe the imaginary tears away, and he hated that part of himself at that moment.

"Legal strategy dictates most of my actions right now, and unfortunately, I can't share much of that with you."

Can't, or won't?

"I wish I could say I had good news for you, but unfortunately it's only going to get worse for a while before it gets any better."

News flash: it already is worse. Worst.

"Mr. Richards informed me that since you and I have not yet obtained our marriage license from the county, we have no legal status as a couple. In other words, we're not legally engaged."

Here it comes.

"Since it's almost a certainty that you'll be called as a witness by both sides, he feels it's best if we continue the policy of not speaking or seeing each other until after the trial."

Which could last months. Years.

"For this and other reasons, I think it's best if we put our engagement and wedding plans on hold, at least until all of this is resolved."

On *hold.*

"I'm sorry to have to tell you this way." Blah, blah, blah. "Love, Stacy."

Love. Ha!

Diamond spit the soggy wad of chewed-up bad news onto the floor of the truck. He emitted a fierce gagging sound and cast a sad glance at Lehigh.

"Too tough for even you to swallow, eh?" Lehigh reached out his hand. The dog licked it, then sat up on the seat for some petting. Lehigh obliged him for a few moments, then started the truck's engine.

"Get in back with Lucky, Diamond," he said. "Time to make room for another beautiful, confident woman in our lives."

He burned rubber peeling out of the parking lot, ignoring the dogs' nervous protests.

***

"Did she return the ring?" Samantha asked when Lehigh finished his story.

"Her note said that she'd have her lawyer send it to me."

Standing across from her desk, he tossed the chewed-up, soggy note onto her desk. He crossed his arms and stared at the view of Mt. Hood's Elliott Glacier through the window of her office, a 1940s-era munitions depot restored to expose the original brick and mortar. Sam remained at her desk, uncrumpling the note and writing on her legal pad, just inside Lehigh's peripheral vision.

"I think it's a play," she said.

Lehigh spun on his heel toward her. "A play? What exactly does that mean, a 'play'?"

"A legal strategy. Knowing Constantine Richards, he's trying to create the appearance of—or the reality of—distance between you. Strain in the relationship."

"Well, if that's what she wanted, it's working." He stared out the window again. "But why?"

Sam stood and walked over to him. "I can think of a couple of reasons. First and foremost, she's right—you're almost certain to be called as a witness. The prosecution will try to impeach your testimony in support of her by pointing out that you're engaged."

Lehigh snorted. "And since we're not anymore, suddenly I'm believable?"

Sam's lips pressed into a thin smile. "If she can create a credible impression that you two are now estranged—and if you assist in creating that impression—your testimony in her defense, particularly to the extent to which it comes during cross-examination by the prosecution, under duress, will have a much stronger impact on the jury."

"I see." Actually he'd struggled to follow her logic, but she sounded so convincing. He took a deep breath and admired the dark crevasses cut into the glacier's snowy expanse. "You said there were other reasons?"

Sam's smile faded. "You won't like these."

Lehigh leaned forward, resting an arm on the shiny fir window casing, his vision blurring. "I haven't *liked* any of this, Sam. Why should this be any different?"

Sam fidgeted next to him, fingers intertwined. "I don't have to continue, if you don't want to hear it."

"No, no. Tell me. It's better if I know." He blinked his eyes into focus and shifted his gaze from the vision of beauty and power in the distance to the one standing beside him. "Shoot."

She placed a hand on his arm. "Perhaps it's best if we sit."

"That bad, huh?" But he let her guide him to a plush sofa perched a few feet away. His arm tingled at her touch. They sat less than a foot apart. He waited.

She drew a deep breath, then locked her big blue eyes on his. "A second reason for the estrangement would be to set you up as a fall guy—to pin it on you."

"No way. I keep telling you, Stacy wouldn't do that!"

Sam ducked her head as if to ward off a blow. "You don't think she would, to stay out of prison?"

"No, I do *not* think she would."

Sam shrugged. "Okay. But Constantine Richards might."

Blood drained from Lehigh's face. That bastard. He just might.

Lehigh leaned back on the sofa, his head tilted way back to rest on the cushions. "So, the other reason you hinted at. Don't tell me it's even worse than that one." He swallowed hard, counted the tiny ridges in the ceiling paint covering what probably used to be cracks in the ancient plaster.

Sam cleared her throat and leaned back partway, resting an elbow on the sofa back, close enough to send a fresh whiff of her subtle cologne Lehigh's way. "It depends on your perspective. But you're right, it's not good."

He shrugged, turned toward his attorney. Her dark red lips parted to reveal even, white teeth, a delicate tongue forming words he did not want to hear.

"The third reason," she said, "would be that she does, in fact, simply intend to end the relationship. Or, at least, the engagement."

A giant lump formed in Lehigh's throat. Swallowing only made it hurt more. "Yeah, maybe not worse than the other reasons." His voice grew raspy, hardly a whisper. "But bad."

"I'm sorry," she said. "I'm not being very sensitive. This must hurt. I just wanted to be as open and upfront with you as I can."

He nodded and squeezed his eyes shut. "She dumped me once before when we were engaged, twelve years ago." He took a slow, steady breath. "Crazy thing is, her reason back then was that I didn't propose fast enough. She was in a hurry to get hitched, then."

"You've been together twelve years and aren't married yet?" Sam asked.

Lehigh laughed and blinked his eyes open. "No, no. She's been married and divorced since then. We just got back together last fall."

"Oh, that's right. She was seeing that Paul van Paten guy when you two, ah…"

"Hooked up?" Lehigh grinned, remembering the early, steamy days of their rekindled relationship. "Paul was pretty unhappy about it. Still is, I guess."

"I've had dealings with him professionally. He's a tough adversary."

"In more ways than one." Lehigh rubbed his sore ribs.

"Which raises another possibility…" Sam's voice trailed off.

Lehigh sat up straight. "What?"

"She could be manipulating Paul, too. Taking you out of the equation to give him the idea that maybe he still has a chance at her."

"Ridiculous," Lehigh said. "The only way that would be believable is if she really did get back with him."

"Exactly," Sam said.

"No way!" Lehigh flared his arms out, palms down. One arm nearly struck Sam in the chest. He yanked his arm back to his side. "She wouldn't. She couldn't. Not after what he's done to her."

Sam's eyes drooped, as did the corners of her mouth. Her full, red lips parted again. He stared at her a long moment, letting the possibility sink in.

"Oh, hell," Lehigh said. "I guess she could." He leaned forward and hung his head over his knees. A delicate, feminine hand rested on his back.

Damn it all to hell. As much as he didn't want it to, that hand…it felt good there.

***

Lehigh could barely concentrate over the next hour as Sam outlined various scenarios and defense strategies. He alternated between anger and sadness at being dumped again—or, at least, at being kept in the dark about Stacy's true intentions—and worry over how her court hearing would turn out. In the rare moments that he paid attention to his attorney, he battled to keep his focus on her words rather than her delicate scent and captivating smile.

"Overall, I think we have each scenario covered," Sam said toward the end of the meeting, "although we'll need to continue investigating to fill in some gaps. Do you have any questions?"

Seated perpendicularly to her, with papers spread over the low table in front of them, Lehigh couldn't recall a single specific thing she'd said about scenarios and strategies. "Uh, no. Except, what can I do to help?"

"Try to stay out of bar fights." Sam smiled and patted his knee. Electric current shot up his leg and spine and back down to his toes. He gazed at her hand, retreating from his leg. A gold band with a bright white pearl—not a diamond—adorned her ring finger. Definitely not a wedding ring. *Probably* not an engagement ring.

Stop it! he scolded himself. The ink on Stacy's "Dear John" note had barely dried, and he was already on the rebound. And to think, six months before, he had been single and happy about it.

"Other than that," she said, "lay low. If the police contact you for any reason, refer them to me without answering any questions. If Paul or his 'friends' come after you again, get away from them at all costs."

"That didn't work out so well last time."

She frowned. "It's going to have to from now on. Remember, if we're right about them, they're trying to impeach or eliminate your testimony in Stacy's defense. Or, worse, put you in the position of bargaining—which means, testifying against her to keep yourself out of jail."

He nodded. Her phone rang. As she rose to answer it, the side slit of her skirt parted, revealing a bit more leg. He shut his eyes and rubbed his forehead. If Paul van Paten didn't kill him, temptation might.

"I see," Sam said into the phone. "Thank you for the update." She hung up and frowned. "That was Constantine Richards' office."

"Is the hearing over?"

"Yes, and it's not good news." Sam sat back on the sofa and folded her hands across her thighs, leaning toward Lehigh. "Stacy has been formally charged with first-degree murder."

Lehigh's stomach did a churning, crashing, whiplashing somersault. Stacy, a murder suspect. "What's next? We go post bail, or…"

Sam pursed her lips and shook her head. "No bail set. The court viewed her as a flight risk. Did you know that she renewed her passport recently?"

Lehigh nodded his head, numb. "We'd been researching honeymoon options—Mexico, the Caribbean, places like that."

Sam frowned. "And saving up some cash, no doubt, to pay for the trip? Well, she's going to need it. Constantine Richards is expensive."

"Which brings us to you," Lehigh said. "What's your fee?"

She smiled and patted his hand. "Oh, don't worry. I'm *much* more reasonable."

***

Lehigh kept his speed a few miles under the limit driving home, made full stops at all red lights and stop signs, and signaled even for the most obvious turns and insignificant lane changes. No way he'd give one of Buck Summers' boys any excuse to lock him up. Unless, of course, he could share a cell with Stacy.

Nah. Even in fantasy, that idea sucked.

He pulled into Stacy's driveway and parked in his usual spot. With her stuck in jail, he felt free to return home, and even his lawyer agreed. Besides, the dogs needed care and feeding. Poor things hadn't eaten or been outside all day.

He tossed a ball for them out in the fenced backyard for a few minutes, then brought them in out of the persistent rain and dried their drenched fur with a rag towel. He fed them in the kitchen. Lucky chewed her food with deliberation, as if savoring every bit, but the puppy gulped down his chow with minimal chewing. Meanwhile, Lehigh made coffee, sorted mail, and tried to settle back in to being at home again.

It didn't work. After half an hour of sitting at his desk, staring at the computer screen, he hadn't accomplished a damned thing, other than deleting a few spam emails. Too many things pressed on his mind—Stacy's situation and her unwillingness to share information being tops among them.

He closed his email program and was about to power the machine down when his eyes rested on another icon on the desktop: "Stacy's mail." She sometimes checked her work email from his laptop on her days off. He hesitated. He didn't want to snoop, but dang it, she hadn't shared any information at all with him since everything went crazy these past few days. He deserved to know *something*.

Then again, what he didn't know, he couldn't testify about.

He closed the laptop and grabbed the stack of bills on the side of his desk to sort through them. Stacy's credit card bill had come in that morning and topped the pile. With her in jail, he'd have to pay it for her, which he could do from their joint account. He opened it. Scanned the page—

And his jaw dropped.

First, the total due shocked him: over two thousand dollars. Half of it was from a single purchase—the wedding dress, for which her mother would reimburse them, eventually. But before that, and for a week after, the bill listed a ton of charges at restaurants, bars, even a motel.

And the date of the motel charge?

The night of Jared Barkley's murder.

Part 3

Romantic Twist

CHAPTER 24

Detective Jim Wadsworth studied his case notes. The case against Stacy McBride seemed solid: means, motive, opportunity, all there. She had no alibi, or even a reasonable alternative explanation behind what she'd been up to with Barkley, other than what he and everyone else suspected: they were having an affair. Cheating.

Except that it didn't quite add up. Not yet.

First, he hadn't found any corroborating evidence of the affair. No love notes, no gifts, no stash of contraceptives in his glove box. Nor did they find anything of the sort at Stacy McBride's place. In fact, what they'd found fit her version of events—a purely platonic friendship—better than the "affair" version.

Second, McBride's motive paled compared to a lot of other people's. Lehigh Carter, for example. He had a strong jealousy motive, and no alibi. Nothing he could confirm, anyhow. Plus he'd gotten into some scrapes lately, both the legal kind and the fisticuffs kind. He'd shown he had the potential for violence in him.

Paul van Paten had even stronger motives: jealousy, revenge, ambition. But his alibi checked out. He'd checked into a vacation rental in Rockaway Beach, Oregon, the Friday before the murder, and checked out on Sunday morning. Because he was still under indictment, he'd checked in as required with the Tillamook County's sheriff's office upon his arrival, and they verified his BMW had been parked outside the house the entire weekend. Witnesses confirmed he'd been playing poker with them all weekend. Not the most reliable of witnesses—the sleazy James Thornburgh, the mouth-breathing Neil Brockton, and another crony or two—but their accounts lined up.

Then there was the gun found in Stacy's bedroom. Could she really be that dumb? More disturbing, nobody could figure out where it had come from. Why would Stacy McBride go through all the trouble of buying it on the black market, then kill Jared Barkley with it, and not get rid of it? What kind of fool would stash a murder weapon in her bedroom? Stacy McBride was a lot of things, but stupid wasn't one of them.

No, he was missing something. Maybe the whole cheating thing had blinded him. Maybe he needed to broaden his search a little bit.

He picked up the phone and called the file clerk on the other side of the building. "Bring me all of Jared Barkley's case files for the past two years," he said. "Yes, I said *all* of them."

***

Stacy tugged at the starched blue cotton pinching her armpits. She'd always imagined that the jumpsuits provided to county prisoners would at least be comfortable, even loose fitting. Maybe they got the size wrong.

She waited for Constantine Richards to settle his long, hefty frame into the undersized folding chair on the other side of the rickety table between them. She wished they could close the door, but the guards insisted that leaving it open was "procedure," and Richards didn't argue, so neither did she. How they could keep their conversation private, she had no idea.

"Let's start with a candid assessment of where we are, shall we?" Richards said. He fidgeted with his glasses, wriggled in his chair, and drew out a report of some kind, a few pages stapled together with the county logo across the top.

"How about we start with what your rates are?" Stacy said. "Don't I have to sign a contract or something?"

Richards removed his glasses and smiled. "That's been taken care of."

Stacy smiled. That man! "Mr. Richards, I should let you know that Lehigh and I haven't yet merged our legal or financial affairs, and I—"

"It wasn't Mr. Carter." He let his gaze rest on her for several seconds. "As you know, I am a longtime acquaintance of your father's, and—"

"My *father*? Impossible. He's broke, or so he claims whenever the subject of my wedding reception comes up."

Constantine cocked his head, and his expression grew curious. "Should I be investigating the senator's credit before attempting to cash his checks?"

Stacy leaned across the table, eyes ablaze. "No. You should tear up his checks. I'm paying for my own defense, and that's not negotiable."

Richards bit his lip, nodded once. "Very well." He opened his briefcase and set a form in front of her, with blanks filled out in his elegant handwriting. "I anticipated you might feel this way. Please look this over and sign…there." He handed her a pen and pointed with a long, manicured finger at the signature block. Stacy scanned the terms, gulped, and signed. Just the initial retainer would wipe out her savings, but she could refinance the house and maybe the veterinary clinic to cover the rest.

Richards studied the county form. "You're charged with first-degree murder, assault with a deadly weapon, assault of a police officer, conspiracy to conceal evidence—"

"And what else? Jaywalking? Terrorism? What other crap did they trump up?" Stacy pushed away from the rickety table. For a moment it teetered, but Richards steadied it.

"The addition of lesser charges is not unusual in cases like these," Richards said. "If they fail to convict on the most serious charge, it gives them—and the jury—alternatives. The only surprise to me is the conspiracy to conceal, particularly since you have no codefendant."

"They're going after Lehigh." The words escaped her before the conscious thought finished forming in her mind.

"Not necessarily. Conspiracy usually involves a willing accomplice, but doesn't require it—only a clear intention on your part. The prosecution is required to disclose all material evidence to support their charges, so we'll know the source of this in a few days. What can you tell me about it?" Richards spread his leather portfolio open on the table and readied a pen above the yellow legal-sized pad within.

"Nothing. I have no evidence to suppress because I didn't do anything!" In her excitement, Stacy bumped the table and nearly knocked it over.

"You've cooperated with all warrants, subpoenas, and information requests?"

"I did what you told me." She crossed her arms, but that stretched the fabric too tight under her armpits, so she uncrossed them.

"Very well. Let's walk through some of your records, shall we?" He opened an envelope and unfolded a sheet of paper: her itemized cell phone bill, with a record of all calls.

Stacy paled. "We're going to look through all of my mail now?"

Richards continued to scan the sheet. "I'm afraid so. We have to counter their data with better data. Their case against you is largely circumstantial—who you were with, where you've been. Most murder cases are. There are almost never eyewitnesses."

"Great," Stacy said. "You're really cheering me up here."

"My apologies if this upsets you. Would you rather we not review it now?" Richards spoke in a slow monotone, but somehow it sounded disapproving.

"No, no. Let's go ahead." She recrossed her arms and ignored the pinching fabric. "What have they got?"

"First, of course, they have the weapon." Richards fished out a photo of the gun the deputies had confiscated from her house and set it on top of his portfolio. "The ballistics report is not yet in, but the weapon does fire the same nine millimeter ammunition used to kill the victim. Whoever fired it, unfortunately, wiped it clean of any fingerprints."

"I'd never seen that gun before they 'found' it in my house. I've never even shot a pistol. Rifles, yes, but—"

"An important point. But it was found in your bedroom."

"I have no idea how it got there."

"No idea?" His bushy white eyebrows arched high on his forehead.

"I suppose I could come up with one, but—"

"Could Mr. Carter have put it there?"

Stacy harrumphed. "Not without telling me. Besides, he already has a gun—a revolver of some kind. And a permit."

Richards jotted down some notes and looked over his glasses at her. "That doesn't preclude him getting another. Now, Miss McBride, do you lock your doors when you leave home?"

Stacy shrugged. "Usually. Ever since we got the dogs, we've been a little more lax. Especially Lehigh. He's still getting used to living near people again."

"But Mr. Carter was away that weekend—*so far as we know.*" Richards emphasized the last five words as if in doubt.

"Yes. So far as…no, I'm sure he was."

"One hundred percent sure?"

"Absolutely."

Richards nodded and a made another quick note on his legal pad. "Secondly, you were the last person seen with Mr. Barkley—just a few hours before his death."

"I–we—" She swallowed hard. "Yes. I suppose so."

"Third, you have no alibi for the time of death."

She bit her lip. "I was at home, in bed."

"Can anyone corroborate this?"

She swallowed harder. "No. As I said, Lehigh was away."

"Fourth, the phone records, and now, statements from witnesses show a pattern of meetings prior to and leading up to the date of his death."

Stacy's ears and face grew warm. She knew she was flushing

red—her fair skin never could hide stress. "We—Jared and I—met to discuss some things."

"Some *things*?"

"Yes."

"Care to elaborate?"

"It was all very innocent. Really. We're just friends."

Richards sighed. "So, how do you explain the motel charges on your credit card for that night?"

"We met there to discuss our...things. We did *not* spend the night."

"So why meet at a motel?"

"We met first at Dot's, but he had some things to show me, and he didn't want to be seen in public doing that."

"Why not?" Richards waited.

Stacy opened her mouth to reply, then shut it again, and thought for a moment. "Certain people would have...it could have gotten ugly."

"Certain people, such as your fiancé?"

"I don't have a fiancé anymore."

Richards paused, his face grim. "Ms. McBride, verbal sparring with me does not help you. I am your advocate, not the enemy. I need you to be as forthcoming as possible."

She nodded. "I understand."

He waited. When no further explanation seemed forthcoming, he cleared his throat. "You can imagine how this would appear to the casual observer...and a jury."

Stacy took a deep breath. As much as she hated to admit it, her attorney spoke the truth. And the truth looked bad. "I guess I need to explain that," she said.

Richards inclined his head forward a notch, then righted it. "It would be helpful."

"Jared came to me over a year ago, when I was seeing Paul van Paten." She folded her hands into a worried knot. "He'd heard that we were getting kind of serious, and he warned me that Paul was...not the most ethical of men."

"Did he come to you in his capacity as a law enforcement officer, or as a friend?" Richards focused his gaze on his notepad rather than on her. It helped.

"The latter. Actually, as more than that. Jared confessed that he'd had feelings for me for years—since we were teenagers. But he was a shy boy, and I was kind of popular, and—well, anyway, we went away to different colleges, I always had a boyfriend or husband or…oh, I don't mean that the way it sounds."

Richards waved it away. "You're not in front of a jury." He cleared his throat. "Yet."

She swallowed the lump of concrete in her throat and worried her interlocked fingers a bit more. "I asked him if he could show proof of anything illegal. He said he couldn't, so—"

"Couldn't because he had none, or because an ongoing investigation prevented him from sharing?"

She shrugged. "He didn't say. But I doubt the sheriff's office was investigating. Buck thinks Paul's the greatest thing since double stuffed Oreos."

Richards smirked and jotted something on his notepad. "Go on."

"I was rather firm with Jared. I loved Paul, and it felt to me like Jared was just bad mouthing him. I told him that was not the way to win my heart, if that's what he was after. So he–he asked what *would* win me over." She blinked moist tension out of her eyes. "He really was very sweet."

"How did you respond?"

She smiled, a sad, weary expression. "I told him to bring me proof."

"Did he?"

"Not right away. For a while, our meetings were purely social. But after I'd left Paul and gotten back with Lehigh, and the sheriff seemed hell-bent on convicting Lehigh for all the bad things Paul had done, Jared raised the subject with me again. This time, he had evidence."

Richards frowned. "I was representing Mr. Carter then. I don't recall either of you coming forward with any such evidence."

Stacy's face warmed. "Jared asked me not to share the information—even with Lehigh. He said if it got out, there...would be trouble. For us, and for Jared." Her gaze dropped to the floor. "And, as it turns out, he was right."

Richards' eyebrows raised on his forehead. "I see. So...*Jared*, now...what exactly did he share with you? Any physical, tangible item that could help corroborate your story?"

"My *story*?" She gritted her teeth. Richards could be so exasperating. "He showed me things—documents, mostly—but I wasn't able to make copies. I just read them."

"And did he share anything confidential that you otherwise could not have discovered since? Something, again, that we could present to a jury?"

Stacy shrugged. "I'll have to think about that. It seems that almost everything he told me came out to the public once Paul got arrested."

"Yet you continued to meet with him until just before he died—long after Mr. van Paten's arrest. Why?"

"He was still investigating. He thought—he *knew*, as it turned out—that Paul's arrest wouldn't end the threats. Paul's connections and his ruthlessness meant that, even in jail, he remained a threat."

"To you?"

She nodded. "To me, to him, and especially, to Lehigh. These people, Mr. Richards—Paul and his friends—they won't be satisfied with putting Lehigh and me in jail. Paul is so jealous and so vindictive...the only thing that will satisfy him is to see both of us dead."

CHAPTER 25

Lehigh made a list of the establishments on Stacy's credit card bill, looked up their addresses and phone numbers, and stuffed her bill into a folder he labeled "Stacy—legal—C. Richards—Privileged." He doubted it would stop prying detectives from snooping, but it might remind him to send it off to Constantine Richards. And if it didn't stop the snoopers, at least they might have to explain why.

He shoved the list into his pocket, rounded up the dogs into the truck, and set out for his first destination.

Dot greeted him with what for her could count as a smile—lips set in a line rather than a frown. "Ain't seen you in a while. Coffee?"

Lehigh nodded and sat at the counter. Some familiar faces, long-ago acquaintances of his parents, huddled in tiny booths around the glass walls of the café. A few glanced at him, gave near-imperceptible nods of greeting, and returned to nursing their own bottomless cups of coffee. He thanked Dot and added, "I've been kind of busy lately."

"So I've been hearing." She set a tiny bowl of creamers in front of him.

Lehigh stirred some sugar and cream into his coffee, sipped the bitter brew, and added more. "Oh, yeah? People must be bored, if all they've got to talk about is me."

Her eyebrows danced upward and back down. "Cops are never bored."

"Cops are asking about me?" He sipped the mixture again, so loaded with cream and sugar he could hardly call it coffee.

"When? Which cops?"

She shrugged and readied the pot to warm up his cup. He covered it with his hand. She frowned and set down the pot. "That detective feller, Watts-his-mouth."

"Wadsworth?"

"That's him. And old Buck, of course."

"What kind of things are they asking?" He sipped the coffee and managed not to grimace. He hoped. He'd had bowls of cereal as a kid loaded with less milk and sugar.

"If I seen you in here, when, who with. That kind of thing. But mostly they ask about your fiancée and that dead cop." She found her opportunity and topped off his cup, leaving no room to dilute it back down with the dwindling supply of cream on the table.

Lehigh sighed and stirred the mixture with a swizzle stick. "And?"

She shrugged again. "They didn't tip very well."

Lehigh smiled in spite of himself and pulled a fiver out of his wallet. When she didn't react, he added a ten, then a twenty. That brought a real smile from her, even a display of her tiny, uneven teeth.

She snatched the cash off the counter. "That McBride girl and that one cop, the good-looking one that got killed? Well, they used to come here every week or so, usually at lunch. That much I told the cops. But what I never told them was, they brought in lots of paper and pictures and stuff. Like they was working on some secret project of some kind."

"Secret project? What makes you think that?" Lehigh kept the cynicism out of his voice, a lessoned learned from long experience with Dot. For every UFO sighting, government conspiracy, and Sasquatch story for which she claimed "proof," she had ten times as much gossip about well-known locals.

"Every time I went over to their table, they'd hush up and cover up their papers and photos." She leaned over and whispered, "But not always fast enough. Sometimes, I saw."

Lehigh opened his mouth in his best act of surprise. "You

didn't! What did you see?"

She nodded, long wags of her head up and down, and poured a few more drops of coffee into his cup, causing it to overflow. She mopped up the mess with a quick wipe of her bar towel and kept her eyes locked on the counter. "Some of them photos, newspaper clips, things like that."

Lehigh took an obedient sip of coffee, causing it to spill more, and giving Dot a reason to hang around a bit longer with her bar rag. "Could you read any of the headlines? Identify anyone in the photos?"

She nodded again, this time a single, slow droop of her head. "I never told them cops any of this. I mighta if they'd a been *friendlier*, but it was all take, take, take. Know what I mean?"

"Oh, I know very well," Lehigh said. He did a mental count of the cash in his wallet. At this rate, he might not be able to afford his coffee.

"You know?" She squinted. "How so?"

"Let's just say, we've done business together, unfortunately." He shot quick glances left and right, for effect, then leaned in to whisper, "We're not on good terms, them and me."

Her eyes grew wide. She spoke in a hoarse whisper. "You on the wrong side of the law again, Lehigh?"

"Yes and no," he said. "They keep busting my ass, but I ain't done nothing wrong."

She nodded. "I like most cops, but not these few. They think they're so dang better'n everybody. 'Specially that Buck fella." She checked the coffeepot, still half full. "I better go make some fresh."

"Wait," Lehigh said. "Before you go. What'd you see in those pictures and headlines that Stacy McBride and Jared Barkley were looking at?"

Dot looked around to make sure no one was watching and leaned over the counter. "It was stuff about you—you know, your house fire and all—and that other guy she used to date.

The *good*-looking one."

Lehigh ignored the slight. "Paul van Paten?"

She nodded. "I got the impression they was more interested in him than you."

Lehigh frowned. "Dot, when did you say these meetings started between them?"

Dot cocked her head, tapped her chin a few times, and said, "I guess around September, October? Maybe sooner. I ain't sure."

Lehigh nodded. "Thanks, Dot. You're a princess."

She smiled, a real, wide-mouthed smile, and hustled off into the kitchen.

Lehigh swiveled around in his seat and got up to go. Out of the corner of his eye he spotted a long forgotten face in the corner—an old high school football teammate, Phil something or other. Less hair, twenty-plus pounds heavier, but the same square jaw and close buzz cut. He waved, and Phil waved back. Lehigh strolled over, held out a hand. "Long time."

Phil took his hand and shook it. "Got a minute?"

"Sure." Lehigh sat down across from Phil, remembering bits and pieces of their shared youth. Phil played cornerback, occasional tailback, and special teams. A starter, but not a star—a teammate who laughed at jokes but rarely cracked a memorable one, went to parties but never hosted, bought rounds when his turn came at places that honored their fake ID's. A regular guy. A lot like Lehigh, actually.

"Haven't seen you around much lately," Lehigh said.

Phil nodded. "Just moved back from Pendleton a couple years ago. After my divorce. You?" He smelled of tobacco—chew, not smoke.

"Been here all along. Running my dad's forestry business now. Sorry about the divorce."

Phil waved it off. "Never shoulda married her. Love the kids, but her family...ugh." He took a long drink from his mug of black coffee.

"Anyone I know?"

Phil shrugged. "You knew her cousin." He leaned in. "Jared

Barkley."

"Oh, jeez." Lehigh winced.

"That's why I called you over." Phil glanced in each direction and lowered his voice. "I talked to his mother a couple days ago—about something other than the little ones, I mean. Seems the cops have been asking her questions about old Jared. Who his friends and enemies were. She called to ask me about you."

"Me?"

"You, and that old flame of yours. Stacy McBride. Did you ever marry her?"

Lehigh gritted his teeth. Unclenching his jaw took effort. "No. We were engaged, but..."

"That was, what? Ten, twelve years ago?"

Lehigh nodded. "Yeah, and then we got back together last fall. I proposed in January. She just broke it off a day or so ago."

"January? Not *this* year?"

Lehigh furrowed his brow. "What do you mean? Of course this year."

"Officially, or just, you know, the 'hey let's get hitched' sort of thing?" Somehow Phil managed to keep drinking Dot's coffee.

"Yeah, officially. I bought her a ring, got on one knee, the whole deal."

Phil's eyes widened and he shook his head. "You say so."

Alarms went off in Lehigh's head. "What are you getting at? Why do I get the feeling this don't square with what his mom told you?"

Phil shrugged. "Well, maybe she got it wrong." He sipped his coffee again. Iron stomach.

"Got what wrong? What'd she say?"

Phil raised his cup, swallowed, signaled Dot for a refill. "She said Jared had been spending a fair amount of time with her lately, and...well, finally, after all these years, he'd fallen in love."

CHAPTER 26

"You sure?" Lehigh's mouth went as dry as the high desert of eastern Oregon. "In love? Not just, you know..."

Phil cocked his head, pressed his lips together, and looked away.

Lehigh leaned in closer and dropped his voice to a low murmur. "Have the cops asked you about any of this?"

Phil shook his head and curled an eyebrow. "You think maybe I should tell them?"

"No!" Lehigh glanced around to make sure no one could hear. "How did Jared's mom come across this information?"

Phil twisted a beefy hand palm up, a mini-shrug. "I guess he talked about her at their batty old grandma's eightieth birthday party a few weeks before he got...uh, before he died. Apparently Grandma asked him—you know how grandmas get—if he'd met anyone special, if he was ever gonna get married, that sort of thing. Hell, he mighta just been trying to shut her up."

"Yeah. Maybe." Lehigh leaned back in his chair and ran a hand through his long brown mop of hair. "Say, Phil, you wouldn't happen to have Jared's mom's number handy? I'd like to give her a call."

"Suit yourself. Hell, if you can stand talking with her, you're a better man than me." He scribbled on a paper napkin and slid it across the table to Lehigh. "You'll have to wait a few days. She's been off with her sister, my former mother-in-law, visiting my kids out in Pendleton this week. But do you think they'd be willing to drive them out here when she comes back tonight? No, sir. They're gonna make me drive out there, wasting time and gas…I'm sorry. You don't want to hear about my family battles."

"It's all right. Thank you, Phil." Lehigh pulled his baseball cap onto his head and held out his hand. Phil shook it.

"It's good seeing you, Carter," Phil said. "You know, you're still a good guy in my book. I heard what the sheriff and that rat, van Paten, tried to pull on you last year. If it was up to me, and a lot of other people around here, you'd be in charge and *their* butts would be in jail."

"I have no ambition to be in charge, but thanks."

Phil gripped Lehigh's hand a bit harder. "I mean it, Lehigh. Don't let them roll you. They've got it coming, and I have a feeling you're the guy who can give it to them."

Lehigh smiled. "You got that right." He tipped his cap and elbowed his way out the door of the café.

***

"So, let me get this straight." Constantine Richards stood and stretched his arms and back, then paced the tiny room, hands folded behind him. "The sole reason for your continued meetings with Jared Barkley was so he could keep you informed about his investigation? That hardly seems like normal police procedure."

Stacy's face reddened. "Well. I guess you could say the visits were also partly social."

"Only social? Nothing more?"

"Well, to me, yes, just social. But to Jared…well, maybe it meant more than that to him." She shook her head. "No, not maybe. The last time we met, he made it clear—he wanted to win my heart. I had to let him down. I was trying to be kind, but I–I'm afraid I may not have been."

"Ms. McBride." Richards stood and paced with his hands folded behind him. "I am trying to construct an image in my mind of how your relationship with Deputy Sheriff Barkley differs from how the prosecutor will characterize it—a secret, budding romance gone awry. So far, you haven't given me much to go on."

Stacy reddened. "We were not romantically involved."

Richards pointed to file folders resting next to his notepad. "Deposed witnesses argue otherwise—including those who, despite your efforts to be discreet, saw you two together the night he was killed."

"They got the wrong impression." She looked away from him.

"Then correct that impression. Tell me what you were doing with him that night—a man who had declared feelings for you—and in the weeks and months prior, without your fiancé's knowledge."

Stacy stared at him, open-mouthed. "Whose side are you on?"

Richards narrowed his eyes. "Ms. McBride, you're going to need to get used to such characterizations—and worse. It will be up to you to counter those allegations with a more plausible alternative."

Stacy drew a deep breath and stood with her back to her lawyer, arms folded across her chest. "I don't know where to begin."

"With the truth, Ms. McBride."

She whirled to face him. "The truth, Mr. Richards, is that Jared pursued me in a romantic way. I knew it—and, though I'm not proud of this, I used him to help Lehigh. And to protect myself from Paul. And Jared—" Her voice broke. "He knew it, I think. But he helped me anyway."

"Specifically, how?"

Stacy sighed. "Jared found witnesses who saw Paul with his two thugs for hire—Brockton and Thornburgh—hanging around in the vicinity of my clinic just before the break-in last fall. He also pieced together the arson at Lehigh's house. The sheriff blamed Lehigh at first, but Jared, working with the fire department, found physical evidence and witnesses that confirmed Paul's involvement. And somehow, he kept Paul from finding out any of this. Things like that."

Richards nodded and took copious notes. "Did he do this despite, or because of, orders from his superiors?"

Stacy spread her hands. "He didn't say, but given that he was meeting with me in secret, I'm guessing it was on his own initiative."

Richards paused in his note-taking. "Because of his feelings for you?"

Stacy reddened again. "I imagine."

"And you? Did you ever return his affections or give him reason to believe you might?"

Stacy knitted her hands together under her chin. "I didn't think so, at the time. I mean, I was grateful, and told him so. Over time our conversations got a little more...personal."

"As in, romantic?"

"No, no. I mean, I never kissed him or anything. Well, once I kissed him on the cheek, a thank you after a particularly major revelation, a long meeting where we talked about...oh, just a lot of things."

Richards glared at her. "I will remind you again. This is not the right time to hide details from me."

Stacy shuddered. "Somehow I knew you were going to say that."

Richards straightened in his chair and folded his hands on the table. "Stacy, I am not here to pry into your private affairs, or to judge you. I am here to provide the best legal representation I can, given your situation, the evidence, and the applicable laws. But I can only do this if I have complete, accurate information. If you fail to provide it, I not only cannot formulate an optimal legal strategy, but I am very likely to formulate a very inadequate one. I cannot—and you cannot— afford to be blindsided by revelations from the prosecution's witnesses for which we have no prepared response."

"I understand, Mr. Richards." She took a deep breath and returned to her chair. She sat and leaned her elbows onto the table. "Jared's investigation into this whole situation uncovered some things about me that he quite rightly concluded would embarrass me and my family should they ever become public. And Paul, by extension, because of our relationship."

Richards nodded. "Go on."

Another deep breath. Her head ached. Telling this refined, elegant man about the foolish mistakes of her youth made her feel dirty. But she could see no other way.

"My father and I had a falling out while I was in college, and he cut me off. I had no money of my own, so I found a job—not an easy thing to do in the down economy around here."

Richards shrugged. "Getting a job is hardly an embarrassment, even for the wealthiest of families."

Stacy swallowed. "This job was. I had no skills, no experience. All I had to offer—so I thought—was..." She let her gaze fall to her lap. "My...looks."

Richards cleared his throat. "You traded on your looks in some way?"

She nodded. Her throat hurt. Tears collected in the corners of her eyes. Oh, the humiliation. "I went to work at one of the, uh, 'Gentlemen's Clubs' owned by Mr. Downey. Just as a waitress at first, but then I learned that even waitresses had, uh, *obligations.*"

"I see. Did you engage in anything illegal, such as prost—"

"No!" Stacy slapped the table. "I had to, well, 'perform.' For men. Individuals. Stripping, okay? In private. Often in costume. Never fully nude, but, well, it didn't leave much to the imagination."

Richards nodded, expressionless. "Did it ever go any further than removing your clothes?"

She balled her hands into fists. "Sometimes...they paid extra. It's technically forbidden, but they...the men...would want to touch."

"I see. Anything else?"

"Um, well, lap dances, things like that."

Richards nodded and jotted down some notes. "Does anyone else know about this? Could any of Mr. Downey's clients identify you, for example?"

Stacy shrugged. "I bleached my hair, wore a lot of makeup, gave a fake name, so I doubt they could. But obviously Mr. Downey knew. And Jared somehow got hold of some photographs."

"How...*compromising* are these photos?" Richards remained matter-of-fact, emotionless.

Stacy shook her head, stared at her feet. "I doubt the amount of skin I showed in those photos would shock anyone who's ever browsed the Internet or a girlie magazine. But, it's pretty clear from the pictures what was going on."

Richards' eyes closed, then opened in a fluid motion. "Which was?"

Bile rose in Stacy's throat. Richards' interest in the lurid details bordered on the voyeuristic. "Do you *really* need to know the details?"

Richards gave his head a light, slow shake. "I'm sure the police have Mr. Barkley's files and will share the photos with me at some point, if they plan to use them. And I can't imagine they would not."

Stacy's face flushed, practically aflame. "Dear God. All of that in open court...my father will have a heart attack. And my mother...she'll—I can't imagine."

"So they're unaware of this activity?"

Stacy nodded. "The details. They know I worked for Downey, but I've convinced them that I kept my clothes on."

Richards sat back and rubbed his generous nose with two fingers. "There is an alternative, of course."

"Alternative to a trial? Like what? Getting the evidence tossed out somehow, or—"

"That is one possibility." He paused. "The other—assuming it is offered—is a plea."

"A plea? You mean admit to something I didn't do? Go to jail for no reason? Forget it. Out of the question!" She stomped over to face the wall of the small room, arms crossed.

"Not even—"

"No! Nothing!" She whirled about. "I'm not going to jail, Mr. Richards. Not for a single day."

Richards glanced around the room, eyes wide. "Seems to me, that sentiment is a few days behind reality."

Stacy slumped against the wall. "This is so crazy, so unreal. I wish I could wake up right now and end this idiotic nightmare. It's a witch hunt, and I'm the witch, aren't I?"

Richards gazed at her a long time. "Ms. McBride, I must ask you. Is there any reason I might need to consider a change in legal strategy—a shift from not guilty to self-defense?"

Stacy's eyes squeezed shut. She took several calming breaths, then reopened her eyes.

"Mr. Richards," she said "if you ever ask me that again, it will be your final minute of engagement as my lawyer."

CHAPTER 27

Gentleman Jim Wadsworth studied the pages in front of him in disbelief.

It all made sense now.

He'd gone back through Jared Barkley's old case files, looking for ideas, connections, even just hints of what else might have occupied the deputy's time on the months—years—leading up to his murder. And he found something startling. A *few* somethings.

Gaps. Omissions. Evidence that ought to have been there, but wasn't. Or it was there, and should have been spotted before.

For instance, in the break-in of the Cascade Animal Clinic, the transcript of the interview with Stacy McBride seemed way too short. And different, somehow.

He compared those interview notes with the printouts of other interviews. On Stacy's, the paper seemed a little grayer, the typeface a little more crisp, than the others. Two others were like that, too: the notes for the interviews of Lehigh Carter and Anne Marie Stapleton, a volunteer at the clinic. Both of them seemed conspicuously light in their references to Stacy McBride.

He pulled a recent memo out of his desk, the one announcing Dwayne Latner's appointment as interim sheriff, filling out the unexpired portion of Buck's term. The print and paper matched the three oddball interviews he'd set aside—Stacy McBride's, Lehigh Carter's, and Anne Marie Stapleton's. Then he compared them to another, older memo from the same file. The old memo differed from the new memo and the "oddball" interviews in the same way: different paper, different typeface.

He suspected that he knew why.

Three months before, the sheriff's office spent some use-or-lose end of year budget authority on new computer equipment and supplies. That included a fancy new laser printer—and a new paper supplier. Buck Summers had specified a particular brand of paper—one that didn't use pulp from any of Lehigh Carter's trees. He remembered laughing at Buck's petty revenge then.

Someone—maybe Barkley, but probably someone else—had reprinted these notes after the new printer and paper arrived.

And why reprint, unless they were different? As in, changed?

If Jim Wadsworth could trust his instincts—and he'd have never made Detective if he couldn't—then he'd bet his morning coffee that he knew which person had edited and reprinted the notes. He had a good guess as to why, too.

He picked up the phone, dialed a four-digit internal extension. A cheery voice answered, "Mt. Hood County Information Systems. Can I help you?"

"I need some backup files from last November," Wadsworth said. "Stat."

***

Lehigh turned off the engine of his pickup, but held onto the keys, still in the ignition. The bright indoor lighting flooded out of the double glass doors of the Sheriff's office, slicing through the dark mist of early evening and reflecting off the handful of vehicles parked near the entrance ahead of him.

Including the hood of a black BMW, at the very least a dead ringer for the car driven by Paul van Paten.

Lucky whined in the back seat of the pickup, a noise echoed a second later by Diamond. He knew that sound—the "I've really, really got to pee" alert shared by dogs the world over—so he pocketed his keys and popped open the driver-side door. The dogs jumped straight up in the air and yelped with excitement. Lehigh grinned in spite of the ache forming in his gut. No matter what his enemies were up to, he could never stay upset when his dogs got playful.

His dogs. Six months ago, he'd have never expected to have thought such a thing.

He hopped out and issued a pro-forma wave of his hand to command the dogs out of the vehicle a half second after they clambered past him. Lucky dashed over to a patch of grass on the side of the building. Diamond lifted his leg next to the rear wheel of a car. Lehigh opened his mouth to shoo him away, then changed his mind when he noticed which car Diamond had chosen.

The black BMW.

"Hey!" A man's voice shouted from the open doors of the building. "Get your damned dog away from my car!"

Lehigh made a slow turn toward the sound of footsteps crunching closer on gravel. Paul, dressed in a black suit with no overcoat, ran toward him in that awkward, slippery way of a man in dress shoes who doesn't want to step in puddles or splatter mud on his expensive clothes. "You hear me, Carter? Get your dog—"

"Gee, Paul, I'd like to stop him, but gee, he ain't been trained yet. I don't know *what* commands he knows. Stacy might know, but, shucks. Ain't it too bad that Stacy can't be here to stop him?"

Paul reached the front of his car at full throttle on a beeline for the urinating dog. Just in time, Diamond finished his business, yipped once, and galloped toward Lehigh's nemesis. He raised his front legs like a rampant lion and landed wet, muddy paws on Paul's crisp white shirt and colorful paisley tie, smearing them with brown goo amidst his victim's angry howls.

Lehigh howled too—with laughter.

"This isn't funny, Carter!" Paul aimed a kick at the dog and missed by two feet, since Diamond had already scampered behind him before Paul's foot left the ground. He bounded under Paul's extended leg and knocked him into a counterclockwise spin, terminated only by the teetering collapse of the well-dressed lawyer onto the rain-drenched gravel.

Lehigh couldn't see what happened next—his peals of laughter forced his eyes shut, and he doubled over, holding his stomach with both arms.

"You won't think this is funny when you get the cleaning bill!" Paul struggled to his feet, made twice as difficult by Diamond, who straddled him and licked his face like a child devouring an ice cream cone.

"Are you kidding me?" Lehigh howled again. "I'd pay twenty bucks to see him do this again right now!"

"I should have killed you when I had the—hey! Get off me, you smelly, rat-infested mongrel!" This time his attacker wore a yellow coat and a snarling face. Lucky, returning from her own private pee party, had jumped up on Paul, but not with the intention of making friends. From her guttural growls, she seemed to want to eat Paul's face off.

Which, Lehigh noted to himself, would be a massive improvement.

Still.

"Down, Lucky. Now!" Lehigh grabbed the older dog by the collar and pulled her back toward his pickup. Lehigh opened the truck and half-dragged Lucky into the cab. Diamond, barking and howling like a crazed wolf, followed a step behind.

"You'd better learn to keep those animals under control!" Paul, who had followed right behind him, pointed a muddy finger in Lehigh's face. "There are laws against this, you know."

"Yeah, you're a real expert at obeying laws." Lehigh batted Paul's hand away and pointed at the sheriff's office building. "Speaking of which, what brings you here? A visit to your parole officer?"

"I'm not on parole, stupid, I'm—oh, never mind. I came because I was invited." His face split into an evil grin. "Care to guess by whom?"

Lehigh shrugged. "What do I care? Half that building's on the take from you. Whose turn is it this time—Buck? Cam Patrick? Or did Dwayne finally make your payola list, now that he's acting sheriff? Bet you didn't see that coming."

Paul laughed. "See it coming? Hell, who do you think made sure he got the votes on the County Commission?"

"You disgust me." Lehigh shut the door to the truck.

"Anyway, Carter, you're way off base. I wasn't invited by anyone wearing a badge. No, this time it was someone on the other side of the black bars. A woman we've both been engaged to. Figured it out yet, stupid?"

Lehigh's jaw slackened. "Not..."

Paul's eyes narrowed and his evil grin widened. "Yes. Your beloved ex-fiancée. Would you like to know what we discussed?"

Lehigh balled his hands into fists, but kept them at his sides. "I'm dying to find out."

Paul leaned in close enough that Lehigh could smell whiskey on his breath. "Our future. And I don't mean mine and yours, Huckleberry."

Only his lawyer's warning and his desire to stay out of jail kept Lehigh from clubbing him. "You two planning on getting adjoining cells or something?"

Paul's grin faded to half mast. "Hilarious, Carter. But you won't be laughing when you take that final long walk to the execution chamber in Salem. And as for Stacy and me? We're gonna watch you fry. *Together*. Wine glasses in our hands." Paul spun on his heel and stalked off to his car.

Lehigh spun toward his truck. He raised an angry fist, ready to bash something metallic, or glass, or anything. He stopped at the image of two happy canine faces steaming the inside of the driver's side window. Colorful tags detailing the dogs' names, inoculations, and "call if lost" information rattled at their collars. Stacy had taken care of all that as soon as each dog had come into their lives. Always thinking ahead, that girl.

Always thinking ahead.

She was like that. Forward thinking. Smart. Strategic.

Really smart.

He stepped in front of Paul's car, already creeping toward the parking lot exit, and held up a hand. The driver's side window descended with a low hum, and Lehigh stepped to the side so he could see Paul's face.

Paul sneered. "What now, loser? You want to fight over losing your woman to me again?"

Lehigh smirked. "Careful around that *woman*, Paul. She's smarter'n you."

Paul twisted his face into a doubtful frown, his eyebrows curled in a clear expression of *Are you crazy?* "Smarter than you, you mean. But that's not setting the bar very high. Hell, even your stupid dogs are smarter than you."

Lehigh shook his head. "Oh, I know she's smarter'n me. I have always known that. I just never before realized how stupid *you* were."

The BMW spit gravel speeding out of the parking lot.

Lehigh opened the truck door and snapped his fingers. The dogs jumped over the seat into the back of the cab. Starting the engine, he glanced at the mutts in his rearview mirror. "No, I ain't gonna go inside after all, dogs. I don't think I could stand hearing Stacy repeat what Paul just said—or deny it, for that matter. But I'm glad he told me, 'cause now I think I know what's going on."

The dogs stared, waiting.

"Either she's playing him," Lehigh said, "or she's playing me. And if that's the case, I need to get the heck out of here." Fighting the urge to race away and draw attention to himself, he looped his truck around the one-way parking lot, past the front doors and the long line of state vehicles with their blue-lettered, orange-background plates. He started to turn away from the building when a bulky figure stepped out of the last vehicle in the line, a blue Crown Victoria with too many antennae. The man held up his hand, not a wave of hello, but the unmistakable signal of a policeman ordering him to stop.

CHAPTER 28

The dogs exploded into an insane chorus of barking in the back of the cab. Lehigh stopped the truck, quieted the dogs the best he could, leaned over, and rolled down the passenger's side window. He recognized the hefty frame approaching his truck.

"Evening, Detective."

Gentleman Jim Wadsworth lumbered over and rested his elbows in the open window. "Evening, Mr. Carter. Got a minute? I got a question for you."

Surprised by the detective's casual approach, Lehigh nodded, trying not to betray the panic he'd felt a moment before. "Um, sure. Shoot." He smiled at the irony. Pappy always warned him: *Never* say "shoot" to an armed man.

"When did you find out that your girlfriend was secretly meeting with Jared Barkley?"

A slow burn heated Lehigh's face and ears. Maybe this wasn't such a casual conversation after all. "After she got arrested."

Wadsworth nodded. "Thought so. Do you know what they were meeting about?"

Lehigh shrugged. "Either they were carrying on something I ought to be supremely jealous about, or—and I hope to hell this is true—she was helping him nail Paul van Paten's ass to the wall for setting me up on those arson and burglary charges."

Wadsworth nodded. "You got a guess as to which it might

be?"

Lehigh shrugged. "If I said I preferred the second explanation, would you accuse me of wishful thinking?"

"I wouldn't, because I hope you're right, too. But we've got some missing pieces, and—well, I wondered if you'd be up for helping me out a little bit."

Lehigh laughed. "Help you? Why, so you can put Stacy on death row? Or me? No, thanks."

Wadsworth patted the air with his hands facing downward, a shushing gesture. "No, no. Quite the opposite. I think if we can show that they were working together, it might help clear her as a suspect. And you."

"I didn't realize I was a suspect again."

"Obviously you haven't been charged," Wadsworth said with a shrug, "but some people around here still seem to think you ought to be."

Lehigh cocked an eyebrow. "And you don't?"

A shake of the big man's head became the precursor to a tiny smile. "Not anymore."

Lehigh drummed his fingers on the steering wheel. "And just who, in your opinion, ought to be?"

Wadsworth averted his eyes and squinted into a sudden burst of passing headlights. "Let's just say, the foxes may be guarding the henhouse...and getting help from the wolves."

***

Lehigh topped up his mug with hot mud from the Mr. Coffee on the kitchen counter and stirred sugar into the brown crud. Somehow he'd made coffee even worse than Dot. Maybe some milk would make it drinkable. He sighed. If only he hadn't emptied the jug into the first cup.

Wadsworth's plea for help still weighed on his mind. A few days ago, the detective seemed as hell-bent as the rest to put Lehigh behind bars. The question he'd raised—whose side Stacy was really on—remained unanswered, and without an answer, he'd be running in blind. Where angels fear to tread, as Maw would say.

Tires crunched on gravel outside. He went to the window. A mint condition 90s-era yellow Corvette pulled in next to his pickup. A five foot three, slightly overweight buxom brunette climbed out, wearing a skirt four inches too short for her age, her legs, and the weather. He grinned. Gotta love Donna Arbuckle, Stacy's best friend since the Stone Age, even if she did show up without calling first.

He opened the door before she knocked. "Long time," he said. An easy grin tugged up the corners of his mouth.

She threw her arms wide and crushed him in a tight squeeze, smacked his back twice, and shook him once. A man hug with boobs. "It sure has been. Can't I come in?"

"Coffee?" He held up his mug, and her head bobbed with enthusiasm. "Anything in it?" he asked.

"Kahlua if you got it, cream if you don't," she said. "Mind if I use your bathroom? I've got wicked cramps, and—oh, sorry. Girl stuff." She disappeared down the hall before he could apologize for the lack of creamer.

"I don't know how you drink this stuff black," she said a few minutes later, seated on the sofa. She sipped the coffee anyway and made a face. "You definitely need a woman's touch around here."

"Yeah, well. That's a bit of a problem right now."

"I know. I visited Stacy yesterday. She said you haven't been by. That just seems wrong."

Lehigh choked on his coffee. "She told me not to. What does she expect?"

Donna smacked his thigh with the back of her hand. "She expects what any woman would. That you'd ignore that and try to visit anyway."

Lehigh scoffed. "Like Paul van Paten?"

Donna groaned. "Yes. Like Paul. Except without being the major butthole that he is."

"I think she puts me in the same boat. Besides, he's convinced that they're an item again—even claims that they're practically engaged."

Donna slammed her cup onto the coffee table. Coffee sloshed over the sides. "Of course he thinks that. He's an idiot."

"But where would he get an idea like that, if not from her?" Testing her. He wiped up the spilled coffee with a T-shirt he grabbed off the floor.

Donna made a face like she was about to spit. "Well, sure. She told him, of course."

"Well, then."

"It was a lie, dammit! Can't you see that? She's using him."

Lehigh stood and faced away from her so she couldn't see him smile. "Your opinion."

"No...well, okay, it is—but it's based on other things she told me."

"Like what?" He considered turning back to face her, but resisted.

"Like, she doesn't know if she can go through with it. Not sure if she really loves him. Things like that."

This time he couldn't stop from whirling around to face her. "She said she loved him?"

"She said she didn't know. She—"

"Oh for God's sake. Forget it, Donna."

"Forget nothing, Lehigh!" She stood inches from him, her face right in his. "Stacy's in trouble—deep trouble. And she's pulling out all the stops to get out of trouble and stay out of prison. She—"

"Including dumping me?" His voice echoed off the walls— probably the neighbor's walls a quarter mile away. "Yeah, I know all about how far she'll go to save her own skin."

"It's not just about her skin. It's—oh, why do I bother? You're so thick!"

Lehigh turned back away from her. "I know it's not just about her. She'll do anything to protect her dear old crooked father, too."

"What does her dad have to do with it? You idiot. She's doing all this to protect *you*. Yes, herself too, but mostly *you*!"

Lehigh stared at her for several seconds. "Okay, I'll bite.

How is this protecting me?"

Donna shook her head. "Your brain is as bitter and screwed up as your coffee. Who do you think the sheriff would rather lock up in county jail—her, with all of her family's money and connections, or you? Who do you think he'd rather face in a courtroom presided over by a judge that her daddy owns lock, stock, and barrel? Who do—"

"Okay! Okay, I get it." He plopped onto the sofa. Donna glared down at him, arms folded across her chest. He dared not look at her. "I mean, I see the argument you're making. What I don't see is proof."

Donna grabbed her coat. "That's because you're not looking for it."

"I've been poking around a bit."

"Poking? That's what she means to you, a little bit of poking around? Gee, aren't you the brave one. Remind me not to call on *you* if I'm ever in trouble." She stood and pulled on her coat. "Thanks for the coffee. I'll see myself out."

Lehigh stared after her yellow Corvette, kicking up mud all the way down the driveway to the street. Donna's timing couldn't have been better. He felt bad about hiding his intentions from her, but the risk of her telling Stacy—and thus, possibly, tipping off Paul—loomed too large.

He hadn't yet followed up on Phil's hot tip, either. Maybe now was the time.

He nodded to himself, picked up his phone, and dialed.

"Detective Wadsworth? Lehigh Carter. Count me in. I'm ready to help. And I think I know where to start."

CHAPTER 29

Lehigh hesitated before knocking on the chipped paint peeling off the wood of the old storm door, wondering instead if he shouldn't tap the clear plastic replacement for what once must have been a large glass pane occupying the center third of the door. No sound escaped from the inside of the house, at least none louder than the creaking of the loose planks on the porch beneath his feet. No lights on, either, but he wouldn't expect any in mid-day.

He knocked, and listened. Ten seconds. No sounds. No lights came on. He knocked again, once, twice—

The door flew open. A thin, elderly woman appeared, wearing a flannel floor-length nightgown and gray slippers that might once have been pink. He recognized her from twenty years before—at that time, a pretty, fortyish brunette cheering on her son from the bleachers, proud and happy—before tragedy had struck the life of Rosalynn Barkley, mother of the recently deceased Jared Barkley.

Mrs. Barkley looked him over, and her lips curled into a snarl. Her pale, withered face contrasted with her fiery, bloodshot eyes and wiry brown curls flecked with silver. She pointed a spotted, crooked finger at him. "You got some nerve, coming here. There's a *reason* I didn't answer your calls."

Lehigh bowed his head. "I'd like to express my regrets for what hap—"

"Get out of here!" She banged the door open. He dodged its crooked arc by backing up a step.

"Ma'am, I understand your being upset, and—"

"Upset? *Upset?* You *understand?* You say I'm *upset,* and you think you *understand?* Good God, you're as stupid as they say!" Her face blushed crimson and her whole body quivered. She reached to pull the storm door shut, but it banged against the crooked doorframe. A screw fell to the deck of the patio from the top hinge. She swore as the door bounced open again, then swayed uneasily in the soft breeze.

"Ma'am, I didn't kill Jared."

She glared at him a second, then her face broke, and tears gushed from her eyes. She raised an arm, pointing at him, then let it collapse to her side. "I know you didn't," she said. "That idiot whore of a fiancée of yours did."

"Excuse me for disagreeing, ma'am, but—"

"Oh, I know she didn't pull the trigger. She's too spoiled and useless to do anything that brave." The old lady spat, clearing the rickety rail surrounding her patio by a good foot and a half. "But it's because of her my Jared's gone. That I know for a fact."

Lehigh bowed his head. "Yes'm. And I'd like to put the right person in jail for it."

"Well, if that don't beat all." She pushed the door wide again. "I'll be honest with you, Mr. Carter. Jared didn't like you much. But he loved that pretty girl of yours, and he'd have done anything for her."

Acid boiled in Lehigh's gut, but he only nodded.

"Personally I thought she was bad, through and through. Spoiled, rich, and pretty. About the worst combination known to God."

He had to grant her that one. "It's caused all of us no end of trouble, ma'am."

"Nobody more than my Jared. How that girl tore him up so…I'm sorry, sonny. I get so worked up, I've forgotten my manners. Would you like some coffee?"

Lehigh met her gaze again. No longer hard and angry, her eyes had softened, and the wrinkles in her face had faded, making her look ten years younger. A fresh flood of tears begged to fall from the corners of her eyes. He swallowed a lump rising in his throat. "A glass of water would be more than kind, ma'am."

"I've got some lemonade. Fresh."

"Like you used to bring to Little League, Mrs. B?"

A smile of mischief came over her face. "You got a good thing, why change it?"

Lehigh's mouth watered. "The best in the county. I'd be much obliged, ma'am."

She waved him inside and shuffled into the kitchen. He sat on a threadbare sofa in the front room, careful not to let any mud fall from his shoes onto her spotless, faded rug. She bustled in with two tall tumblers of pale yellow liquid, pulp floating amidst crushed ice cubes.

"Just squeezed it this morning. Hope it's sweet enough."

He sipped the drink. Intense citrus tartness, balanced by a soft sweetness, and cold as the Arctic. "This is amazing," he said. "Thank you."

She smiled. "My husband, Theo—God rest his soul—used to tell me I ought to bottle it and make us millionaires." She laughed and shook her head, clamped her lips shut, close to tears again.

"I remember Mr. Barkley," Lehigh said. "He used to umpire our games. Always gave me a little wider strike zone when I pitched."

"You were a little wild even then, Lehigh." She choked out a laugh, and the dam broke. Tears spilled down her face again. "Kindest man I ever knew. Damn those people who took him from me so young! Damn this cursed family!"

An eight by ten inch brass picture frame rested atop the TV, the lone item in the room that sparkled. Not a speck of dust blocked the image of the young, dark-haired man in the beige uniform of Mt. Hood County's finest. Next to it, a glass box contained a purple strip of fabric attached to a gold shield. Lehigh took a long look at the photo to make sure that it was Theo rather than Jared in the picture, so closely did father and son resemble one another.

"He was a fine man, ma'am." One of the few cops that even Pappy respected, Theo Barkley died in a fatal crash in pursuit of armed fugitives before Jared reached the age of ten.

"Now, I'll die alone. I just pray to God they find Jared's killer before I go." She sighed. "I have a feeling it won't be long now."

"Ma'am." Lehigh stood and rested his hand on the weeping woman's shoulder. "I owe your son a great debt. He kept me out of prison with his investigation last fall, when everyone else was ready to lock me up and throw away the key."

Her shoulders shook with sobs, but she placed a frail hand over his and nodded. He waited until she stopped crying to speak again. "The detectives say you won't talk to them."

"Those idiots! Pah!" She spit on the chipped linoleum floor. "Useless as teats on a bull. They ain't got no interest in finding the real killer, because them, and their cronies, are the ones who gone and done it." Her eyes blazed into his, her face flushed red. "I got no proof, so don't even go asking. I just know what's in my heart, and when I know, I ain't wrong. Just like when Theo was gone and they didn't want to go looking for him until the end of his shift. I knew he was down in that ravine, I knew it!" She wept again, face toward the floor.

"Yes'm." Lehigh squeezed her hand. "I trust your instincts, truly I do. But a jury, they need facts. I aim to find those facts, and I'll need your help."

She wept for another minute or two, still holding Lehigh's hand. Then she looked up at him, resolute. "Bring your Maw over."

Lehigh blinked. "My Maw? Ma'am, she's not—"

"I'll talk to your Maw. You can come if you want, but I ain't talking to no one unless she's here." She took her hands off his and shifted her body away from him.

Lehigh took a deep breath. "I'll talk to her. But we've not been on good speaking terms lately."

"That's your problem. I got my own to worry about."

"True enough." Lehigh stepped toward the door.

"One more thing." He stopped and she pointed a long finger at him. "Tell her to bring pictures of Augie."

Lehigh swooned. Oh, dear Lord. Not that. Not Augie.

CHAPTER 30

Pappy leveled out the row of light brown tobacco shreds in the paper trough with the end of a matchstick. He used the slow, deliberate strokes of a man who had all day to do nothing, the easy habits of the long-since retired. He set down the match, rolled the paper into a perfect thin cylinder, then sealed it with a quick lick of his tongue.

"No," he said without looking at his son, seated across from him at the chipped Formica-topped kitchen table. "I won't do it to her."

"But Pappy—"

"You heard me." He set one end of the cigarette in a corner of his mouth and lit the match one-handed. Inhaled. Exhaled a cloud of blue smoke. "I won't do that to your Maw."

"She won't even have to know about the pictures—"

"She'll know." He inhaled again, took the cigarette out of his mouth, held the smoke in for several seconds. "Just like she'll know you were here without me telling her."

Lehigh slouched into his chair. "It might even be good for her."

Pappy's hand slammed the table, hard enough to knock ashes out of the overflowing ashtray onto the Formica. "Don't you *ever* tell me what's good or bad for her! Don't! You! *Ever!*" Smoke surrounded his face as he spoke, as if flowing out of his pores. He got up and grabbed his cane, but didn't tap the floor with it so much as carry it like a drum major's baton into the living room.

"Pappy, the cigarette…you know how Maw feels about you smoking in there."

The lit butt landed on the checkerboard vinyl tiles at Lehigh's feet. "Take care of that for me," Pappy said.

Lehigh scooped it up and tossed it into the ash tray on the table. He followed Pappy into the living room.

Pappy stood in front of a faded brown and white photo on the wall. The cherublike face of a two-year-old boy with curly brown hair smiled back at him, a face still pudgy with baby fat. Laughing, for all eternity, with deep dimples decorating his plump cheeks.

"It never stops hurting, does it?" Lehigh said.

Pappy turned sideways toward him. Wetness sparkled on his grey stubble. The old man's hard gaze softened. "No, son. It never does."

Lehigh couldn't remember the last time he'd seen Pappy cry. Probably when Augie died over thirty years before. He stepped closer and put his hand on Pappy's shoulder. Returned it there after Pappy slapped it away. They stood there a long moment, and another. And—

A woman's voice shattered the silence. "What in hell's bells is going on in *here*?"

Pappy stood rock still. Lehigh whirled to face Maw, her hands on her hips in the doorway to the kitchen, lips set in a line. She wore a blue and white layered ankle-length dress that flared out from her waist, making her look several times larger than the reality of her tiny stick figure.

"Pappy and me were just talking."

"Talking? In there? Why?" She shuffled into the room and stopped. Pappy still hadn't moved, still stared at the photo. Her voice grew soft. "You two were talking about Augie?"

Pappy nodded. She faced Lehigh. "You haven't asked about Augie since you were in high school."

Lehigh nodded. She must've just come from church. Services always seemed to help Maw's mental clarity, however briefly. Outside, a car's tires crunched gravel, the noise growing softer by the second. He hadn't noticed it coming in. Her ride to church, no doubt. Pappy had stopped going ages ago.

Pappy studied Maw's face, then glanced at Lehigh. Something changed in his expression. He seemed hopeful, resolute. He signaled Lehigh to keep quiet, reached out for Maw's hand, and drew her closer. "Rosalynn Barkley wants to talk to you about Augie. She wants to see a picture of him."

"What's Rosie Barkley got to do with Augie?" Suspicious, but curious rather than angry. She let Pappy pull her over to the photo of their baby son.

"Her boy's the deputy that died." Pappy tugged her closer. "She needs someone who can understand."

Maw glared at Lehigh. "You told her about Augie?"

Lehigh shook his head. "Everyone knows about him, Maw. It's been thirty-five years."

Her lip quivered. "But nobody ever asked to see his picture before."

She turned away and wrapped her arms around Pappy. They both stared at the picture for a very long time.

***

Lehigh waved blue smoke away from his face and shot a wincing glance at Pappy, seated next to him in a matching rusted metal chair on the widow Barkley's front porch. How the old guy could consume so much tobacco and not break into massive coughing fits, Lehigh could never explain. He gave silent thanks to Maw once again for curing him of the habit at age twelve. After catching him lighting up behind the old woodshed, she forced him to smoke an entire pack in one sitting. Or try to. He'd turned green and puked his lungs out less than halfway through. Ever since, the thought of a cigarette touching his lips evoked an intense gag reaction.

"What do you suppose they could be talking about in there?" he asked. "It's been two hours."

Pappy shrugged and, with no hands, shifted his cigarette to the other side of his mouth. "Women. They don't need nothing to talk about. They just talk." He wiped spittle off his chin.

"I've never known Maw to talk five minutes without having to fix, clean, beat, or cook something," Lehigh said. "Remember when she had our phone removed? It never occurred to her how that might affect our business operations."

"It occurred to her." Pappy grinned. "She just didn't care."

"She didn't care about how it'd affect my love life, that's for sure," Lehigh said. "Because of it, I missed out on taking Rhonda Fairbanks to Senior Prom."

Pappy cackled around puffs of his cigarette. "Oh, on that little item, she cared. In fact, I'd wager she'd say 'mission accomplished.'" His body shook and laughter escaped his mouth amidst clouds of blue mist.

"I adored that girl. I would have married her."

"So would've any boy who wasn't half blind. But your Maw hates two things when it comes to girls, and Rhonda had two of the biggest."

Lehigh grinned. "I'm sure there's a story of your own in there somewhere." He poked Pappy on the shoulder. "What's her name?"

Pappy shook his head.

"Come on, Pappy. I know there's a girl involved. Who was she?"

"Mary Ellen O'Shea," Pappy said. "And that's all you're ever going to—"

"Don't *mention* that redhead's name." Maw appeared in the doorway.

"Once every forty-two years," Pappy said. "I think it's okay." He leaned over and whispered to Lehigh. "Oh, yeah. One other thing she hates: red hair."

Mrs. Barkley stepped past Maw onto the porch. "Would you gentlemen like to come inside for a glass of lemonade? I have a few things to show you."

***

Lehigh leaned over the kitchen table, its surface covered

with photographs, news clippings, and memorabilia from Jared Barkley's life. He ignored the headlines about Jared's college football exploits, except one, in which Stacy occupied the foreground, dressed in her Oregon Ducks cheerleader's outfit a few steps in front of a jubilant, mud-splattered Jared after a hard fought victory over Stanford. Instead he focused on more recent items: articles about arrests he'd made, cases he'd solved, and awards he'd received.

The latter included a glowing citation from the County Board on cracking the George McBride bribery scandal. A news clipping detailed how he'd solved Lehigh's arson case. "I didn't know he'd won awards for this," Lehigh said. "Look at this story. It says he spent months investigating Senator McBride."

The widow Barkley sighed. "Years, more likely. Anything to do with the McBrides, Jared seemed to take a special interest, from his very first days as a deputy."

Lehigh sifted through the clips and photos. "Why's he so interested in them?"

"Not them, so much as her." Mrs. Barkley tapped a photo of Stacy from high school, or so Lehigh guessed. Her "big hair" days.

"He was obsessed," Lehigh said.

"I told him to forget about her, a hundred times if I said it once," she said. "But he couldn't leave her alone."

Lehigh moved to the end of the table to a stack of yearbooks and journals. "Stacy never mentioned him much. When she did speak of him, it was as if he was a stranger, really." He opened the yearbook from his high school graduating class year—Jared's junior year—and scanned the inscriptions on the inside cover.

"Page seventy-three of that one," Mrs. Barkley said. "Yeah, he was too shy, and she was too popular to notice him much. He kept a distance."

Lehigh flipped to page seventy-three—the cheerleaders' page. Stacy had signed next to her photo, "Jerry, thanks for a great season—knock 'em dead next year. Luv, Stace! XOX!!!"

Heat rose in Lehigh's face. "She noticed him enough."

"Enough to get his name wrong," the widow said.

Lehigh shrugged. "We all called him Jerry at school. He seemed to prefer it." He turned to the football team's section, saw his own handwriting in the margin: "JB, nice pass against Twin Falls. Lee." Jared, then second string quarterback, stole the starting job late in the season with a long touchdown throw to a wide-open Lehigh to beat their archrivals. He kept the job long enough to lead the team to the conference championship. Jared was the school's hero for a time—and probably caught the eye of more than one cheerleader.

He closed the yearbook and opened one of the journals. "How is it you ended up with all of his stuff?" Lehigh asked.

"Jared's apartment in Clarkesville doesn't have much in the way of storage space," she said. "Every few months, he hauls stuff over here. Hauled, I should say." She choked up and stifled a sob. Embarrassed, Lehigh turned away from her and flipped through the pages of the journal.

"Some of that's liable to be personal, son," Pappy said. "You might want to ask first."

"It's okay," Mrs. Barkley said. "By me, anyhow. There might be things in there Lehigh don't want to see, though, as the fiancé of Stacy McBride."

"Such as?" Lehigh paused in his scan of the pages. So far all he'd seen was the typical musings of a mopey, shy teenager.

Mrs. Barkley crossed her arms. "Girl's got a bit of a past."

"I'll bet," Maw said. She hadn't spoken in over an hour.

Lehigh nodded. "I know."

"What kind of things does it say in there about her?" Maw shuffled over next to Lehigh and craned her neck to peer around him at the journal's open pages.

Lehigh closed the book. "Best if you didn't hear—"

"She was a stripper," Mrs. Barkley said. Pappy's eyebrows arched high. Lehigh started to protest, but Maw's accusing glare deflated his halfhearted attempt in a heartbeat. His eyes drooped back to the page.

Maw snorted. "I knew it," she said. "Miss Goody Two Shoes with all her money and family influence. Hah! Putting on airs and taking off her clothes. I hate her daddy something bad, but when this comes out, I'd hate to *be* him even more."

"She was young and desperate," Lehigh said. "She's different now."

"Yeah, now she's all grown up." Maw made a face, like she'd just eaten a bad turnip. "A grown-up crook, just like her daddy."

Lehigh counted five before answering. "That ain't fair. What she did was perfectly legal."

Maw jabbed a chipped fingernail on the pages of the journals. "So you *knew* she was a tramp and still hitched up with her? God help you, boy."

Lehigh grabbed the stack of journals and shoved them under his arm. Facing away from Maw and toward Mrs. Barkley, he asked, "Mind if I take these home and look through them? I, uh, don't want to overstay my welcome."

Mrs. Barkley scowled. "For how long?"

He shrugged. "Can I bring them back to you next weekend?"

Mrs. Barkley waved a dismissive hand. "Sure. Don't mess 'em up, though. It's all I have left of him."

"I won't."

She wagged an accusing finger at him. "And no taking them to the cops. Them bastards would never give them back in one piece."

"I promise."

Maw hustled over to Pappy and whispered in his ear. Pappy straightened and nodded. "Well," he said to the women, "why don't Lehigh and I take off while you two gals visit a little longer? We men have some business to discuss."

Lehigh mouthed a question at Pappy: *Business?*

"I'll make some tea," Mrs. Barkley said. Maw followed her into the kitchen, complaining about "boys always getting into some kind of trouble."

Pappy grinned. "Good work, boy. I ain't seen her so happy and clear-minded in years."

Lehigh smiled and hefted the journals higher on his hip. "What say we go find us some trouble, old man?"

***

Deciphering Jared Barkley's inconsistent scrawls and unique, self-styled shorthand for hours on end gave Lehigh a serious headache long before dinnertime on Monday. Worse though, was the effort it took to keep his head from spinning at the revelations in the books' pages.

The man was obsessed.

He dialed Jim Wadsworth's number and sauntered to the medicine cabinet. Before he'd located any aspirin, the detective answered.

"I have good news and bad news." Lehigh found the aspirin and popped the cap one-handed. Nothing childproof in Stacy McBride's house.

"Give me the good news first," Wadsworth said. "I've had a lousy afternoon."

"I have enough evidence to put Barkley's real killer away for good." He filled a Dixie cup with water. "And it isn't my fiancée."

"Who? And what kind of evidence?"

Lehigh swallowed the aspirin and washed it down with a gulp of water. "That's the bad news. I can't share that with you—yet."

Part 4

Trapped

CHAPTER 31

Wadsworth slammed the phone into its cradle and cursed Lehigh Carter from the one end of Oregon to the other. That fool! All he had managed to do was make the detective's day that much harder—and probably ruin his weekend, too.

Carter hadn't revealed much, other than to confirm what Wadsworth had suspected already. Barkley had investigated off-book on a number of fronts—Senator McBride's dirty politics, which led to Paul van Paten's illegal campaign financing schemes, the break-in at Stacy McBride's clinic, and the arson at Carter's mountain home. He'd enlisted Stacy McBride's help, and their secretive behavior had aroused Paul's jealous suspicions about who she'd been seeing. She'd left Lehigh exposed as bait—a dangerous game that nearly got him killed…and, eventually, did get Jared killed.

Motive pointed to Paul van Paten. Yet he'd somehow kept his fingerprints off all of the actual crimes, literally and figuratively, with the exception of his weakness for personal run-ins with Lehigh Carter. Even then, he'd come up with enough doubt-inducing objections, counterarguments, and procedural technicalities to escape punishment or even serious investigation.

Which didn't really add up.

Which meant, he'd had help. From the inside, both at the district attorney's office and inside the Sheriff's own hallowed halls. Cheaters and liars everywhere. And that just stunk.

A knock on his office door broke his concentration. Buck

Summers' voice filtered through the cracks. "Jim? I need an update on the McBride case."

"On the phone, Buck." Wadsworth picked up the receiver and speed-dialed his home number.

"Hang up. This is urgent," Summers said.

"Just a sec." His wife answered on the third ring. Wadsworth raised his voice a bit. "But Doctor Doskey, on page seven of your report, you said the results were inconclusive!"

Gwen Wadsworth sighed. "How long are you going to be?" She knew this game well, though she never liked to take part. Gwen was *too* honest sometimes, to the point where she wouldn't even help Jim escape unwanted meetings.

"Okay, I can hold while you check that," Wadsworth said, again in a loud voice. "Just for a minute, though—I've got someone at my door."

"Call him back, Jim," Summers said from the hallway. He rattled the door handle. Locked. He rattled it again. Wadsworth smiled. He loved his private office, even if it was too small.

"Make sure it's no more than a minute," Wadsworth said into the phone. A loud clunk in his ear told him his wife had dropped the phone down on the end table a bit too hard.

"Open the door, dammit!" Summers rattled the handle again. "That's an order!"

"What's that, Doctor? I couldn't hear you over the *noise*," Wadsworth said. "I see. Well, that raises some serious questions, and the public's not going to stand for any ambiguity on this here *Barkley* case." He spoke in a loud voice to make sure Summers would hear. Heck, Gwen could probably hear, and she'd probably left the room. The door rattled again. Still locked, but just to be on the safe side, he opened the coroner's report and scanned it. "How long after he got shot do you suppose he lasted, based on the hemorrhaging? Ah, I see." Under two hours, according to the report. "Can't you get a little more precise? Uh, huh. I see. But what about—"

Heavy footsteps faded down the hallway. A door slammed

shut a moment later. Wadsworth hung up, grabbed his coat and hat, opened the door a crack to make sure the coast was clear, then slipped into the hallway. He hustled away from Buck's office, turned the corner toward the exit—

And nearly crashed into Buck's massive frame, leaning on one elbow against the water cooler.

"Going somewhere, Detective?"

"Uh…to the coroner's office." Wadsworth slipped an arm into one sleeve of his coat. "He has an updated report I need to pick up."

"Does he now? Well, that's curious." Buck straightened, as best as a man that round can straighten. "I'd ask why he doesn't just email it to you, but perhaps this would explain why." He rapped on the door of a meeting room behind him. The door opened, and a bespectacled head appeared—the head of the County Coroner, Dr. Herman Doskey.

***

Seated in Cascade Legal's narrow, stuffy waiting area late Tuesday afternoon, Lehigh fought the urge to slouch once again in the uncomfortable metal-framed chair pressed up against the wall. The wretched chair surprised him. He remembered the furniture in her private office as stylish and comfortable, even plush. The wait also surprised him—he'd never had to wait to see Samantha Pullen before. Then again, he'd never shown up without an appointment, either. He drummed his fingertips on the sealed, large yellow envelope in his lap.

"I'm sure it will be just a few more minutes," said the young man seated behind the sleek glass-topped reception desk. He offered a highly practiced, insincere smile that let Lehigh know that the kid hadn't the slightest idea of how long he'd be waiting. "Can I get you a cup of coffee, or water, or…?"

Lehigh resisted the urge to snap at him, or even to roll his eyes. He held up the half full water bottle already delivered ten minutes before by the same eager young man. "I'm good. Thanks."

"Perhaps if you could share with me the nature of your business—?"

"I told you. I'm a client. I need to update her on a few things. *Urgent* things." Lehigh fixed a stare on the kid's forehead, one of Pappy's tricks that made a person feel that they were both the center of attention and insignificant at the same time.

"Yes, Mr. Carson. I understand."

"Carter."

"Excuse me?"

"My name's Carter. Lehigh *Carter.* Not Carson."

"Of course, I'm sorry." The receptionist went back to whatever he'd been doing on his computer and didn't look the least bit sorry.

A few moments later, the receptionist's desk phone buzzed. He pushed a button and spoke into his headset. "Yes, Ms. Pullen. A client is waiting to see you—a Mr. Carson—"

"Carter!"

"Carter. Yes, I'll send him in." The kid hung up, brushed a few stray hairs away from his forehead, and resumed typing.

Lehigh stood. "So, I can go in now?"

"It'll just be a mo—"

"Screw you." Lehigh strode past him and pushed open the door to Samantha Pullen's private office. She smiled up at him from her desk and waved him into a chair. Lehigh pulled the door behind him to shut it, but the protesting receptionist pushed it back open and glared at him.

Sam spoke into her cell phone. "Seven o'clock is perfect. I'll grab a bottle of wine. Okay. Bye-bye." She hung up and smiled again at Lehigh, and the room brightened like someone shined a spotlight on it. "It's all right, Aiden." The receptionist glared at Lehigh, then backed out of the room, pulling the door closed behind him. Sam gestured Lehigh into a chair. "To what do I owe this unexpected pleasure?"

Lehigh sat in the much more comfortable chair of Sam's

private office and held the large yellow envelope where she could see it. "I've uncovered some evidence in the Jared Barkley case that could exonerate Stacy."

Her eyebrows furrowed. "Stacy? What about you?"

"Me too, but I don't need it. I was in Portland, remember?" He shifted his weight forward. He hadn't expected such a skeptical response. He expected her to reach for the envelope, but she seemed to ignore it.

"Until we find that motel employee you described—who is now, I've learned, a former employee with no available contact information—we have no corroborating witness for your alibi. You're not out of the woods yet, as far as the police and prosecutors are concerned—and therefore, me, too." She folded her hands, leaned forward, and lowered her voice. "You have to be careful, Lehigh. Now, how did you come across this evidence?"

Lehigh relaxed. He liked this better. "I did some asking around. It seems that Stacy and Jared—"

"Asking around? Lehigh, please. Don't go playing private detective. It could be very risky for you legally, and very dangerous."

Lehigh smiled at her. "I appreciate your concern, but I can take care of myself pretty well. Those city boys don't scare me none."

She frowned. "This is no time for bravado. We need you to lay low and not go around calling attention to yourself. You could very easily make a mistake that gets you arrested—or worse."

"Arrested? How? For what?"

"Compromising a police investigation, for starters. Tampering with evidence. Withholding evidence. Have you shared any of your findings with the police?" She pulled a file folder out of a drawer in her desk.

"Not yet. I wanted to talk to you first."

"Good. I want to hear it. Let's set up an appointment for tomorrow afternoon."

"Tomorrow?" Lehigh tossed his hands in the air. "Why not now?" He handed her the envelope. "You might want to read that."

"I can't right now. I'm booked up." She made a quick note on the outside of the envelope and set it on the corner of her desk.

"Oh, *that's* right. You have to go buy *wine*. Don't let my *legal* situation get in the way of your good time." He stood and took a step toward the door. She stopped him with an edge of steel in her voice.

"That was uncalled for." She glared at him, then stood. "Make an appointment with my receptionist. I need to work on another case right now."

Lehigh stared, openmouthed. "You're seriously kicking me out of your office?"

"I have another appointment. Besides, it looked to me like you were leaving anyway."

He nodded, one long, slow toss of his head. "I see."

"Lehigh. Don't be offended. It's not personal."

"Yeah." He half-turned toward the door, then stopped and faced her again. "But you see, I kind of had the impression that it was. Personal, I mean."

"In what way?" She had already busied herself again at her desk.

He dropped his gaze to his feet. "In the way that you seemed to be taking a personal interest. In me, and in my case."

"I see." She nodded, rolled her tongue around inside of her mouth. "Well, you're not the first client I've had who's gotten that impression, so clearly I'm communicating something wrong." She sighed and strolled around her desk, gathering her thoughts. "Mr. Carter—Lehigh—I like you. You're a nice guy, a fierce and loyal fighter for your fiancée, or girlfriend, whatever your current status. You're smart, and tough, and even charming at times. But." She stared at her desk for a long moment, then glanced back at him. "Even if things were…*different*…even if you were someone I could be interested in…ethically, I couldn't get involved with a client."

"What's this? A lawyer with ethics?" He tried on a grin, but it failed at half mast when she didn't smile back.

Instead, she took a breath, bit her lip, then cocked her head to the side a bit. "I hope you know me well enough to say that I am exactly that. But, all that aside. Lehigh, let's just say I'm…" A long pause as she seemed to choose her words carefully. "*Taken*. Okay? And so are you. And that's a good thing, for both of us. Let's leave it at that, okay?"

Lehigh stood still, stunned by the directness of Sam's speech. Of course she was taken! A beautiful, accomplished, intelligent woman like her wouldn't stay single in Mt. Hood County for ten minutes. "He's a lucky guy," he said.

Samantha burst out laughing.

"What's so funny?" Lehigh asked.

"Nothing. Nothing. You're a lucky guy too, Lehigh." She stepped toward him and took his hand. "Do me a favor, okay? Stay out of harm's way, and keep yourself in one piece so you can keep fighting for that fiancée of yours."

Lehigh nodded. She squeezed his hand, gazed into his eyes, and for a moment he thought she would change her mind. But she turned away, and he left the office without looking back at her.

And as for her advice to stay out of trouble…he ignored every word.

CHAPTER 32

Lehigh pulled into the Roadhouse parking lot at low speed and proceeded at a crawl down the line of cars parked at haphazard angles along the front of the building. He allowed himself a wry smile. If these guys drove and parked this badly *before* getting to the bar for happy hour, he didn't want to be on the road with them a couple of pitchers later.

With all but one of them, that is.

He found the black Beamer around the corner of the building, nestled between an oversized SUV and a mini-pickup jacked up on even more oversized all-terrain wheels. He parked across the rear of all three vehicles, blocking their exit. He planned to leave ahead of them anyway—*just* ahead of them.

"All righty then," he said to the dogs before getting out of the truck. "Here goes nothing." They stared at him in awe, as if he'd just written and delivered the Gettysburg address. He gave them treats from the glove box and left them chewing happily in the back seat.

He strolled through the front door as if he owned the place and sat at the bar without a single glance at any of the patrons. No need to go looking for his quarry. They'd find him, soon enough.

Babs, the silicone-enhanced barmaid, dressed in her usual low-cut tank top and painted-on jeans riddled with rhinestones, faked a smile, and set a coaster in front of him. "Welcome to the Roadhouse. Just in time for happy hour."

"Shot of Jack Black, beer chaser." He ignored her gravity-defying breasts and twirled around in his chair to face the billiards tables. In the corner, a couple of familiar faces stood behind cue sticks, and another familiar face leaned over a table, sizing up a shot.

The face he sought. Paul van Paten.

"Six off the seven, far corner," Paul said. Two clicks of colliding ivory later, the solid green ball plunked into the designated pocket.

"Lucky," Lehigh said.

Paul's face froze and his eyes locked onto Lehigh. Dark tousled hair covered half of his creased forehead. A curled sneer split the handsome face's lower half. "Think you can do better?"

"I don't waste my time in pool halls," Lehigh said. "Unless I'm searching for punks."

His drinks appeared at his elbow. He slammed the Jack in a swallow, then half the beer.

Paul sauntered around the table toward the bar, pool cue gripped at the waist. Too high of a grip to use it as a weapon. "Well, you're out of luck. The only punk in here's about to leave."

"You should settle your bill first," Lehigh said. "T'ain't good to stiff the waitress." Someone sniggered at the unintended double meaning.

Color rose in Paul's face, visible even in the dim light of the bar. "Did you have a reason to come here, other than to ruin my day?"

Lehigh shrugged and finished his beer. "Isn't that a good enough reason?"

Paul's buddies closed in around him. Curly-haired Thornburgh and the big blond, Brockton, stood to one side, pool cues in hand. An athletically built African-American, almost as tall and broad as Brockton, closed off the other side. "We don't want trouble," the black man said in a soft voice.

"Unless you do," Thornburgh said. He giggled, a nervous

laugh.

"I don't have business with any of you," Lehigh said. "Except van Paten."

"You have business with him, you have business with us," Brockton said. "Right, guys?"

"Shut up, Brock," Thornburgh said. "Paul can decide for himself if he needs us. What's the word, boss?"

"Stay put for now." Paul pointed to Lehigh's empty glasses at the bar. "Now, Mr. Carter, as a lawyer I feel obliged to advise you of Oregon's strict laws about driving under the influence of alcohol. My guess is that you're getting close to the legal limit already with those two drinks. If you left now, there'd be no reason for us to alert the local authorities about a dangerously inebriated driver on the highways. But if you stay..."

Lehigh chuckled. At least a dozen empty long-necked brown bottles littered a small table next to the billiards rack, with at least as many shot glasses scattered among them. "Am I to believe you boys had no part of all those dead soldiers over there?"

"Ben here's our designated driver." Paul indicated the tall black man with a nod of his head. "As for the rest of us...well, we might be a little loose and ready for action. If that's what you want."

"Good." Lehigh stood face to face with Paul. "Because I've had it with you, you coward. It's bad enough you hire red meat like these boys to do your fighting for you. But to let a woman take the fall for your crimes—that's unconscionable."

The three men behind Paul muttered in angry voices. Brockton pushed forward, fists raised. Paul stopped him with a raised hand. "You're up to something, Carter. Coming in here, baiting us like this. I'm not falling for it. Stand down, boys."

Lehigh snorted. "Yeah, I'm up to something. I'm up to my ears with your crap, that's what. Do you know where I just came from? Huh? No? I'll tell you. Stacy's lawyer's office. He just prepared a statement for her to sign. It's going to end Jared Barkley's murder case right now. You want to know what it says?"

Paul's smart-assed smile faded a bit, and his eyes widened. "Let me guess. She's turning state's evidence against you."

"Close." Lehigh pushed through the crowd of men to the door, then glanced back at them over his shoulder. "It's a confession."

***

Lehigh made it halfway to the truck before Paul caught up with him and spun him around. "You'd better be lying, Carter!"

Lehigh sighed. "I wish. But no. Nice work, by the way, getting an innocent woman to take the fall for you. What's next for you? Kidnapping babies?"

"I just talked to her this morning. She didn't say anything about confessing."

"Not to me, either. Apparently she only talks to her lawyer about such things." Lehigh pushed past Paul toward his truck.

Paul ran past him, pulling keys from his jacket pocket. He stopped short when he reached his blocked-in car. Again he spun to face Lehigh.

"Is this your idea of a joke? Or is that how they teach you to drive in the sticks? Move this hunk of junk, or I'll—"

"What? Ram me? Doubt it. It'd cost more to replace your dented bumper than my whole truck is worth." Lehigh stopped several feet away and stood with his arms crossed. "This screws up your plan, doesn't it, Paul?"

"It screws everything up. You're the one who belongs in jail, not her. And when I get through with you, you'll wish you *were* in jail."

Lehigh cocked his head. "Oh, really? Funny. I noticed you pulled all the right strings to get yourself out of stir, but you let Stacy rot in county lockup for days on end. Why's that?"

Paul shook his head. "You're even more stupid than I thought. She's charged with murder one, hayseed. She's got reason and resources to flee. They don't let people like that out."

Lehigh spit between Paul's feet. "If you wanted her out, she'd be out, just like you. No, you *want* her in, so she can't create trouble for you. And if she has to go down, well, you don't mind—so long as it ain't you. And you've got her so warped, so confused, she's doing this to protect you. Out of—" He choked on the words, despite his having rehearsed them for over an hour. When he spoke again, his voice sounded raspy and thin. "Because she loves you, dumbass."

"You don't believe that for a minute. And as for the rest—you don't know what you're talking about."

Lehigh shrugged. "Call her lawyer. He'll tell you."

Paul whipped out his phone. "I will do just that." He pounded a few keys, then held the phone to his ear. Lehigh sauntered to his truck and got in.

Now, it was up to Constantine Richards.

***

Lehigh didn't wait to find out if Stacy's lawyer—or more likely, his secretary—would play along well enough to fool Paul. Besides, providing a distraction right then seemed like a good idea—pull Paul's attention away from any inconsistencies or holes in Lehigh's story. He started the truck's engine and burned rubber racing out of the parking lot. The dogs whimpered and hunkered down on the back seat.

Sure enough, Paul followed, phone jammed to his ear. Lehigh kept an eye on him in his rearview mirror. Paul appeared animated, alternating between yelling into his phone and listening with his mouth clamped shut. Lehigh even took a few detours to make sure of Paul's intention to follow him and not think too much about where they were going.

Or, how fast.

Or that Paul, in his haste to catch up to Lehigh racing out of the Roadhouse parking lot, had forgotten to buckle his seat belt.

At the designated location, Lehigh pushed his speedometer well over eighty miles per hour—in a fifty mile per hour zone.

Sure enough, Paul kept pace. When the highway opened up to two lanes in each direction, Lehigh kept to the left, as did Paul.

After taking a blind corner a few seconds before his pursuer, Lehigh swept the truck into the right lane and dropped his speed down to fifty. Paul zoomed around the corner and flew past, still yelling into his phone, then braked.

But not before getting caught in the speed trap staffed by none other than Detective Jim Wadsworth.

The red and blue lights flashed even before Paul passed the detective's car, already idling on the side of the highway, partially hidden by a couple of overgrown shrubs. A quick burst of the siren announced the success of the snare, and Paul, shouting and pounding the steering wheel, stopped on the shoulder a couple of hundred yards down the road.

Lehigh drove past the infuriated, half-inebriated lawyer, and waved.

CHAPTER 33

As fun as it had been to mess with Paul and ruin his evening, that was only step one of the night's plan. Step two would be much trickier—and carried far more risk.

Lehigh returned to the Roadhouse Grill, where Thornburgh and Brockton loitered around the pool table, still clutching their pool cues—but not to sink ivory balls into corner pockets. Instead, staggering drunk, they used the long sticks as crutches, to keep from falling off their bar stools.

"You got some nerve, coming back here," Thornburgh said without getting up.

"I got nerve wherever I go." Lehigh signaled to Babs for a beer and stood across the pool table from them. "Where's your other buddy?"

"You mean me?" Ben's large frame cast a growing shadow from behind Lehigh. "Don't turn around. You just keep having your conversation like a gentleman. I repeat, like a gentleman."

Lehigh nodded. He hadn't come here to fight, so being surrounded didn't create problems...unless they had other plans.

"Just thought I'd come by to give you a message from Paul."

"Ha!" Brockton downed his whiskey. "Like he'd tell you anything. Why wouldn't he just call us?"

"He got detained." Lehigh's beer appeared and he took a swallow. "The message is, don't wait up. Unless you, too, decide to drink and drive tonight."

"Paul got a dewey?" Thornburgh's eyes widened and he set down his drink on a table covered in peanut shells. To Brockton's questioning stare, he said, "D–U–I. Driving under the influence."

"That ain't the worst of his problems." Lehigh took another sip. "It appears he needs an alibi for the night of Jared Barkley's murder."

"Paul wasn't nowhere near Elk Creek," Brockton said. Thornburgh shot him a furtive, wide-eyed glance, but the big blond kept talking. "He was with us."

"Sure, sure. 'Course he was. But, uh, where were you?"

"We was on the coast, playing poker," Brockton said.

"Just the three of you?" Lehigh scratched his cheek. "Seems kinda like a small crowd for poker."

Silence hung in the air for a beat. Then, from behind, Ben's rumbling baritone. "Sometimes we like small games."

Lehigh nodded. "Yeah, me too, sometimes. So, just the three of you, right?"

Thornburgh and Brockton nodded. "That's right," Ben said. "So?"

"Then where was Paul?"

Empty stares.

"He'd have made four, right?"

Brockton staggered around the pool table, dragging his walking stick behind him. "You think you're pretty smart, don't you?"

Thornburgh grabbed his arm from behind. "Brock, easy now. Remember what Paul said."

Brockton shook off his friend's grip. "I don't care. This one needs to be taught a lesson."

Lehigh took a step backward and lowered his beer glass, readying it, if need be, to splash Brockton in the face with it. "S'matter? You don't like math?"

"I don't like *you*." The big blond drew the stick back like a batter preparing to hit a fastball. Thornburgh grabbed the shank before Brockton could swing it forward.

"None of us like him, Brock. But van Paten said hands off him until, uh…you know."

Brockton blinked, shook the cane free, glanced at Lehigh, but leaned his would-be weapon against the pool table. "Oh, yeah. The broad thing."

"The 'broad' thing?" Lehigh sipped his beer. "I take it you charmers mean my ex-fiancée? Yeah, her confession creates a problem for you guys, doesn't it? Makes it hard to frame me for it now."

"It complicates matters a bit," Ben said from behind Lehigh.

"But," Thornburgh added, "you're going down, my friend."

Lehigh stepped to one side so he could keep all three men in view. "I don't see how. I was out of town when Barkley was killed."

"Yeah. So was Paul." Brockton sniggered. "Doesn't mean you couldn't hire it done, too."

"*Too?*" Lehigh frowned, acting as best he could like a man deep in thought, rather than one celebrating inside for Brockton's slip-up. "You mean, like the real killer done?"

"What he means," Thornburgh said, "is that if you were smart, like, uh, well, if you were, you could hire people to, um…keep an eye on things."

"Yup. Could." Lehigh nodded. "Responsible people. People who were in town, of course. But not you guys, because you were all at the coast playing poker, right?"

"Hey, we—uh, yeah." Brockton frowned. "Hey, Thorny. He's right. We got a problem."

"You've got a bigger problem than you think," Lehigh said. "Namely, your 'boss' is going to sell one or more of you down the river if his frame job on me doesn't work. Which it won't, as you've just figured out. Because if you goons were watching me, then you weren't at the coast—and neither was Paul. And who, by the way, was watching him?"

The three men glanced at each other. Ben's eyes grew wide. "Dudes," he said. "I can't go back inside. There's guys in there that—"

"Shut up!" Thornburgh pointed a chubby finger at Ben.

Ben pushed his way forward and smacked Thornburgh's hand away. "Don't tell me to shut up. I ain't your slave. Paul's neither. And I ain't taking a fall for anyone."

"You think so, huh?" Lehigh made direct eye contact with Ben. "Who do you think *is* going to take the fall? Not Paul, that's for sure. And these two guys are old chums. Neither one's gonna sell out the other. Who does that leave?"

Ben glared at him, his large eyes growing to the size of white saucers against his dark brown skin.

"He's blowing smoke," Thornburgh said. "Don't listen to him."

"One of these things is not like the others," Lehigh sang, hoping he got the old kids TV show tune right. "One of these things just doesn't belong…"

"That's you, Carter," Brockton said. "*You* don't belong. *You're* taking the fall. *You're* going down."

"Shut up, you idiot!" Thornburgh said.

"No, it ain't me," Carter said. "See, the sheriff's already given up on me. He's got Stacy, and now she's engaged to Paul again, and Paul don't want a jailbird wife, so how's he gonna get her free? He's got to give them one of you. Let's face it, you're expendable. And it's the only way." He nodded at Ben and sipped his beer. "I'm afraid that's real bad news for you, partner."

"I ain't doing time for no rich lawyer!" Ben said. "He can do his own damn time!"

"*Shut! Up!*" Thornburgh scampered over to Ben and grabbed him by the shoulders. "He's baiting you!"

Ben shook him off. "No. I've already been baited—and now I'm on the hook. Well, I'm cutting the line, right now." He pushed Thornburgh backward. The smaller man bounced off the pool table and a few chairs before Brockton caught him. Laughter resounded from around the bar.

"Well," Lehigh said, "I'm about ready for a refill on my beer. But this place, it's kinda noisy." He locked eyes with Ben again. "Thinking I might want to go someplace quieter, where folks can talk, if they wanna."

"You stay put!" Brockton pushed off of his cane and lunged at the space between Lehigh and Ben, as if he couldn't decide which one to grab. Ben dished out a quick chop to Brockton's neck, and the big blond sprawled face first onto the floor.

"You want some of that?" Ben stared at Thornburgh. The smaller man shook his head no. Ben gestured to a chair. "Then park your ass down and don't even think of following me." He spun on his heel and strode out the door.

"Fellas," Lehigh said, slapping a fiver on the table, "don't forget to tip the barkeep. Oh, and I don't think Paul will be back tonight. Make sure you cover his drinks, too."

He made it to the parking lot in time to catch up to Ben's white El Camino before it pulled out onto the highway. Ben rolled down his window and said, "You know that sports bar in Twin Falls?"

Lehigh nodded. "It's the only bar in Twin Falls."

"Meet me there." He pulled away without waiting for an answer.

CHAPTER 34

Lehigh jogged to his vehicle. His phone chimed, but he ignored it until he reached highway speed. Then he pressed Call Back.

"You're doing great," Wadsworth said. "But we need specifics. Try to get more detail."

"Easy for you to say," Lehigh said. "If these guys find out I'm bugged, they'll rip me to pieces and feed me to my own dogs. And, trust me, my dogs would go ahead and eat me." In the back seat, the dogs each barked once, as if to confirm their appetite for his lean muscles.

"Just keep doing what you're doing and they'll never suspect."

Lehigh sighed. "Make up your mind. Do you want me to keep doing what I'm doing, or ask more detailed questions?"

"Both. Are the other two following you?"

Lehigh checked the rearview mirror. "Doubt it. Brockton's taken a beating already, and Thornburgh doesn't go anywhere without his muscle. Or, for that matter, without his brains—and Paul's still with you, right?"

"Yeah, but he's not talking. He called his lawyer and zipped his lip tight. We'll hold him on the DUI until the morning, but if we don't have anything more solid by then, we'll have to let him go."

"You will," Lehigh said. "But if I go too many more rounds of drinks with these guys, I'm going to need a driver—or else

I'll end up in the cell next to Paul."

"We'll be close by. Call us if you need us."

Lehigh caught up to Ben's El Camino about a mile before they reached The Stadium, a run-down shack across from an equally run-down amateur sports complex in Twin Falls. Declining lumber sales meant reduced sponsorships, fewer games, less post-game celebration, and therefore, less maintenance on the shabby structure. Lehigh had snuck into The Stadium with a few friends after a high school football game there more than once. He wondered if the same blonde barkeep worked there, the one with the crazy laugh to match her spooky grey eyes. She'd known damn well that Lehigh and his friends were under age, and served them anyway—watered-down drinks, but the boys couldn't really complain.

He found Ben settled into a corner booth, already halfway through what looked and smelled like whiskey on the rocks. A second drink sat sweating on a cocktail napkin in the open seat opposite him. "That's for you," Ben said. "It's the house drink—water that once got introduced to bourbon."

So, maybe it wasn't just because they were underage. Lehigh toasted him with it and took a sip. Ugh. Not just watered down, but the cheap stuff. Same old Stadium.

"Paul might kill me for this," Ben said. "Even just being here with you is dangerous."

Lehigh nodded. "No one's forcing you. If you want to take your chances with Brockton and Thornburgh—"

"Those idiots? I might as well be dead." Ben finished his drink and signaled for another. "I'm just not sure why I should trust you."

Lehigh's arm itched where the tape holding the wire in place had come loose. His sweating probably didn't help that any. He smiled at Ben. "Would you believe that I stand for truth, beauty, and justice?"

"Truth, no. Beauty, yes—I've seen your girlfriend. Justice, time will tell."

Lehigh sipped his drink. "Fair enough. And in your experience, what does Paul van Paten stand for?"

Ben made an ugly face, a sneer mixed with a frown and an urge to spit. "Paul van Paten stands for Paul van Paten."

A deeply tanned feminine arm reached past Lehigh and set a shot glass of slightly darker amber liquid in front of Ben. "Anything for you, hon?"

Lehigh turned. The blonde with the crazy laugh had aged far more than the twenty years that had passed, largely due, Lehigh guessed, to excessive sun worship and too many cigarettes. Dark shadows framed her sad but spooky eyes, and thick pancake makeup worked overtime to hide deep lines forged by long-forgotten laughter. She looked like she hadn't smiled in ten years.

"I hear you make great coffee," he said.

"Enough cream and sugar in it, sure," she said. "Better yet, I can add some rum, or some Seagram's. Maybe some Bailey's." She set another square napkin on the table.

"Just the coffee, thanks."

She jotted a note onto a tiny notepad and squinted at him. "You look familiar. Didn't you used to play football?"

"A long time ago," Lehigh said.

"Not so long," she said. "I remember you liked PBRs. Hey, did that dark-haired gal ever hook up with you? I used to see her in here every so often."

"What dark-haired gal?"

"That cheerleader. The rich gal. Daddy's some sort of lawyer, or politician. Tracie something or other."

"She comes in here?"

The waitress wiped a spot of water off the table near Lehigh's glass. "Not so much lately, but a long time ago, yeah. With different guys, but she'd always ask about you. Then, she kind of disappeared, until about a year ago, when she started coming back."

"Alone, or—"

"Nope, never alone. No girl's crazy enough to do that. She was with a guy—a tall, good-looking fella. Real well-dressed." She made a sour face, and shuddered.

Ben grinned. "Hey, Carter, look at that. We're in luck. She don't like good-looking guys."

She continued to shake her head. "Not guys that mean."

Lehigh turned so he could get a better look at the waitress and to hear her better over the clinking of glasses at the bar. "Did you ever see him do anything to her?"

"Ever? Ha! Like, *every* time, just about. It's not like he tried to hide it. Always said mean stuff, told her she was fat—imagine! Her! And he got a little physical. Nothing too brutal, no punches or anything like that, but he'd grab her arm, shake her, things like that. Once they had a loud fight, and she was heading to the ladies' room, and he drags her out the door by her ponytail. The creep. If I'd have been ten years younger, I'd have done something. God forbid the *guys* in here would ever do anything to help a woman. Anyways, you want a PBR?"

Lehigh shook his head. "I'll stick with the coffee. When's the last time either of them came in here?"

The waitress paused, hand on her chin. "Little over a week ago. The lawyer, I mean. Him and another fella. Pretty late on that Saturday night. Maybe eleven o'clock?"

Lehigh's senses went on full alert. That put Paul in the area when Barkley was killed—not, as he'd claimed, playing poker on the coast. "Who was the other guy?"

"Blond-haired guy. Kinda muscular, a little bit scary looking. Walks with a limp and a cane."

"Brockton," Ben said.

"Yeah. Brock, he called him. They seemed to be looking for something, or someone." She turned to Ben. "Another one?"

"Please."

She scooted away, humming some old country song off-key. Lehigh leaned closer to Ben. "So they were here that night—right?"

Ben shrugged. "I don't know if they were here or not. But I'll tell you where they weren't. They were not at the coast with me. Except at check-in on Friday night, and check-out on Sunday. The rest of the time, they were gone. All three of them."

Lehigh scratched his chin. "How did they get back and forth? In Paul's BMW?"

Ben snorted. "No way. They drove Thornburgh's big ol' beast back to Portland, and split up into separate vehicles from there. Paul left his precious Beamer behind to 'prove' he'd been there the whole time. Man, you should've seen him when he handed me the keys. 'Easy around corners. Wipe your feet before getting in.' You'd have thought I was babysitting his kid for the first time."

"Paul has a kid?"

"Figure of speech. Yeesh." Ben gave Lehigh a searing stare.

"One more thing," Lehigh said. "Did they talk about stopping anywhere, say for gas or food?"

Ben thought for a moment. "Paul said he wanted to make it to Portland for dinner. Some crab shack where he planned to meet a guy. At the time I thought he was hiring a private eye or something."

"Why's that?"

The big man shrugged. "He mentioned that the guy was a former cop. Oh, and he said something about the guy costing him a lot of money."

"Any idea who it was?"

"Nah. I never met him, never heard his name. Funny thing, though."

"What's funny?" Lehigh's whole body tensed, his senses on alert.

"When he said that thing about the guy costing him a lot, Thorny and Brock laughed their butts off."

Lehigh cocked his head. "How exactly did he say it?"

Ben lifted a shoulder, dropped it. "He said the guy would be 'big bucks.' I don't get the humor, but—"

"Big bucks?" Lehigh stood and slapped two twenties on the table. "Thank you, my friend. Your drinks are on me tonight."

Ben held up a hand. "Thanks. But where are you going? And what are you grinning like that for?"

Lehigh grinned. "I'm going to the jail to free my fiancée.

Because I know who Paul's secret partner was in the murder of Jared Barkley."

***

Lehigh had just started his engine when his cell phone chimed on the seat next to him. He answered, shushed the dogs, and put the phone on speaker.

"Good work, Carter. Although you've created a problem for us." Wadsworth's strained voice carried a high-pitched note of worry.

"Understood. Is he there?"

A heavy sigh on the receiver sounded like static. "Both 'he's' are here—or were, last time I checked. In fact, they were together."

Lehigh froze a moment and had to jerk the wheel to stay in his lane. A driver passing in the other direction blared his horn at him. "When you say 'were'…"

"Yeah. We're checking. It seems my boss wanted some one-on-one with the suspect. Now I know why."

Lehigh pounded the steering wheel. "You mean to tell me they were alone? Paul and Buck? Are you cotton-picking kidding me?"

Commotion in the background interrupted Wadsworth's reply, followed by muffled conversation. "Take your hand off the mouthpiece and let me hear," Lehigh said, swerving his truck out of the other lane again. Another near miss.

"Sorry. I just got the word. They released Paul van Paten from custody a half hour ago and dropped all charges. Even the DUI. Guy blew a damned point-one-five, almost twice the limit, and he's free to drive home!"

"Holy mackerel!" More wheel pounding. "This gets crazier every minute."

"There's more bad news." Wadsworth's voice grew grim. "You didn't hear this from me, you understand? I could lose my job. And a lot worse."

"Hear what from you? Detective, what the hell's going on?

Wadsworth blew a loud breath into the phone. "Buck

Summers put out an all-points—on *you*. You're to be arrested on sight."

"Crap! Can't Dwayne countermand the APB? I mean, Buck's only a contractor, and—"

"Not anymore. Haven't you heard? He's been reinstated—not as sheriff, but as First Deputy. In fact, he's now my boss. Named to that post by none other than Acting Sheriff Dwayne Latner."

"Oh, great." Lehigh rolled down the window and spit onto the roadway. The bad taste lingered. "So glad I helped you guys out today."

"Sorry, Mr. Carter." Wadsworth's voice fell. "I'm going to talk to him now. Our guys will call in a moment to arrange getting that wire off you."

"And then what? They arrest me? No, thanks. I think I'll take my chances on my own. How long ago did Paul leave?...Hello?...Hello? Wadsworth? You there?"

A triple beep and a dial tone signaled the end of the call. A few moments later, a black BMW appeared ahead, heading straight toward him.

CHAPTER 35

The gap between the two cars closed quickly. The BMW straddled the center line, leaving only half of a lane on either side before the steep shoulder dropped off into thick stands of trees. The BMW's motor raced, accelerating. Two figures occupied the front seat: Paul van Paten and Buck Summers, their faces clearly identifiable through the glass.

"Here comes the long, chubby arm of the law," Lehigh muttered. Lucky poked her nose through the bucket seats. He pushed her back. "Lay down, dogs." They obeyed, for a change.

He had two options, neither good. He chose the more dangerous one.

He edged his truck closer to the center of the road, his tires perhaps an inch away from the yellow stripe separating the two lanes. Then he floored it.

On the passenger side of the BMW, Buck's face contorted, mouth open, jaw working. Paul stared ahead, arms locked on the wheel. Buck reached across, his face red. Paul struggled, and jerked his arm free of the ex-sheriff's grip. But he hadn't let go of the steering wheel.

The BMW swerved, its nose pointing to Lehigh's left, tail right, with the body of the BMW skidding forward along the center line. Lehigh yanked his wheel right, tapped the brakes—

It wasn't enough. The back ends of the two vehicles collided. The truck whipped around counterclockwise and the air bag crushed Lehigh into his seat. Still the truck spun left, with Lehigh's foot locked onto the brake. The air bag deflated, and the truck's spin slowed to a stop. Something warm flowed down Lehigh's face and his nose hurt like hell. Somewhere in the back, the dogs whimpered and clawed their way back onto the seat.

He blinked, clearing his vision. His truck sat crosswise on the highway, facing the shoulder of his own lane. Some fifty or so yards away, on the truck's passenger side, the BMW's rear end faced him, its driver's side crinkled like foil, and its back left tire stuck out at a crazy angle. He glanced in the rearview mirror to discover that the pickup's back end looked even worse. The windows were gone. Tiny trapezoids of blue-green glass littered his lap, the seat, everything.

His cell chimed somewhere on the floor. He ignored it, tried restarting the stalled truck. No go. He smelled smoke and gasoline.

Smoke and gasoline!

He struggled with his seat belt. Stuck! He yanked at it again, smacked the buckle with his open palm. It stung, but didn't help. Off to his right, two figures stumbled from the BMW. The temperature in the truck's cab seemed to shoot up. Sweat poured down Lehigh's face. "Dogs," he said. "Get out. Out!" They stared at him with uncertain expressions. "Go!" he said, pointing to the glassless opening where a window had once been. "Out!" Lucky climbed into the opening on the driver's side and jumped out. Diamond scampered after her. Moments later, their tails disappeared into the trees on the side of the highway.

"Better stay back. I smell smoke." Paul's voice drifted in through the shattered window.

"I think he's stuck in there," Buck said. They'd stopped walking toward him, Paul a few feet behind Buck, neither closer than twenty yards away. "Look, something's leaking under his truck. I think it's gas."

"Poor guy." Paul laughed. "You got a cigarette?"

"This is a hell of a time for a smoke," Buck said. "You're

liable to blow that truck sky high."

Paul laughed again. "That's a risk I'm willing to take."

Lehigh yanked again on the seat belt. Still jammed. Paul stepped in front of Buck, reaching into his pocket. "Well, lookie here. Matches, from the bar *Carter* was in earlier tonight. I guess I'll just have to satisfy my urge to smoke without tobacco."

"Paul, don't do nothing crazy."

Lehigh gave the seat belt one final, futile tug, then moved on to Plan B. He untangled the shoulder strap from his torso and leaned sideways on the seat so he could reach the glove box. He flipped the latch—no use. Locked. He pulled the keys from the ignition, fumbled for the right key, and jammed it into the hole. The contents spilled out onto the seat and floor.

"Paul, think about this," Buck said. "It's already gone too far. You got your revenge with Stacy. Killing Jared was a mistake, but we can still pin it on her and Carter. But that's it. No more, okay?"

Lehigh pawed through the papers and clutter that had, moments before, been in his glove box. Where the hell was that thing?

"I'm not done!" Paul shouted. "What if Stacy walks? What if this jack-hole stumbles onto something and links Jared back to us? No. He dies, and takes the blame with him to his grave. And we have the perfect opportunity to do it right here. I say we do it!"

Lehigh gave up on the detritus covering the seat and pawed around, half blind, in the glove box. There were a few things still in there, mostly papers and tissues.

"He can't link it to us. We're clean. You made sure of it."

"Shut up. If he's listening—where the hell did he go?"

Lehigh located the jackknife in the glove box and pried open the long steel blade. Sharp and always ready to cut metal if need be, as Pappy taught him. He lifted the seat belt away from his waist an inch and slid the blade along its edge. In one swipe he cut a third of the way through the tough cloth.

"He's laid out on the seat. Knocked out, I think." Buck's

voice strained as if he was exerting himself physically—perhaps, Lehigh hoped, to restrain Paul's advance. That couldn't last. "Call your muscle to come get us and your car out of here before somebody comes."

Another slash of the blade, and only an inch of fabric remained.

"No. I'm finishing this. Now!"

"And I say we stick to the plan!"

Grunting and unintelligible shouts edged closer. Lehigh sliced through the last inch of the tough fabric, yanked the driver's side door handle and kicked the door open. He sprawled out and rolled on the ground several feet to the side of the road, the open knife still in his grip.

A loud thud near the truck drew his attention. The heads and shoulders of Paul and Buck appeared over the truck bed. Buck's body sagged against the truck, then convulsed in response to a sharp movement of Paul's right arm. Buck doubled over. Paul pushed him to the ground, visible to Lehigh underneath the truck's chassis.

"You love him so much, you can burn with him," Paul said. "You're nothing but dead weight anyway." His foot drove hard into Buck's midsection. Buck's body convulsed again. A shoe to his head laid him out cold, face down to the ground.

Paul jogged back to his car and opened the trunk. Lehigh crawled around the far side of his truck and pressed his driver's side door closed, then crept around the truck's tail end. Paul closed his trunk and walked back toward the pickup carrying a bright red plastic gas can.

Lehigh slid under the truck, hoping Paul either couldn't see him or wouldn't bother to look for him there. He scooted up toward the front, next to Buck's body lying on the ground beside the truck. Buck's torso rose and fell in a regular breathing rhythm. Alive, but unconscious.

About ten yards from the truck, Paul slowed his pace and tugged at the cap on the gas can. After a few moments, a "swoosh" sound rewarded Paul's efforts. He continued unscrewing the cap as he walked toward the truck. Lehigh scooted out behind the truck and crouched, waiting, watching, holding the knife by its tip.

Six feet from the truck, Paul stopped, pulled the cap free, and tilted the can forward. Gas spilled onto the ground, the hood of the truck, and Buck's still form. He emptied the can and tossed it into the bed of the truck, then reached into his pocket where he'd stuffed the matches.

Out of nowhere, angry barking filled the air. Paul stopped, hand still in his pocket, and whirled around. A bright yellow flash of fur sailed toward him, snarling, all teeth and claws slashing at his face. Paul used his free hand to bat the dog away. Lucky landed on her side, yipped, rolled, and ran. Moments later, Diamond dashed through, nipping at his heels. Paul kicked at the air, missing, and the puppy scampered over to the still-prancing Lucky, barking at a frequency that could pierce eardrums. Paul screamed at them, unintelligible syllables of rage and frustration, then rotated his body back toward the pickup.

Lehigh could wait no more. He stood, aimed, and threw the jackknife. The knife tumbled end over end through the air on a slight downward trajectory. Just in time, the tip of the blade swung around and lodged deep into Paul's right thigh, inches below Paul's right hand, still stuffed in his pocket. A red torrent gushed down his leg, and from his mouth came a blood-curdling scream loud enough to be heard in Portland.

Paul stumbled, but righted himself. He made a weak grab at the knife handle with his left hand. His hand slid off. He grabbed at it again with an open palm, again failing to get a grip. On his third attempt, he missed altogether, his arm swishing past his blood-soaked leg. He staggered, spun, and collapsed against the hood of the pickup.

Lehigh sprang from his crouch, arms wide. His shoulder plowed into Paul's midsection and his arms wrapped around Paul's knees, his own legs driving. Momentum pushed all four hundred pounds of humanity several feet away from the truck, airborne, until Lehigh landed on top of Paul on the pavement.

Paul issued a loud grunt, then another ear-piercing scream. He pushed Lehigh off of him. Lehigh's head grazed the pavement, probably scraping a serious amount of skin in the process, and he rolled to the side of the road.

"My leg! You rotten bastard, you stabbed me in the leg!" Paul clutched his thigh, wrapped his bloody fingers around the handle, and pulled the knife out with a violent yank. Fresh blood gushed from the wound in his thigh. He struggled to his feet, still holding the knife, and stumbled toward Lehigh, unsteady on his feet, but rage filling his eyes. Behind him, the dogs crouched, growling, teeth bared.

"Put the knife down, Paul. It's over."

"It isn't over until I say it's over!" Paul stumbled toward him, knife raised high. Lehigh rolled into a low crouch and hooked the back of Paul's knee with a stiff boot. Paul's legs crumpled again, and he landed with a thump onto the pavement.

This time Lehigh took no chances. He stomped on Paul's hand, freeing the knife, and kicked it away. Paul grabbed at him with his free hand, screaming in rage. Lehigh shook free, took one step back, and planted his left foot. "I've been wanting to do this for a long, long time," he said.

Lehigh swung his right foot forward with brutal force. His instep met the bridge of Paul's nose with a loud, sickening crunch. Paul's head flew backward, followed by the rest of his body, and he flopped unconscious onto the pavement, into the waiting, face-licking tongues of Diamond and Lucky.

"Nice one," said a voice behind him. "You should have been a place kicker instead of a tight end."

Lehigh turned toward the voice. "Actually, I was a wide recei—"

He stopped short the moment he spotted the revolver in the hand of former Sheriff Buck Summers.

"Stay put, Carter."

"Buck. What are you doing? Put that away."

Summers shook his head. "Put your hands up, Carter.

You're under arrest."

"Buck. Seriously."

"Hands *up*, I said!"

Lehigh shook his head but lifted his hands into a goalpost pose. "I'm sure you have some specific charges in mind, like, oh, I don't know, saving your stupid life?"

"Reckless driving, assault and battery, reckless endangerment, resisting arrest—"

"Resisting? Are you high? I stayed right here, and saved your butt from burning along with my truck. I'd have thought you'd be at least a tad bit grateful." Behind him, the dogs resumed their high-pitched yelping.

"Grateful, my butt. You're going down for Barkley's murder, too. All of it. Now put your hands on the truck's roof and spread 'em. And shut them damn dogs up, would ya?"

Lehigh sighed and raised his voice over the dogs' racket. "This is such a waste of time, and such a bad move for you. You know I heard every word you and Paul said a few minutes ago."

Buck laughed. "So what? No one's going to believe you. Your word against mine and Paul's, and need I remind you, I'm an officer of the law. Now, get." He waved the gun toward the vehicle. The canine racket subsided, replaced by the sound of paws pounding pavement, then swishing through grass.

"Nobody's gonna have to believe me." Lehigh shuffled over to the truck, rested his hands on the cab's roof, and spread his feet.

"They ain't gonna believe your girlfriend, neither, if that's what you're thinking."

Lehigh shook his head. "No need."

Buck patted Lehigh's right side, then his left. He stopped when his rough pats pushed the wire into Lehigh's skin. He yanked Lehigh's shirttail high over his waist and yanked on the wire. Lehigh's skin burned where the wire ripped out of the tape holding it to his skin.

"What the hell is this?"

Lehigh chuckled. "It's like you said, Buck. Nobody's gonna

believe me when I say you and Paul killed Jared. But they'll sure as hell believe *you*."

Moments later, snarling and barking filled the air once more, joined by the angry voice of a large man being smothered in fur. When Lehigh turned, Lucky had Buck pinned to the pavement, teeth bared. Next to her, Diamond held Buck's gun in his mouth. In the distance, red and blue flashing lights appeared over the rise of the highway, followed by the sound of sirens.

Lehigh grinned. "Good dogs. I think our work here is done."

CHAPTER 36

"Great job, Carter." Gentleman Jim Wadsworth extended a beefy hand to Lehigh. They shook, and Wadsworth held on a moment. "I misjudged you at first. I thought you were a cheater."

Lehigh shrugged. "I misjudged you, too, Detective. I guess there's been a whole lot of that going around."

A sudden clatter of noise erupted through the thin walls of Wadsworth's office. They waited until the shouting stopped. Lehigh smiled when he recognized Dwayne Latner's voice among the hubbub. He didn't sound happy.

"I'm going to personally see to it that none of this stays on your record." Wadsworth gave Lehigh's hand one final firm shake and released his grip. "That goes for your fiancée, too."

A knock on the door startled Lehigh. A male voice followed. "Detective? Is Mr. Carter in there?"

"Yes, he is. Come in."

The door opened and Deputy Roscoe's face appeared. "His fiancée wants to see him."

Lehigh sighed. "She's not my—"

Stacy pushed past Roscoe, wearing a denim sundress, a welcome change from her prison pajamas. "Who says I'm not? You getting cold feet again, mister?"

Her lips covered his before he could answer. Her arms wrapped around his back and neck, and her legs wrapped around his waist. He couldn't breathe, but he didn't care.

Somewhere behind him, Wadsworth's office door banged

shut, and two pairs of footsteps faded down the hallway.

***

Standing in a sunlit meadow a few hundred yards from the ashes where his house once stood, Lehigh reached back as far as he could, then whipped his arm forward. A bright yellow tennis ball rocketed out of his hand and sailed a good forty yards, bouncing a few feet ahead of two yelping canines, racing for reasons known only to dogs to be the first to reach it. For that task, the winner—which, it turned out, would once again be Lucky—would be rewarded with the privilege of returning it to Lehigh and Stacy, only to be thrown again.

"I still don't see what Jared's journals had to do with anything," Stacy said. "It was the taped conversation between Paul and Buck that convinced the grand jury—when they tried to burn your truck. What else really mattered?"

"Everything," Lehigh said. Lucky dropped the ball at his feet, and Diamond snatched it up and darted off into the field. Lucky followed in hot pursuit. "Jared documented all of his evidence about the arson in there, knowing, somehow, that Buck was in on the cover-up. He kept copies of the original interviews in there, which apparently Buck altered later. He even had old computer logs in there, showing who changed the files, and when. He was thorough."

"But that's the arson. How did that connect them to Jared's murder?"

The dogs returned, and somehow Lucky had stolen the ball back from Diamond. She yipped a warning at the younger dog and laid the ball at Lehigh's feet. "My turn," Stacy said. She picked up the slobber-covered sphere and whipped it twenty yards into the trees on the side of the meadow. "That'll keep them busy."

Lehigh laughed. "For a minute. Anyway, Jared also found—and kept—a record of the money trail that connected him, and Brockton, and Thornburgh—the political payola, the payoff for the arson, all of it. And, those records led to the greatest find of all—the one that almost got one of us sent to prison for the rest of our lives, or worse." The dogs returned, and Lehigh whipped the ball into the meadow again.

"Don't keep me in suspense," Stacy said. "What find? What was so great?"

"The gun," Lehigh said. "The one that they 'found' in your house during the search? Thornburgh bought it at a pawn shop in Hood River a few weeks before. How Jared found out, I don't know, but he knew about it, right down to the serial number. The only thing he didn't know was what they planned to use it for.

"He also overheard the deputies, Patrick and Flynn, talking about planting it somewhere, but of course at the time they hadn't decided where, because the murder hadn't happened yet. Once Paul's thugs used it to kill Jared, it magically appeared in your house during a warrant search. Little did they know, Jared had the whole thing mapped out in advance in almost as much detail as they did. The only thing he didn't count on was being the victim—which, so far as we can tell, was the only thing they *didn't* plan."

"Because," Stacy said, "the original plan was to kill you."

"But I was surrounded by thousands of people at a convention, in Portland of all places, which they didn't count on. And then I wouldn't stay put long enough for them to get a shot at me, I guess."

"What they didn't know, and I did," Stacy said, "was that Jared had decided to make his move, to arrest them that same weekend."

Lehigh nodded. "When he found them, they must have panicked, and Jared paid the price."

The dogs returned, this time with the ball in Diamond's mouth. Stacy shook her head. "Too much drool. I'm done." Lehigh chuckled, grabbed the ball, and fired it into the woods.

"I'm surprised they got that sloppy," Stacy said. "Paul and his cronies, I mean, not the dogs."

"I'm not," Lehigh said. "At least when it comes to Thornburgh and Brockton. Those idiots tried to bribe me last year, thinking I was Paul. They were the weak link in the operation. Oh, and it didn't help matters that the bartender at the Roadhouse got tired of being Brockton's punching bag, so she confirmed Ben's story about them being in town the weekend Jared was killed. Not just Brockton, but Paul and Thornburgh, too. So much for their alibi."

"Let that be a lesson to the men of the world," Stacy said.

"I'd never hit you."

"I know," Stacy said. "Although I'm pretty sure there were times over the past few weeks when you were tempted to strangle me."

Lehigh grinned. "Counselor," he said, "on that, I plead the fifth."

She grinned back. "You're doing a lot of that lately." Her grin faded. "Um, speaking of counselors."

"What?" Lehigh picked up the ball and tossed it again.

"You never spoke much about your lawyer."

He avoided her gaze. "I haven't seen you much since I hired her."

"She's a pretty gal."

"You know her?"

"I saw her through the window the day I tried to surprise you and got arrested in my underwear. Long story, don't ask. What's her name?"

"Pullen. Samantha Pullen. She's not so pretty, really."

Stacy laughed. "Holy cow." She laughed more, then doubled over laughing.

"What's so funny?"

She struggled to get her laughter under control, but it took nearly another minute before she could stifle her giggles. "Your face...your expression...looked so guilty!" She doubled over laughing again. The dogs returned, running in circles around her, barking.

"Hush, dogs!" Lehigh held up a finger to quiet them. It worked, sort of. "And why would I feel guilty about anything?"

"Oh, Lehigh. Come on. She's a beautiful woman, and—

well, the way I was acting, I wouldn't blame you if you were tempted a little. And you *were* tempted, weren't you?"

"I wouldn't say that. I mean, sure, she's *kinda* pretty, but—"

"Oh, come on. Heck, even I'd be tempted by her, if I swung that way."

He grinned. "I'm glad you don't."

She stepped closer and placed her hands on his waist. "Speaking of which—if I'd known her name sooner, I wouldn't have worried."

"What are you talking about?" Lehigh leaned back a little. "You just got done saying I ought to have been, you know, attracted to her."

Stacy shrugged. "Wouldn't make any difference if you were or weren't." She grinned as his expression grew even more puzzled. "Lehigh," she said, "Samantha Pullen's name gets tossed around at the sheriff's office—a lot. And not favorably. They're a pretty conservative group down there, and they don't like her one teeny tiny bit. Do you know why?"

He shook his head, more confused than ever.

"Lehigh, did Sam Pullen ever mention that she was in a relationship?"

"Uh, huh. Why?"

She grinned. "Did she ever mention with whom?"

He shook his head again. "Why? Do I know him?"

She practically squealed with delight. "No, Lehigh. You don't know *her*."

For the first time in years, Lehigh blushed.

CHAPTER 37

Lehigh stopped the truck, engine idling, at the far end of the long gravel drive. Three figures occupied the front porch in the distance. Pappy, in his usual overalls, smoked a cigarette in his old rocker by the front door. Maw clutched a broom in both hands, standing next to him in a plain, light blue housedress. The third figure, sitting in a chair next to Pappy, looked vaguely familiar.

"Is that Mrs. Barkley?" Stacy asked.

"I'm thinking it is," Lehigh said. "Crazy."

"What's crazy? That she's left her house, or that your parents have company?"

"Both." He let the truck inch forward. Lucky and Diamond sniffed at the windows in back, open just a crack. "Settle down, dogs," Lehigh said. "Don't get your hopes up."

Stacy ruffled Lucky's fur and tried without success to avoid Diamond's slobbery tongue. "They need to be let out."

Lehigh shook his head. "Not until I'm sure Maw's broom isn't loaded with buckshot. She'd as soon cook 'em for dinner as let 'em pee in her yard."

He stopped in back of the two vehicles already parked on the grass near the end of the drive and took Stacy's hand. "Here we go again."

"I'm ready," she said.

They walked hand-in-hand to the porch. Pappy and Maw sat motionless, eyes fixed on the younger couple. Mrs. Barkley stood. "If I'm in the way, I'll—"

"You're all right." Maw chewed something with her lips open, probably her own tongue. "It's just my younger son."

"I recall," Mrs. Barkley said. "Hello, Lehigh. Hello, Miss McBride."

"Please, call me Stacy." They took the steps with slow deliberation. Lehigh kept one eye on Pappy, the other on his mother. Maw stood guard on the top step, still clutching her broom. Two steps down, Lehigh and Stacy stopped, her hand squeezing his almost hard enough to break it.

Maw squinted at Stacy, long and hard, then turned her gaze to Lehigh. She leaned on her broom handle, searching his face. Lehigh's hand grew clammy, and Stacy's fingernails dug into his skin. Lehigh shifted his weight from one foot to the other, and back again. A cool breeze sifted through warm rays of sunshine breaking through fluffy clouds. A pair of crows cawed and wings flapped overhead. The breeze subsided.

Maw's gaze flitted back to Stacy for a moment, then to the thin void of space between them. "Well," she said, "the roast is about ready. I suppose we ought to go wash up."

Pappy smiled through a thin veil of smoke and waved Lehigh inside.

"Thank you, Maw." Lehigh tugged Stacy's hand forward. She let go, held her arms wide.

And hugged Maw.

Lehigh's heart jumped, and he sucked air in between his teeth. He reached for Stacy to pull her away before Maw could kill her...

And found Maw's arms wrapped around Stacy.

"Take care of my boy," Maw said, eyes closed. "He needs him some spoiling."

"I will." Stacy pulled back, arms still at Maw's side. They held their intense gaze and loose embrace a few moments longer. Maw stepped back and smacked Pappy's knee. "Go on, Caleb," she said, and spit a black wad of what once might have been tobacco over the porch rail. "Get your hands washed."

Pappy nodded. "I'll be along. You go pull the roast out and mash those 'taters."

Maw bent, kissed Pappy's forehead, and disappeared behind the swinging wooden storm door, broom in hand. Stacy started to follow, but Pappy stopped her with an upraised hand. "Hang on a moment. Miz Barkley wants to jaw at you for a minute." Stacy took Maw's seat, and Lehigh sat on the rail.

Mrs. Barkley gazed into the house after Maw and smiled. "That dear woman. What a beautiful soul." She sat on a folding chair next to Pappy. "I thought when I lost Jared, I had nothing else. Theo's gone, my boy's gone—my life may as well be over. The only thing I had left was to see his killer brought to justice." Her eyes met Stacy's. "At first, I thought that was you."

"I know." Stacy dropped her gaze. "I…I think I understand."

"You'll never understand. What it's like to lose everything…" Mrs. Barkley halted, her hand to her mouth. "I hope not, anyway. And I hope I never have to endure what you've been through, either. False accusations, jail…I–I'm sorry."

Stacy wiped away tears. How Mrs. Barkley held them in, Lehigh couldn't fathom. Made of steel, these women.

Mrs. Barkley turned to Lehigh. "I want to thank you for helping me. I might never have recovered if you hadn't knocked on my door."

Lehigh bowed his head. "Much obliged to you, ma'am. I don't think Maw's been in such good spirits since—"

Pappy coughed into his palm, glaring. Lehigh took the old man's silent direction and bowed his head. "I just hope you two stay in touch."

"We will." Mrs. Barkley stepped close and pressed dry lips against his cheek. She whispered into his ear. "Your Maw loves you more than she can ever show." She stepped back. "I'd best go help with dinner."

"I'll help too." Stacy held the door open for Mrs. Barkley, then turned to go inside. Pappy blocked her path with his cane. "A moment, young lady."

Stacy waited in front of him, hands folded. Pappy smoked the last quarter-inch of his hand-rolled cigarette and crushed it under his boot.

"I don't trust rich people," he said. "Your Daddy—I never voted for him. Not once."

Stacy smiled. "I voted against him once or twice myself. Don't ever tell him I said so."

Pappy smiled, a broad gap-toothed grin, and cackled. Harsh aromas of tobacco followed the laugh out of his mouth. "You served time in jail when he could have probably bought your way out. I respect that."

Stacy blushed. "In retrospect, I wish I hadn't."

Pappy nodded. "I respect that, too." Stacy held out her hand. Pappy enveloped it in both of his. He blinked twice and swallowed. "So, young lady. You gonna keep your name, or take ours?"

Stacy looked down at her feet, then at Lehigh. They'd broached the subject only once, months before, and she'd dismissed the idea out of hand. "You know," she said, "I was married before. And I didn't change my name then."

"I know. It's why I'm asking."

She stepped closer to Pappy and pressed her free hand around his. "I think," she said, and took a deep breath, "that we've all heard enough of the McBride name in Mt. Hood County. I'd be proud to take the name Carter…if you'll have me."

Pappy's eyes narrowed, and his lips curled upward again. "That I will…Daughter."

They held hands for several more seconds.

Mrs. Barkley reappeared at the door. "Stacy, we'd love to have your help with the salad, if you wouldn't mind."

Stacy glanced at Lehigh. He nodded, and two women disappeared inside the house.

Lehigh sat back on the rail. "Pappy, we—"

Pappy held up an index finger. "Hold on, son. Company."

Wheels crunched gravel behind Lehigh. He turned to spot a blue Crown Victoria roll to a stop behind his truck, blocking him in. Detective Wadsworth emerged a moment later.

"You in trouble again, boy?" Pappy asked.

"Not that I know of."

"That's usually how it works, son." Pappy leaned on his cane and stood. Lehigh turned and stood by his side on the front step to greet the detective coming toward them.

"Afternoon, gents." Wadsworth tipped his hat. He faced Lehigh. "Mind if I bend your ear over something for a minute?"

"He's about to have dinner." Pappy's voice dipped a few registers, almost to a growl.

"My apologies. I'll come another day." Wadsworth turned to leave.

Lehigh stopped him with a raised hand. "What's the issue, Detective?"

Wadsworth brightened. "I've got a proposition for you. Call it a job opportunity."

"Whatever it is, take it," Pappy said. "Oh, hell, son, don't stare. You and I both know you ain't making ten cents running that forestry business, and now you're getting married, and— well, son. You need a job. Desperately, I might add."

"In all my days, I've never before seen you agree with a man in uniform so fast." Lehigh descended the porch steps. "Well, Detective, what's the job? Sheriff's office needs some timber cleared?"

Wadsworth shook his head and chuckled. "Mr. Carter, you've already done a fine job helping us clear out the dead wood. And as a result...well, we don't even *have* a sheriff anymore."

"What happened to Dwayne?"

"Suspended, pending investigation. He went along a little too willingly with Buck's schemes." Wadsworth dropped his gaze, seemed to grasp for words.

Lehigh nodded. "So let me guess. That leaves you, next in line. And as Acting Sheriff, you're looking to hire some deputies." He glanced at Pappy with a sly smile. "Still think I should take the job?"

"Not exactly." Wadsworth kicked at the dust at his feet. "I'm not offering you a job as a deputy. I can't exactly *offer* you any job, technically."

"Then I'm confused, Detective," Lehigh said. "What *are* you offering?"

"My endorsement." Wadsworth folded his arms across his body. "You see, I declined the County Commission's offer to make me acting sheriff. It's never a job I wanted—too much politics, paperwork, and management crap."

Lehigh spread his hands wide. "Now I'm completely lost."

"If he's that confused," Pappy said, "maybe you shouldn't endorse him after all, Detective."

Stacy, Maw, and Mrs. Barkley emerged onto the porch. "Dinner's ready," Maw said. "Evening, Detective. Endorse who, for what?"

"Endorse Lehigh," Wadsworth said. "For sheriff."

"Sheriff? Me?" Lehigh laughed. "I've spent the last six months fighting you guys to keep my sorry butt out of your jail—mine and Stacy's. Now you want to hand me the keys?"

"Hey!" Stacy said. "Who's calling my butt 'sorry'?"

Wadsworth grinned, then got serious again. "Mr. Carter, I can't think of anyone I'd trust more for this job. Please consider it."

"It just doesn't seem likely I'd have any credibility with the deputies," Lehigh said.

"The guys—and gals—in uniform will come along, in time," Wadsworth said. "In the meantime you'd have the trust of the County Board, me, and the voters of Mt. Hood County. For now, that's all that really matters. Like I said, it's all politics."

"I hate politics."

"It's also a lot of police work," Stacy said.

"Which I'm sure I'd also hate." Lehigh chuckled. "What a crazy idea."

"Not at all." Mrs. Barkley descended the steps in slow succession, resting both feet on each step before taking the next, until she reached Lehigh. "You did some pretty good police work finding Jared's killers."

"Exactly," Stacy said. "And you were awfully proud of it. All those stories you've been telling me…you seemed to have a real passion for it."

"That's because I wanted you out of jail," Lehigh said.

Stacy rolled her eyes and stepped to the side of the porch, punching numbers into her cell phone.

Mrs. Barkley took Lehigh's hand and pressed it between both of hers. Her eyes moistened. "I'd be proud to offer you my endorsement, if that helps. I'm sure Jared would approve. As would Theo."

"Wow." Lehigh looked from face to face, finding hope and excitement in each.

After a few moments, Maw nodded her head. "Do it," she said. "Make your Pappy and me proud." She wrapped a bony arm around Stacy, who was talking in a low voice on her cell phone. "And you gotta do something for a living. You can't expect this pretty girl to support you forever."

Stacy returned Maw's hug and lowered the phone from her jaw. "That's right," Stacy said. "Not if I'm going to be busy raising all those grandkids."

"*Grandkids?*" Lehigh staggered up the steps. "Stacy? Are you, uh—"

"Not yet," Stacy said. "How could I be? I've only been out of jail a week." She slipped out of Maw's arms and into his. "But I think we should get right on it, don't you?"

"Maybe you could at least get married first," Pappy said.

"Speaking of which," Stacy said. "My father wants a word." She spoke into the phone again. "Here he is, Daddy."

"What the—?" Lehigh sputtered unintelligible protests but accepted the phone Stacy offered and held it to his ear. "Yes, sir?"

"Lehigh, my boy," Senator McBride's voice boomed from the phone, "I've been wanting to come by and thank you for helping my daughter out of her little scrape with the law. What you did was stand-up and proper, son. Stand-up and proper."

"Well, thank you, sir," Lehigh said. "I'm most obliged."

"Not at all, not at all," McBride said. "It's the least I can do for the man I am *proud* to call my future son-in-law. Her mother and I can't *wait* to help plan your reception."

Lehigh's jaw dropped to his knees. "We'd be most appreciative, sir."

"But the number one reason for my call," McBride said, ignoring, apparently, that Stacy had called him, "is to support and endorse your decision to serve our county. You're a local hero, young man, and I'll do everything in my considerable power to assist you in this endeavor."

Lehigh swayed, lightheaded. "Well, if that don't beat all," he said finally. "I mean, uh, thank you."

"You're welcome. We'll talk more soon, but I need to go. The people's business waits for no one."

Lehigh handed the phone back to Stacy and turned to face Wadsworth. "Detective," he said, "I think you, and the rest of the county it seems, have talked me into it. I accept your endorsement."

"Now," Maw said, drawing the porch door open, "let's eat!"

ACKNOWLEDGMENTS

The Mountain Man Mysteries series has been in the works for nearly a decade. Many friends, colleagues, and family members—too many to count or even remember—have contributed ideas, feedback, critique, encouragement, and love. I thank you all.

But special thanks goes out to those whose support really pushed me when I needed it to get this story published. They include:

Angela Carlie, Randall Houle, Kelly Garrett, Suzie Harvey, and Paul McKlendin, all members of the North Bank Writers Group, whose chapter-by-chapter critiques made this story better on a weekly basis;

My Beta Readers, Kelley Tyner McAllister, Patsy Silk, Brigette Hendrickson, and Dominique Rossi, for their invaluable late-in-the-game feedback;

Patsy Silk and Janice Hussein, whose keen editing eyes caught many errors long after my own eyes glazed over. If errors remain, they are my fault, not theirs;

Steven Novak, for an amazing cover design;

The Willamette Writers Group, the best bunch of writers around;

Patricia and Donald Corbin, my mother and father, who made me love books, and who always encouraged my love of writing;

All of the many furry critters who have made their way into my life and heart, each of whom show up on these pages, one way or another; and,

Renée, the kindest, most patient, most beautiful person I've ever known, whose smile lights up the darkest night and brightens even the sunniest day…I love you.

ABOUT THE AUTHOR

Gary Corbin is a writer, actor, and playwright in Camas, WA, a
suburb of Portland, OR. His creative and journalistic work has
been published in *BrainstormNW*, the *Portland Tribune*, The
Oregonian, and *Global Envision*, among others. His plays have
enjoyed critical acclaim and have been produced on many
Portland-area stages.

Gary is a member of the Willamette Writers Group, 9 Bridges
Writers, the Northwest Editors Guild, PDX Playwrights, and
the North Bank Writers Workshop, and participates in
workshops and conferences in the Portland, Oregon area.

A homebrewer as well as a maker of wine, mead, cider, and
soft drinks, Gary is a member of the Oregon Brew Crew and a
BJCP National Beer Judge. He loves to ski, cook, and root for
his beloved Patriots and Red Sox, and hopes someday to train
his dogs to obey. And when that doesn't work, he escapes to
the Oregon coast with his sweetheart.

CONNECT WITH GARY CORBIN

Keep up to date with the latest at
http://www.garycorbinwriting.com.

Follow me on Twitter:
http://twitter.com/garycorbin

Follow me on Facebook:
https://www.facebook.com/garycorbinwriting

Follow my Amazon Author Page
(and review this book!)
http://smarturl.it/GaryCorbinAuthor

Favorite me at Smashwords:
https://www.smashwords.com/profile/view/GaryCorbin

ALSO BY GARY CORBIN

The Mountain Man's Dog

Book One of The Mountain Man Mysteries

Lehigh Carter, a humble forester in Oregon's Cascade Mountains, fears two things: women and dogs. Then his former fiancée, Stacy, convinces him to adopt a stray—and to rekindle their romance. When he accidentally witnesses her father receiving illegal contributions to his gubernatorial campaign, Lehigh's simple life gets entangled in the complex world of politics, arson, romance, and pet ownership.

Lehigh never really meant to adopt the dog. But his ex-fiancée, Stacy McBride, convinces him to do it, with a promise to help. Their rekindled romance angers her father, state senator George McBride, who sees her backwoods suitor as a blemish on his carefully created political image. It also sets off a chain of events that entangle Lehigh in a life-or-death conflict with the senator's hardnosed campaign treasurer, Paul van Paten, who had his own plans for Stacy's future.

The Mountain Man's Dog is a briskly told crime thriller loaded with equal parts suspense, romance, and light-hearted humor, pitting honor and loyalty against ruthless ambition and runaway greed in a town too small for anyone to get away with anything.

Available in hardcover, paperback, and all eBook formats
at garycorbinwriting.com, Amazon.com,
Smashwords.com, CreateSpace.com,
and at your favorite local retailers.

ALSO BY GARY CORBIN

Lying in Judgment

A man serves on the jury trying a man for murder —the murder that he committed!

Peter Robertson, 33, discovers his wife is cheating on him. Following her suspected boyfriend one night, he erupts into a rage, beats him and leaves him to die...or so he thought. Soon he discovers that he has killed the wrong man—a perfect stranger.

Six months later, impaneled on a jury, he realizes that the murder being tried is the one he committed. After wrestling with his conscience, he works hard to convince the jury to acquit the accused man. But the prosecution's case is strong as the accused man had both motive and opportunity to commit the murder. The pressure builds, and Peter begins to slip up and reveal things that only the murderer would know—and Christine, a flirty and intelligent alternate juror, suspects something is amiss.

As jurors one by one declare their intention to convict, Peter's conscience eats away at him and he careens toward nervous breakdown.

Lying in Judgment is a courtroom thriller about a good man's search for redemption for his tragic, fatal mistake, pitted against society's search for justice.

Available in hardcover, paperback, and all eBook formats
at garycorbinwriting.com, Amazon.com,
Smashwords.com, CreateSpace.com,
and at your favorite local retailers.

FORTHCOMING

The Mountain Man's Badge

Book Three of The Mountain Man Mysteries

In the third installment in the thrilling Mountain Man Mysteries, Lehigh reluctantly accepts the challenge of serving as Mt. Hood County's interim sheriff and is immediately confronted with the county's second murder of the year. Stacy's former employer, Everett Downey, had many enemies—including former Senator George McBride, Stacy's father. When the evidence forces Lehigh to arrest George, it threatens the viability of their brand-new marriage. But his search for the truth behind the murder leads Lehigh to discover he has made powerful enemies of his own who will stop at nothing to preserve the corrupt system that keeps them in power.

Expected release: March, 2018

The Incident

Valerie Dawes carries emotional scars from being molested in her youth by a family "friend." After realizing her dream of becoming a police officer at age 22, her unresolved anger over "The Incident" boils over in confrontational situations with suspects, causing her to pull the trigger a little too quickly. When her senior partner shows her how to cover up such transgressions, she gets caught in a callous pattern of taking retribution for her childhood trauma against the violent men on the street—and an increasing recklessness that puts her life, and everything she stands for, at serious risk.

Expected release: Fall, 2018

FORTHCOMING

Lying in Vengeance

Sequel to **Lying in Judgment**

Two months after serving on the jury trying a man for the murder that he committed, Peter Robertson's worst nightmare comes to fruition: Christine, his beautiful and charming fellow juror, knows his dark secret and uses it to blackmail him. The price of her secrecy: Peter must kill again, this time to stop Kyle, the man who torments Christine and threatens her very existence.

Their sizzling nascent romance gets interrupted when Kyle kidnaps her. Peter's daring rescue provides him the opportunity to commit the awful deed. Peter refuses, however, only to discover that his best friend Frankie may have committed the act in his place. Or was he framed?

Peter's relentless search for evidence to clear his lifelong pal forces him to confront his demons and risk his own freedom—and his life—as he battles the ruthless, manipulative, and resourceful woman who always seems one step ahead and knows his every move.

Expected release: Fall, 2017

Check the free sample chapter from this book
in the following pages!

Excerpt from

Lying in Vengeance

by Gary Corbin

CHAPTER 1

Peter Robertson bolted upright in his darkened bedroom. Carlos Santana sang his 1970s hit "Black Magic Woman" on scratchy, poorly-amplified speakers. How, Peter wondered in his melatonin-aided stupor, could a band thirty years defunct be broadcasting a live concert in the second-floor bedroom of his eighty-plus-year-old Portland bungalow? And why on such awful sound equipment?

Something lit the corner of his bedroom with a flickering glare. His stupid cell phone. He reached for it and noticed the bright red digits flickering at him from his bedside alarm clock. 3:15 a.m. What idiot would be calling him at this hour?

Then the song snippet repeated, and he remembered creating and assigning that ringtone two months earlier to a woman in his phone's contact list that he'd prefer to forget. The woman who made his life miserable, sleep next to impossible, and nightmares inevitable for weeks after the close of the Alvin Dark murder trial. The woman who'd threatened to blackmail him into doing horrible things after realizing what horrible thing he'd had to live with for the six months leading up to their ill-fated meeting on that jury.

"Christine?" he said into the phone. It kept playing music.

Dammit! He pushed the "Answer" button, and the music stopped.

"Well, good morning, Sunshine," she said, all chipper and happy. She sounded like she'd been up for hours, probably drinking double espressos and scheduling Twitter messages to promote her various clients' brands. "Have you missed me?"

"Do you know what time it is?" He propped two pillows up against the headboard and sagged into them. Closing his eyes didn't help: he only imagined every detail of her pretty face in front of him, from the thin, black eyebrows and long lashes to her trademark bright red lipstick. He opened them again and stared into the blackness of his bedroom.

"It's breakfast time in New York," she said. "Which means it's mid-morning for you—about nine-fifteen, right?"

"Try three-fifteen." Peter rubbed his temples with his free hand. "You got the time change backwards."

"Oh, silly me," she said. "I'm sorry." She didn't sound the slightest bit sorry. He thought he heard her laugh, even. "Well, now that you're up, let's get that dinner planned that we talked about—what was it, a month ago now?"

"Two months."

"You're *so* right. Time does fly when we're busy, doesn't it?"

Peter scowled and turned onto his side. Monday morning was earning its awful reputation. "Christine, what do you want?"

"I just told you. I want you to buy me dinner."

"I'll mail you a gift certificate to Arby's tomorrow. Good night."

"Don't you dare hang up on me!"

Peter's finger paused an inch above the "End Call" button. Even with the phone held a foot in front of his face, he heard her throaty warning with perfect, chilling clarity. He signed and returned the phone to his ear. "I'm still here."

"Good." Amazing how her voice could transform from dark and dangerous to soft and sexy without missing a beat. "I thought we could go back to Pazzo's, for old times' sake.

Remember our first date there? You were so nervous."

"It wasn't a date. We had lunch. And it wasn't our first anything. We'd had lunch together before."

"Yes, but at Pazzo's, you paid, like a true gentleman, courting the object of his desires."

"I was *not–*" He stopped himself. To be honest, he *had* been courting her—at the time. "How about someplace new?"

After a beat, she countered, "A place we've never been…? Say, perhaps, *Florentino's*?"

His blood froze in his veins. He'd known, deep down, as soon as he gave her the opening, she'd remind him of the restaurant where, eight months before, he'd followed Marcia, his now ex-wife, and her lover, triggering events that changed—*ruined!*—his whole life. The scene of, if not the crime per se, at least where it all had been set in motion. Where the victim, his lover, and his enemy all worked and quarreled. The victim whom he'd later mistaken for Marcia's lover, whom he'd confronted, beaten, and –

"S'matter? Cat got your tongue?"

He shook himself out of the foul memory. "No. Not there. Not Florentino's." His hoarse voice took him aback, increasing the chill spreading across his naked body despite the summer heat. "I'm never going back there."

"Fine. I tell you what—surprise me. I'll be back in town later this week. Pick me up at my office Thursday at six."

"Thursday I have plans."

Her voice grew hard. "Make new plans."

She hung up without saying goodbye.

***

Christine Nielsen hung up the phone and smiled. Peter's buttons were so easily pushed.

But then again, so were hers.

She took a bite of the scrambled eggs on her plate, gooey and runny and pale. Another hotel chain that watered down egg batter to save money on top of their ridiculously inflated prices. If Leicester-Howe, LLC ever turned the corner on profitability, she'd insist on better accommodations on these hellish trips. She'd also remember, tomorrow, to order her eggs over easy. Even a runny yolk beat a plateful of this goo.

Her phone chimed, a pleasant tone, soft and melodic. Caller ID showed the name. She hit Ignore. It rang again. She pressed Ignore a second time, And a third, when the caller persisted. Even 3,000 miles away, she didn't want her day ruined by the man who had, for three awful years, abused her, physically, mentally, and emotionally—and then had continued to badger her since. She made a mental note to ask the tech guy how to block calls on this phone, issued to her only days before she jumped on the red-eye to JFK. He'd offered twice, and she'd declined, knowing that what he really wanted was an excuse to hang out in her office and stare at her legs—which would lead to an unwelcome invitation to drinks after work, which she'd declined a dozen times before. As odd and unattractive as she found him, however, it might be worth it to be rid of Kyle and his harassment.

She charged the breakfast to her room and exited the hotel to the already oppressive heat and humidity of Manhattan in July. She needed to walk about six blocks to her client's office—long New York blocks rather than Portland's tiny two hundred foot squares. She might just melt away to nothing. Which she might have preferred over meeting with this group, an obnoxious, greedy bunch of financial advisors who prided themselves on cheating small investors, going low-bid on out of town ad firms like hers, and paying consultants late, if at all. But the market had tightened up in recent months, and she needed the work.

Her phone chimed again, and the display said "Caller ID Blocked." Probably the clients, wondering why she wasn't twenty minutes early. She answered in her bright, chipper Clients-Are-King voice. "This is Christine Nielsen."

"Hello, baby."

She hung up. That rotten scumbag Kyle had called from a different phone, probably thinking she'd blocked his earlier calls.

Forget the tech. She needed to meet with Peter Robertson, soon.

***

That bitch!! How *dare* she hang up like that, without so much as a hello. Rude, as usual. Kyle had no idea what he ever saw in her.

He glanced at the photo on his dresser, the two of them together in Hawai'i. She looked pretty damned good in that bikini. Even better when it came off.

Oh, yeah. *That's* what he'd seen in her.

He hit redial—like, really *hit* redial, literally smashing the phone with his fist. But the call went straight to voicemail. And again. And again.

She'd pay for that. *Damn* her.

He rolled off his bed, a California king with an iron head and foot rail, one they'd used many times when they'd done the dirty deed. Truly dirty, too, the way he liked it: ropes, blindfolds, hot wax—she'd always preferred things a little rough. Or so she always said whenever he asked, until walking out on him. Then she was all, "Oh, honey, you hurt me." What crap.

He pulled on a pair of chinos, foregoing the boxers lying on the floor. They probably still had the scent of that useless blonde bimbo he'd thrown out, sobbing, at 2 a.m. Like it was *his* fault she didn't climax. In his experience, a woman's pleasure had nothing to do with what filled the space between her legs and everything to do with what filled the space between her ears. And that one had nothing.

He flipped a comb through his own blond curls and made a mental note to get on Gillian's schedule for a trim. Maybe a little touch-up on the roots—they showed a little dark brown, that mousy color that came on in his early 20's that he so despised. So very un-California. He envied his idiot brother Earl in this regard, one year younger and as blond as Kate Upton—even his chest hair. Unlike Kyle's. He rubbed his free hand over his muscular chest and added a spa visit to his to do list. He hated stubble, or any sort of body hair. If he had religion, that was probably it.

That, and avoiding Earl. For the last fifteen years, he'd succeeded at that, ever since Kyle left the foster home in which they'd spent their teenage years. Earl had left him a message once to tell him that their foster parents had died and left everything to their "natural" babies. He'd deleted the message—and with it, he hoped, every last trace of that unfortunate period of his life.

He trudged downstairs, brewed a cup of chai and sat on the deck of his two-story condo overlooking the dark northern California coastline. The majestic beauty of the ocean, the moonlit beach, the mountains in the distance to the north—on a normal day it had the power to calm his agitated soul. But today his frustration lingered. She had a way of getting under his skin, even when she'd flown a continent away from him.

Which he knew, because he always knew exactly where she was, who she was with, and what she was doing.

Every moment.

Every day.

Made in the USA
Charleston, SC
24 January 2017